Purely Academic

A novel by D.W. Rosenthal

DEDICATION

To my wife Addie who makes Em look like a wimp.

ACKNOWLEDGMENTS

There are several people who provided outstanding support and education when I needed it. Valerie Elliott guided me to the newspaper articles about local Oxford treasure and taught me how to use the ancestry websites. Professor Osama Ettouney patiently explained rapid prototyping and direct metal laser sintering. Rod Gillis, Numismatic Educator with the American Numismatic Association validated my coin facts and ideas. Sharon Attaway and her husband Rand helped me to find my way in the publishing maze. A whole cadre of friends, colleagues and relatives encouraged me.

Chapter 1

Timing and balance are everything, especially in a golf swing. I hadn't been playing much, and so I was particularly pleased as I drove the toe of my putter precisely three inches into Les's temple.

I always liked that putter. Lots of guys change putters more often than they change their underwear. Not me. I've had the same Ping Anser 2 putter for over 20 years. I liked the way it looked as I stood over a putt. Most of the time, I could see "the line" and set the ball moving in the right direction. None of those big mallet heads, or belly putters or any of that foolishness for me. Nope. The straight lines of my Ping with its pointed toe, no frills, no nonsense, had come through for me on many a hole... And this was the pressure stroke of my life.

I didn't really know if I could pull it off, but as I said, timing is everything and mine was running out. Everything depended on that one swing of the club. My life. My wife's life. Everything. Funny the things that go through your mind at a time like that. I mean, I knew it wasn't really a golf swing – it was more like a baseball swing, but as I stepped into it I was gauging the distance and I kept thinking, "Keep your eye on the ball!" And, somewhere in the back of my head, I was hearing my old friend and golf partner saying, "Keep your grip pressure constant." "Unknown professor steps to the tee... One shot to win the U.S. Open..." Craziness.

Technically, it wasn't a great swing, but under the circumstances it was the best I have ever made. I took one big step across the living room and swung with everything I had. Turned the toe of the club in, focused on his temple and drove it in, up to the hosel. I don't know if I said it out loud or to myself, "Now here's a message you'll really like…" It was just sort of there in my mind.

I was surprised at how little noise it made. I half-expected it to be louder, kind of like a wood block. Maybe that's a bit cartoonish, but I had worried about it, a lot. In the end, it wasn't really much of a sound at all. It was about the same sound that you get when you thump a cantaloupe in the grocery store. There was also a kind of crunch to it, but that may have been just the feeling through the shaft of the club. I don't know, and I didn't have time to think about it.

He wasn't moving. The momentum of the swing had knocked him sideways in the easy chair he'd been sitting in, but he had not fallen to the floor. I'd worried about that, too. It was a big old, over-stuffed easy chair at the corner of the living room. My wife never liked that chair. If things worked out, she'd love it now. As it was, it absorbed my target and held him as it had held me innumerable evenings as I dozed off in front of the fireplace, the warmth of the room and good bourbon eclipsing whatever book I had allowed to slide into my lap.

His gun had slid down beside him and was now slightly wedged between his thigh and the cushion of the chair. I couldn't tell you what make or model it was. It was a hand gun, an automatic of some sort. It was flat, black and nasty. I'm not a stranger to guns. I've owned several during my lifetime. I'm not an expert, either. I can shoot, but I'm not going to win any contests. Anyway, I guessed

6

that this was a 9 millimeter or something close. I wasn't going to spend a whole lot of time checking or taking notes.

I picked it up, checked to make certain the safety was indeed off, and quickly and as quietly as I could crossed the living room, and the entry foyer. The carpeted living room was one thing, but the foyer was ceramic tile, and even with the Nikes I was wearing, I wanted no noise. None at all. I really didn't think that it would matter given Ray's circumstances, but why take the chance?

The gun was in the cocked and locked position, a round in the chamber and ready to fire simply by pulling back the hammer and squeezing the trigger. I positioned myself a few feet outside the first floor half-bathroom, estimated where the toilet was, and put four shots through the door to where I figured a person would be seated. Then, for good measure, I put two more through toward where one might stand at the sink. The door was closed, so I couldn't be sure where he was, and I damned sure wasn't going to open the door to find out. "Gee, let's go into the wounded lion's den to see if we got him!" Yeah, right.

Backing away from the door, I released the clip and checked the count. Four more. Oh, for the record, I was right. It was a 9 mil and it happened to be a Browning, not that it matters. As I backed into the living room I slapped the clip back into place, and pulled back the slide cocking the gun. I saw no signs of life from my "friend" in the chair, but again, I didn't plan on taking any chances. I'd have enough chances later. I made sure that I was well out of reach of any sudden lunge, and carefully took a two-handed stance, aimed, and put one right through the side of his head. Well, maybe we'd have to get a new chair after all.

Nobody ever thinks about how loud a gunshot is in a confined space. My ears were ringing, and I wasn't at all certain that I could hear subtle movements. If Ray were still alive in the bathroom, he'd be coming out after me. Given the size of the bathroom, I don't know how he could still be alive, but time was precious and I had things to do. There is a little hallway or alcove, just a few feet leading to the bathroom. Being careful not to show myself in front of the door, I tossed all of the dining room chairs and a couple of barstools into the space and piled up a nice little barricade. Nothing that would stop anyone, but it would make enough noise that I'd hear it. I hoped. To help my chances, I ripped a piece of tape from the drawer where we kept empty containers and added a pickle jar to the very edge of the barricade. If the pile moved, the jar would fall and shatter itself, and probably my remaining nerves.

I checked my watch. God! Less than two minutes had passed since my "tee shot". It seemed like forever. At the outside I had twenty minutes. Max. In twenty minutes the other two members of their "team" would be back, my wife between them. Somehow I didn't think that they'd appreciate what I had just done. There's just no pleasing some folks.

Chapter 2

My name is John Douglas Richardson, and I am Professor of business at Miami University. That's in Oxford, Ohio, not Florida. I know, you are confused already so let's get this cleared up and we'll move on to other things. Miami University is in Ohio. It is named after the Miami Tribe who lived in this region when the school was founded in 1809. The city of Miami, Florida was named by alumni of my university to honor their alma mater. They were engineers who built the railroad down the east coast of Florida for Henry Morrison Flagler in the 1890s. So, don't call us "Miami of Ohio". We had the name first. Get over it.

Anyway, I teach business at Miami and have for about 30 years. That makes me a relative newcomer. Let's just say that we have a wonderful tradition. It is a beautiful school, with outstanding students and an international reputation.

Oxford is a small town of about ten thousand full-time residents, supplemented by about fifteen thousand students during the school year. We are located about an hour north of Cincinnati, an hour southwest of Dayton, and right on the Indiana-Ohio border. In the old days, the border meant that there was a certain amount of lawlessness that was fostered by the differences in jurisdiction and such. Who'd have thought that would come home to roost two hundred years later?

I met my wife here. She was a graduate student and we couldn't stand each other. I thought that she had a lousy attitude and she thought that I was a revolving son of a bitch. We were both right. She actually graduated from Miami. I ground my way through Wharton at UPenn and Darden at UVA. After a while we decided that a relationship based on mutual disrespect was worth keeping and we worked our way south from there. Other than the fact that she married me, I'd have to say that she is the smartest woman I ever knew, except maybe for my mother.

The name on her diploma is officially Rita Samms Richardson. She hates that name. Claims it sounds like an elderly schoolteacher. If you want to really get her goat, call her by her given name. Her friends and colleagues call her "Samms". I call her Molly Mae and I couldn't really tell you why. I just do. I've called her that for so long that it doesn't really matter anymore. She is Molly Mae, or "Em" just because she is. She is Professor of History here, by the way. She studied under Dr. Phil Shriver, past President of Miami University, and distinguished professor of history. His area of expertise was local history, say over the past couple of hundred years. Em heard him lecture and fell in love with him and the subject, so she followed in his footsteps. Did I mention that she is smart?

I guess you would say that I am presentable. I'm not handsome, and I'm not ugly. I'm a little over six feet tall, and I weigh a bit over 200 pounds and I'm about as much out of shape as you'd think a sedentary academician approaching 60 years of age would be. I have light brown hair, well, graying, and it doesn't stay where it is supposed to very much. Mostly it goes where it will, and so I tend to keep it medium length just to add to the directional surprise. My eyes are blue, and I need reading glasses. I read a lot. No surprise there.

I tend to dress casually. I used to wear a three-piece suit to class every day. Thank goodness I gave up on that foolishness years ago. Now I wear khakis and a nice shirt on teaching days or days when I have a meeting. Occasionally, some official business will come along that requires me to wear a suit. Generally, I try to avoid such things. Still, I recognize that some situations require the proper protocol and uniform and I begrudgingly acquiesce. But, I pout. Whenever I can, I even the score by wearing jeans and flannel. One of my colleagues refers to my drab flannel shirts as "lesbian" and I am proud to agree.

I teach strategy. That is, I develop the skills of analyzing complex situations and deriving logical and creative solutions. I'm known to be a harsh task master to my students. I am not an easy grader, and I ask a lot from my classes. I figure that they are here for an education and I intend for the students and their parents to get their money's worth. I have high expectations of my students, and myself. I am told that I am intimidating. I can't understand that at all. I am really very sweet.

Em, on the other hand, is mean as a snake. I think it is because she is the youngest in her family and the only girl. She is just over five feet tall, weighs just over 100 pounds, and to quote P.T. Barnum, "… is made of whale bone and rubber." She has auburn hair, and green eyes, and I think that should tell you something as well. When she is angry, her eyes become an odd shade of yellow. Kind of like that weird color just before a tornado hits. If you ever see her eyes that shade, run! I speak from experience.

She is one of the leading authorities in her field and is highly respected in academic and popular circles as well. She is well published, and her ability to ferret out real history is uncanny. That is, Em is not about reading other folks' papers and hypotheses and rehashing the common wisdom. She is about interviewing octogenarians, uncovering attic documents that haven't seen the light of day in ages, and digging up interesting connections among unconnected people, places and things.

She gets great student evaluations, and wins teaching awards. While my students find me intimidating, her students find her to be inspiring. While I am said to be challenging, she is known as motivating. What a crock! She is just way, way better looking and female. Did I mention that I love her very much?

Chapter 3

We live a couple of miles from campus, outside of town. We have about sixteen acres that are about half woods and half open field. Our driveway is almost a third of a mile long, and the nearest neighbors are farther than that. There are a couple of ponds and with the isolation, and cover and forage and water, we have a lot of wildlife to observe. That is about as exciting as it gets. My idea of a good time is sitting on the back deck, overlooking the woods and pond, and watching the deer come up to the bird feeder. Most folks worry about squirrels. Not me. I have deer eating my birdseed... BIG deer, and how they manage to perch on the bird feeder is a wonder.

I have a spotting scope set up in a window so I can observe the birds and deer up close and personal. I keep a couple of pairs of big 12X50 binoculars at hand as well, not to mention the lightweight pair I keep at the office. My colleagues accuse me of using them to watch the coeds, but I actually do use them to watch the birds. I've been watching wildlife and identifying and classifying birds, mammals, reptiles, amphibians, insects, sea shells, shore life, fish, plants, fungi, stars, rocks, fossils, and everything else that I can catch sight of since I was a kid. That is how my mother and father raised us.

I guess you would say that I am a naturalist. I am not a militant tree-hugger or anything. I don't belong to any groups. I don't go to protests. I have not spiked our trees. Nor have I had my legal name changed to "Moonbeam". I have a "life list" of all the different bird species that I have identified, but if I forget to write one down I won't have to seek psychiatric help for traumatic stress.

Em does not approach things in the same way. She does not share my enthusiasm for identification, naming, classifying, etc. I think that she is as perceptive and alert to her surroundings as I am, but she is content to enjoy the moment of the thing. I'll spend an hour trying to determine if it was a Coopers Hawk or a Sharp-shinned Hawk, and then read about the distinguishing features and worry over it. Em will say something like, "Cool! He has orange stripes!" I'll work through two or three reference books and my dog-eared Newcomb's Wildflower Guide to figure out what plant it was that we saw on our walk. Em will smell it, and say, "Pretty!" Of course, more often than not, she is the one who spotted whatever it was in the first place.

When the weather is nice, I sit out on the deck and work the crossword puzzles and the Cryptoquips, or Cryptoquotes, and the Jumble, and the Sudoku and sip decaffeinated coffee, black. Depending on the newspaper, I work my way through the bridge column and the chess challenge. Wow! Be still my heart! I don't know how I stand the excitement. When the weather is lousy, I sit in my easy chair in the living room and work the puzzles and sip my decaf. Woo-hoo!

Em's idea of a good time is to sit at the kitchen counter and work on-line. She plugs in her lap-top, fills her coffee with artificial junk and begins dissecting data bases, and photo archives, and manuscripts and such in search of history. It is astounding what the digital age has done for her field.

14

Somebody finds a document or a photo and either takes a picture with their phone, or scans it into a pdf file, and there it is for all the world to see. She has colleagues all over the region, and for that matter, the world. So, with cell phones and email and electronic files and all of the handwriting encoding and decoding and character recognition, she is just as happy as if she had good sense; just sitting there at the kitchen counter.

We go out sometimes, but not often. Usually, we go out to lunch together on Saturday. There are a handful of places in town that we like, and depending on our mood, we'll go to one or the other. When we do, we almost always order the same thing: Skippers for a gyro platter, regular for me and chicken for Em, Wild Bistro for the noodle bowl. Kona for the kitchen sink salad, at least until they changed the menu – bastards!

We almost never go out in the evening. There are the obligatory departmental dinners and student presentations, and the occasional seminar, of course. I can't remember the last movie that we saw in a theatre. The only thing that we do on a regular basis is we share season tickets for Miami's hockey team. One of my colleagues and his wife go on Friday nights, and Em and I go on Saturday nights. Em grew up a Rangers fan, and I grew up watching the Blues. She knows her hockey and is a fierce supporter of our team. I am too, for that matter.

We are not socialites by any stretch. We have friends and colleagues, but we don't have guests to the house very often. We are not party-goers. Em and I are in complete agreement that making chit-chat at a cocktail party is what purgatory must be like. If you add dancing and loud music, you have completed our vision of hell. Besides, we see our colleagues almost every day. We have lunch with them, I with mine and she with hers. We have the various functions throughout the school year, the end-of-semester parties and such. Home is a haven to which we can retreat.

So, most nights we stay in for a quiet dinner. I do most of the cooking. It is a creative outlet for me. That is another reason that we don't go out very much. Once I have had a dish, I can pretty much duplicate it. Then I futz with it and add my own touches, and generally improve on it. So, why go out and spend a small fortune on a dish that won't be as good as what we could be eating at home for a fraction of the price and hassle? Not to mention the ambience... Where else are you going to watch deer at the bird feeder? And, Em can have a glass of wine, and I can have a double Wild Turkey and not have to drive.

After dinner, Em fires up her lap-top. I'll turn on the TV and watch a sporting event or a classic movie. Em is nuts about the show, HOUSE. In the absence of something of value on TV, I'll read. I read a lot. At the normal crunch times in the semester, I'll retire to the office and grade papers, or work on my own research and writing.

We tend to be seasonal. The school year will do that to you. In August we are getting ready for classes to begin. Mid-terms come in October, and big papers roll in on the first of December. Over Christmas break we usually try to find someplace warm where we can relax, add a few recipes from untried restaurants, and I can play golf or we can go fishing. Same cycle for the spring term, only add in

16

spring break. Again, we usually head southward while trying to avoid our students. Classes are over by the beginning of May and we have the summer to work on our projects and research and my golf swing.

I am not a great golfer. At one time I had a single digit handicap, but that was a number of years ago. As I have aged, and my sedentary lifestyle has caught up with my lower back, my swing has shortened. I still love the game, and I can still break bogey most of the time. It just isn't a competitive thing for me anymore, which is good. Age adds perspective and humility and subtracts distance. Pride, however, prohibits moving to the white tees. Incidentally, I walk. It is an essential part of the game. If I ever get to the point that I need a cart, I'll give up the game. I cannot tell you the level of righteous indignation I can generate as I see a couple of pampered twenty-year-olds drive by in a golf cart as I am manfully striding down an adjoining fairway. I console myself by thinking that if ever they are in one of my classes and are border-line between two grades, they shall receive the lower out of sheer principle. Carts, indeed!

During the summer, I get out to play at least once a week, often with an ex-student or a colleague, or a recruiter who wants to hire our students. I love playing with my ex-students. I get to catch up on how they are doing, what is going on in their business, and make sure that I am still connected and relevant in my teaching. I also love watching them absolutely kill the ball. One of my favorites averages over 320 yards off the tee! He destroys it! Of course, I also delight in rolling in a couple of putts to beat him. "Drive for show – putt for dough!" Not competitive... right.

So, all in all, we lead a pretty mundane existence. We are a couple of academics, living outside a small town in southwestern Ohio. Homebodies, and we like it that way, or did.

Chapter 4

It was just after dinner on Monday night. Em was cleaning up, and I was trying to decide between a Reds-Brewers ball game and game three of the Stanley Cup finals. It was the third inning and the Reds were already down a couple of runs. Detroit was leading the Cup series, as usual, and I wasn't too excited about watching that, either. Decisions, decisions.

Dinner had been a minor triumph, if I do say so. It had been some time and I was in the mood, so I had prepared Spaghetti a la Caruso. Spaghetti a la Caruso has a red sauce with sautéed garlic and onion, red wine, mushrooms and diced chicken livers. Done properly it is to die for! I had acquitted myself well, but it was not my all-time best, so maybe just enough to be severely wounded for, but not unto death. I had added a tossed salad with romaine, a few of the sliced mushrooms, calamata olives, and marinated artichoke hearts all dressed with my own home-made Italian vinaigrette, and garnished with freshly sliced tomatoes. I had picked up a sour-dough baguette on the way home, and we were in business! Em sipped a glass of cabernet, "Sunny Slope" from Imagery vineyards in Napa, one of our all-time favorites. I sipped my usual Wild Turkey. We were celebrating the end of the semester and the beginning of the summer. What a way to go!

As I fiddled with the channel selection and Em put the dishes into the washer, the "dog alarm" went off. That is, Sadie, the remaining canine member of the family, had a fit of massive barkalation, thus indicating an intruder to our realm.

19

I should have introduced Sadie before. Our best guess is that she is half German Shepherd and half Basset Hound... Yep. Think about it. Either a male German Shepherd wedded beneath his station, literally, or some male Basset used a step ladder. Weird, either way. The result was Sadie, the sweetest, most opinionated and smartest dog in the world.

We got Sadie the same way we got all of our animals, although we were down to one dog and two cats. Sadie was a "rescue". One of our students found her in a ditch at the nearby state park. She was worn out, emaciated, covered with mange, and could no longer stand up. Somebody had dumped her on the roadside in the park and she had done her best to live off the land. She lasted for some time, but couldn't cut it as a wolf or coyote. When the student found her, she weighed just over thirty pounds. She now cuddles at a comfortable sixty-five.

When we first brought her home from the vet, she was apprehensive and scared and desperately wanted to believe. We spent untold hours with her and finally convinced her that she had a place forever. She wolfed her food and challenged anyone or anything to come between her and her livelihood. We had other dogs at the time and after a few growling and hackles episodes, they realized that they needed to leave her alone at dinner time.

Unfortunately, she had not lost her idea that anything that was catchable on the hoof was fair game, and so she went after Intrepid the cat. She did not go after him with the idea of "oh, cool – me dog, you cat, me chase..." She went after him with the idea of "me dog, you protein!" Intrepid did not take kindly to this assessment and abandoned his claim on the house and ever after lived in the barn. Sad, but he became "Lord of the Barn Mice" and lived to the ripe old age of 18.

The other dogs were older when we adopted Sadie and although at one time we actually had five dogs of various shapes, sizes, dispositions, and configurations. We had horses until just recently, and would undoubtedly have more. For the past fifteen years all of our animals had been "rescues". We aren't looking, but our view is that if an animal needs us, we'll be there. It is both sad and a blessing that people tend to outlive their animals. The love gets concentrated, but the pain of their passing is very real. Now we were down to just the Sadie-Whomper, plus a couple of cats. Knowing Em, it wouldn't be that few for long.

You see, Em is the "Voice of Radio Free Animal-dom". She comes by it naturally. Her mother used to feed slugs. I swear. Animals are innocents. People are flawed. When the hurricane hit in New Orleans and we saw the devastation on the news, I said, "Molly Mae, we have to give some serious money for the relief effort. Not just in the hundreds, but we have to write a serious check." She agreed wholeheartedly. The following day she wrote a check in the thousands to the SPCA. She could not have cared less about the people, but the animals needed help. Her comment: "The people should have had enough sense to clear out. The animals didn't have a choice. It wasn't their fault that they were owned by idiots!" She had a point.

So, the years of the other dogs had caught up with them. Heartbreakingly sad, every time. We loved those guys, a lot. But we were down to just Sadie, and Marty and Joe the cats now. That was enough to keep us occupied and we weren't looking for another beast, although whenever one needed us, we'd be there, whatever the denomination. Not even a question.

Sadie set up the "there is someone coming" bark-fest, and I abandoned the remote and headed for the front of the house. Anybody who knows us knows to come to the utility room door off the garage. The front door is so infrequently used that it literally has spider-webs spanning it and we just really don't pay attention. Nobody comes to the front door.

Nevertheless, a young couple came to the front door and rang the doorbell. I could see them through the glass panels at the sides of the door. They were, I would guess, in their twenties. The male was wearing dark pants, not dressy but kind of in-between. He had on a standard blue, button-down shirt, Arrow-like. Black belt, black shoes. Medium hair, not short, not long, dark, but not black. I'd guess that he was just under six feet tall, but the front stoop is a few inches lower than the entry, so I'm giving you just an impression. He was slim but not overly so. Didn't think much about it. Seemed friendly enough.

She was similarly unintrusive. Attractive enough in her way. She had brown hair, about three-quarter length. She was about five-six, or so. Certainly taller than Em. She also looked to be in good shape, neither fat nor emaciated. Somewhere in-between. She wasn't wearing much make-up, and her expression was one of friendly expectancy, like she hoped that this would be a good exchange. She was wearing dark slacks as well, a greenish knit top of some sort, short-sleeved, with a v-neck. Nothing provocative, no deep cleavage or anything, nor was she overly-endowed. I have a tendency to notice. But, I swear, I use my binoculars in the office to watch birds. I swear.

All in all, they appeared to be a married couple, middle class, nice enough, well-dressed and innocuous. Frankly, I expected them to be missionaries, or latter day saints, or earlier day saints, or just possibly someone wanting to talk about the deplorable state of the educational system and how we needed to have another levy of some sort to throw money at the problem so that young people would no longer use golf carts. Who knows? They rang the door-bell and, of course, Sadie went nuts barking and forcing her way between my legs and the front door. I kneed her back and opened the door a bit and said, "Hi, can I help you?

He kind of half-smiled, and she said, "Hi, we are the Mallorys. We are moving into the Newsom's house up the street. We noticed that you have a barn, and we have a young daughter who just loves horses. We wanted to ask if we might bring her by to see them?"

This is not an altogether unheard-of request. Frankly it is pretty commonplace. Horses are like swimming pools. They are an attractive nuisance. You have to have fences around both, and kids from all over want to come and wallow in each, and everybody believes that it is the social

23

obligation of the owner to allow such communal, smiley-face nonsense. Of course, if little Biffy happens to get bitten, or stepped on, or drowns while no one is watching, then it is all your fault, and we'll sue you to within an inch of your life, but what of that?

Thinking to myself, "Oh, God. Here we go," I stood back and invited the Mallorys into the entry and turned and said, "Em, we have guests from up the street." I closed the door, and of course Sadie was all over them, jumping up and down, and barking. Now, you have to realize that Sadie has a vertical leap of about an inch and half and was in no way a threat to anyone. She was excited, but would calm down in a minute. I loved the way that her basset-length ears flopped up and down, and she was smiling as only she could.

Em appeared from the kitchen just in time to see Mr. Mallory pull a gun from behind his hip and put an abrupt and violent end to Sadie's happy life.

Chapter 5

Just like that. One second we are standing in the entry with a new young couple from up the street and the next our ears were ringing and the sweetest dog in the world was dead. Total shock. It seemed like forever before it even registered as to what happened. I mean, there was no lead up. There was no indication whatsoever. There was no hint. Just the stark crash of a gunshot and the numbing, inescapable "can't be".

I stood there and gaped. This did NOT happen. Everything slowed to non-moving time. I saw Sadie just drop. Not thrown backward like in the movies or anything. She just dropped where she stood. There was no explosion of blood, no smashing into walls. She just dropped. I believe I adroitly said, "Wha?" and stood there like a total dope, at least until he clubbed me on the side of the head and dropped me to the classical six-point stance, followed quickly by the moaning, lying on one's side, holding one's head stance.

He stood directly over me and pointed the gun at my head, I think. I wasn't in much of a position to judge. As I was in excruciating pain from having a heavy metal object smacked up against my skull, I neglected, like most major-league umpires, to put myself in position to call the play. I didn't even have the excuse of hiding behind union membership for my lack of perspective at that moment.

While all of this was going on, Em said something akin to, "Aar-eegh!" and threw herself down on Sadie. She began to call over and over, "Sadie, honey! Sadie, lamb! Oh, dear God. Sadie! Honey!" I'm certain that Sadie heard her. Sadie had been deaf, or almost so, for years. Her basset ears encouraged infections and despite Em's Herculean efforts to keep them clean and dry and clear, they managed to deteriorate. Still, I know Sadie heard Em Not a doubt in the world.

And I heard the bitch, "Mrs. Mallory" begin to shout, "Dr. Richardson! DR. RICHARDSON! That was to show that we mean business! We have a gun to your husband's head and we will kill him RIGHT NOW if you don't straighten up! GET THE HELL UP AND BACK INTO THE LIVING ROOM RIGHT NOW! NOW! MOVE! WE'LL KILL HIM! NOW MOVE!"

It vaguely penetrated my consciousness, what she was saying. HE hadn't said a word since he introduced them at the outset. I heard the words, but the meaning didn't register… Yet. I was in a lot of pain, the sharp kind like when you stub your toe or hit your thumb with a hammer. Not the deep, dull kind when you lose awareness, but still enough to get your attention and keep it focused on the pain and nothing else.

For Em, I can only imagine. One minute she is doing dishes from a meal celebrating the end of the semester, and the next her dog-child is dead at the hands of two horrors that have appeared from another space-time continuum. Monsters who are now screaming at her to MOVE or they'll shoot her husband without so much as a thought of consideration or pity… and they had proved their point. How she had the presence of mind to actually have her muscles obey a rational command, I do not understand. In any event, she moved.

"Mr. Mallory" unceremoniously grabbed my arm, lifted and shoved me into the living room as well. I seem to recall being run into the back of the couch, then lifted again and half thrown over the side of the couch to the floor.

The sharpness of the pain was giving way to a kind of heaviness, and an ache that said, "Brother, are you going to need Advil by the handful!" As the acute pain subsided, I was able to gather myself sufficiently to register the horror on Em's face, and the electric tautness of her body. The adrenalin had kicked in and she was rigid with energy for which she had no outlet. Yet. If they gave Em even half an opening, their demise would be excruciating, trust me.

"Mr. Mallory", on the other hand, was calmly wary, and my immediate reaction was, "He has been here before." Oh, I don't mean in our home or whatever. He had done things like this before. This was old hat. He knew exactly what he was doing, what to expect, and how to handle it. He was an old pro. Killing a dog was just part of the deal, and not a big deal at that.

"Mrs. Mallory" had a different "feel". She was energized. Her eyes were a bit wider than they should have been. She had an air of energy about her. She, too, had been in this situation. She, too, knew what she was doing. The two of them had worked together as a team before. You could see it in the way that they positioned themselves. They kept their distance, especially from Em, and covered each other's moves. The difference was that she was enjoying this. He was all business. She had a hint of a smile going, and an air of conceited entertainment. At that moment I began to truly understand evil.

And just to make the game complete, at that point I heard the utility room door open. You know, the one that regular folks used. His eyes shifted just long enough to register that, yes indeed, this was expected. Her eyes never left Em. So, in walked Les and Ray. Now, I have no idea whether they were really named Les and Ray. That is what they were called all of the time that we had the honor of their acquaintance. By the way, Mr. and Mrs. Mallory gave up that cognomen, and reverted to Britt and Zach. Whatever happened to "Bill" and "John" and "Mary" and "Sue"? Real names for real people? Sign of the times, and it occurred to me that it gave me verification of their ages. As a teacher I had watched the balance of names shift over the years. These guys were probably twenty-somethings. We never heard "Mallory" again, and it won't hurt my feelings if we never do.

Let's see. Les. Les was about the same age. I'd guess mid-twenties, maybe late twenties. Les looked as if he had never met a beer that he didn't like... and consume. He was maybe five-ten, and he probably weighed in at about 250. He was one of those people who wasn't so much fat as just big. I assume that his relatives were big, too. He probably played football and was a lineman somewhere, but not first string. He had sandy hair, cut short but unruly. He was lightly complected and actually had freckles and rosy cheeks. He seemed to be somebody that you could kid around with, and if you bought him another beer, you were probably a friend for life. His shirt was half un-tucked, and wrinkled. He was wearing khakis. An all-around nice kid, except for the flat-black semi-automatic in his hand.

Ray was... a mess. He was about six-three or four, probably weighed about 170, and all of it was grease, acne, angles and attitude. I think he filed his teeth. Oh, there were no outward signs. He had no tattoos, no piercings, at least where we could see them. Now that's an ugly thought. He reminded me of Ichabod Crane, but if he came up against the Headless Horseman, I'd put my money on Ray. Oh, and he smelled. He was unpleasant and appeared to be waiting for an opportunity to pull wings off of flies, debauch small animals, and in general make a one man plague of himself. I'll betcha he'd ride a cart on the golf course, too... probably on the greens.

Britt now addressed herself to me. "Get up off the floor, professor! You haven't been hurt that badly, yet. Sit next to your wife and keep your mouth shut. I really don't want to hear all of the stupid, standard questions and protests." As I scraped myself off the living-room floor and levered myself onto the couch, she went on. "That's a good professor. Now both of you lean back and put your feet up on the coffee table. I'm sure that is something you'd *never* do, but just this time it will be all right." Em and I complied, and as I settled against her, I could feel the electricity. She was pumped, and shaking. I held my head with my right hand, and searched and found her right hand with my left. I squeezed it for assurance that I did not feel, and she darn near crushed mine with her return grip.

Britt the Bitch… That had firmly cemented itself in my mind as an all-one-word designation. I won't bother to spell it out every time, but believe me, it is there all the same. So, Britt nodded in the direction of the stairs and to the den, and said to Les and Ray, "Check it out." To us, she said, "Sit back, and wait. Say nothing, and do not turn around." She crossed to my favorite easy chair and sat, but on the front of the seat, keeping her feet under her. Zach was behind us somewhere, and I could only keep track of him by watching her eyes.

Anyway, she was unerringly correct. I wanted to ask, "Why?"… "What are you doing here?"… "There must be some mistake!"… "You didn't have to shoot Sadie!"… "Please don't hurt us!" And, of course the dumbest of all, "Who are you?" But now that I had a moment to think, and the pain had now turned into a massive ache, my brain lurched into operation. I hoped she didn't hear the grinding as I tried to find first gear.

I missed on the first try. My initial thought was robbery. We are not wealthy, but we have a nice home and we live off a cul-de-sac and our driveway is 1,500 feet long. Our next-door neighbors are several hundred yards away through a curtain of trees. We are outside the city, and the Township police are infrequent visitors to the area. Easy pickings. We have some household cash, and Em has a pretty fair assortment of jewelry, enough that we actually do have a safe. Our art collection is even more valuable, at least at retail, but one would have to really know art to recognize it.

As I said, I missed first gear. This was dumb. Britt had called Em "Professor Richardson" and she had called me "professor" as well. She knew *exactly* who we were. Furthermore, why rob the place when we were at home? We are gone most days. All they would have to do is drive a van down the driveway, walk around the back, bash in a window or force a door and have at it. They were far too calm, and clear of purpose to have been so stupid as to have arranged a robbery while we were at home. Why create the confrontation?

Ah… First gear at last. They wanted the confrontation for some reason. Okay, who did I give a lousy grade to this term? Oops, slipped back out of gear. All right, who would be willing to commit kidnapping to obtain something from us? Even without shooting Sadie, which ought to be punishable by the most excruciating slow torture unto death ever to be inflicted, they had detained us at gunpoint. That is probably kidnapping, technically. They had assaulted me, I think "aggravated" comes into play, but I'm not a legal expert. They had assaulted Em. All of that adds up to big problems. The biggest issue was that I had absolutely no clue as to what they might want. I think I mentioned the word "mundane" before. We have *nothing* worth all of this. Good job of getting to first gear, but that doesn't help if the car is headed the wrong direction. Oh, and the word "yet" regarding hurting me… that had just registered.

Chapter 6

We sat in the living room on the couch, with our feet up on the coffee table, silent, waiting, as instructed. Em and I held hands, and her grip was causing me to lose any semblance of blood flow to my hand, I'll tell you. Britt sat upright on the edge of the easy chair in the corner, the gun in her hand held loosely, but ready at an instant. I assumed that Zach was "at ease" somewhere behind us, in the dining room. We could hear shuffling noises from the rest of the house. Doors opening, doors closing. Sliding doors moving, then shifting of clothes as hangers scraped along rods. Drawers sliding open, then shut. Cabinets banging shut.

After an eternity, meaning about twenty minutes in real time, Les returned to the living room and flopped into the chair opposite Britt, and reported in. "Checked the garage, the den, the kitchen, pantry, laundry room, bathroom and entry hall closet. Oh, there's a closet under the stairs, too. Looks like a combination Easter Bunny, Santa Claus and ToysRUs under there. They got some great stuffed animals! Anyway, nothing to worry about. There was a pellet gun in the hall closet. What a piece of junk! I took all the knives and scissors and carving forks and all out of the kitchen, anything sharp, and I put them with the pellet gun. Normal cleaning chemicals, and stuff. The wine cooler in the pantry is cool! Hey, that's funny. And, it's jammed! I'll bet since they have a cooler, some of them are real good! Oh, and there are home baked cookies in the cookie jar, too. I tested them, so you don't have to worry."

Britt said nothing during this rambling report, and merely sat and watched as if this was standard operating procedure, and it probably was. Les drummed his fingers on the arm of the chair and looked around the room, and bounced a couple of times in his chair. His short sleeves revealed his meaty forearms which rested on the upholstery while his fingers danced a bored cadence. He was big and freckled, and one got the impression that if he wanted something to move, it would.

Another eternity passed, and Ray appeared. All of a sudden he was there. He had not made a sound coming down the stairs. He had not made a sound crossing the tiled entryway. He simply appeared like an odiferous wraith and stood before us to announce his findings from upstairs. His report was a simple, "This is it."

I am sorry to say that he was carrying two hand guns, a shotgun, and a semi-automatic rifle. Not a huge arsenal, but that was the lot. He had missed nothing. He deposited them in front of Britt and without a sound he made a second trip and just as soundlessly he appeared with the ammunition supply, the letter opener from the upstairs office, as well as the assorted scissors from the bathroom. Britt indicated with another head tilt, and Ray and Les gathered the weapons and ammunition and the rest and disappeared out the laundry room to the garage. I wish that I could say that they had missed something, preferably a squad of Marines, or a SAW or a box of grenades, or at least a trained pet asp, but sadly they got it all.

Britt broke the silence, "I'm surprised at you two. All those guns! Tsk, tsk. Professors are supposed to be pacifists. Your colleagues would be shocked and very disappointed in you. What is surprising, though, is that I didn't know about the shotgun. Looks like it's sawed off; you know that's illegal? What would you be doing with that, hmm? Well, so long as we found it. Wouldn't do to have it show up later, eh? Still, that one wasn't on the list. What fun, kind of like a treasure hunt! I wonder what else we'll find before we're done?"

I was disappointed about the guns. It would have been nice to say, "Excuse me, I have to use the potty upstairs," and return with a twelve-gauge shotgun loaded with buckshot. Her talking continued to build up my limited store of information, however. She "knew" about some of the guns and did not know about the shotgun. The twelve-gauge shotgun had belonged to Em's dad. Somehow Em had kept it when he died. It was, indeed, sawed off, and a finer looking weapon one never saw. Pump action, with one in the chamber and five in the sleeve, it could do some serious damage. I'd have given anything to have it in my hands right then.

She *knew* about the other weapons. All of the others we had purchased ourselves, and ammunition for them, of course. If true, that meant that she had access to either credit card records or gun records, or had interrogated people who knew us well, or all of the above. Whatever the source, it meant that she had somebody providing her with information that a twenty-something was unlikely to just blithely stumble into. Somebody had some pull, or some money, or both. To quote Butch Cassidy, "Who ARE those guys?"

We heard the laundry room door to the garage open and close, and then some of the saddest sounds I'd ever heard, one last jingle of Sadie's collar bling and a few muted scrapings as they picked up the remains of the silliest and most beautiful dog in the world. Em silently sobbed and I gritted my teeth as my eyes clouded with tears. One more door closing and Les and Ray reappeared and dropped Sadie's collar on the end table. "Ready," said Ray. Les happily added, "You want anything while we're out? We could stop by UDF; they got a sale on pints. How about a beer run? We could turn this into a party."

Britt's eyes narrowed, and her voice was quiet. The look that she gave Les erased the smile from his face like she had hit the delete button on his computer keyboard. "Don't even," Britt said. The quiet tone of command, and the implied threat in just those two words spoke of power and the willingness to use it. Les's reaction was one of pure fear, fear of something real. Britt had either punished him for some infraction previously, or he'd seen it done. Either way, it was coming together. Britt was the leader, these folks had been together long enough to establish her position, and she was strong and mean enough to have Les, at least, fear her.

Ray was impassive through this exchange. He stood against the wall, paying little attention to any of it. He said nothing, showed no emotion, and simply waited. I have no idea what Zach was doing or thinking. He maintained a position out of sight. Only Britt's occasional glance over our heads indicated that he was still there. And, she was nasty and sneaky enough to be faking us out just for the pleasure of it.

Britt simply said, "Go unload."

Les looked a shade relieved and Ray simply turned and moved away. In all they made three trips. The first trip sounded like luggage. They banged their loads on door frames and on the washing machine as they tried to make the cramped turn between it and the hot water heater, just as I had every time we came home from a trip. I could hear them trudge up the stairs and then one hefty thud as one of the cases fell on its side.

The second and third trips appeared to be groceries, quite a lot of groceries, it seemed. Again, I could hear the rustling of the sacks, plastic not paper, as they brought them in and put them on the counters in the kitchen. I couldn't get an accurate count of the number of bags because they just clumped them down like we all do. But, there were more than just one or two bags per hand, and they made two trips. That added up to a bunch of groceries.

Ray reappeared at the archway at the edge of the living room and the entry and said, "It's all in." Les remained out of sight, possibly not wanting to get into any more trouble.

Britt nodded, "Get going then."

At any rate, Tweedle Dum and Tweedle Dee disappeared toward the garage, the door slamming behind them. We heard the overhead garage door open and a car start, back out, then the overhead door came back down and there was silence again. We could see out the front windows that some kind of dark colored sedan, Em could tell you the make and model, retreated out the driveway followed by my Toyota. What were they possibly going to do with a ten-year-old Toyota? It wasn't worth a lot at this point. It made no sense to me at that moment.

We had been sitting in silence now for, I don't know, maybe the better part of an hour. There were only two of them now, and I was starting to think foolish thoughts. I was also starting to get cramps in my legs. You try it! Put your legs up on a coffee table or hassock or something and don't move them and after about a half hour, see what you are feeling. I started to uncross my legs and Britt snapped to seated attention instantly. "Don't move, professor. Just sit back where you were."

I'd had about enough. My head was throbbing. I was bleeding earlier, but it had stopped, I think. My legs were beginning to ache from being in one position, and I was tired of just sitting. I'm not a patient person, and not used to being bossed, except by Em. "Excuse me," I said, as plaintively as I could. "I'm nearly sixty years old and my circulation isn't what it used to be. I need to move my legs a bit. I'm also in a lot of pain, and I'm a bit dizzy and I am starting to feel nauseated. I need to move to a more comfortable position. Please, I am not *trying* anything."

Britt's eyes narrowed with the same cold threat as they had with Les's "beer run" offer. I half expected to have my head whacked from behind with the barrel of Zach's gun again. After a moment, her features relaxed a bit. "Yes, your legs would be hurting about now," she said. With a

37

glance over my head and a silent message passed, she said, "All right, professor. You may put your legs down. Listen to me carefully. Do not move suddenly. You may sit forward. Zach has *you* targeted. Need I remind you that Zach is a very good shot? Think hard about how easily he dropped your dog, Sadie wasn't it? Not a whimper, just instant death. That can be yours as well Dr. Richardson. And that will leave your wife, alone... with us. Do you understand?" She paused and glared for another moment, "I see that you do. You may move now."

I squeezed Em's hand, and released it. I slowly uncrossed my legs and used my hands to balance on the couch as I slowly bent first one and then the other leg and put my feet on the floor. I put my right hand on the back of the couch and the other on the front of the seat cushion, and pushed my way to an upright sitting position at the front edge of the couch. As I "ootzed" forward, I turned a bit to my right as I used my right hand for leverage, giving me the opportunity to glance back into the dining room. Sure as shooting, Zach was there, half seated on the dining room table, relaxed, the gun in his hand. Silent. Watching.

Another piece snapped into place. She knew Sadie's name. She knew we had a dog. How? Credit card information? Vet bills? That wouldn't explain knowing Sadie's name, though. Wait, yes it would. Our vet bills had all the medical results, the name of the 'patient' and even an electronic photo. But, how would they get hold of them? They handed them to us as hard copy when we paid at the end of a visit. Prescriptions? Dog license! That is a public record, I suppose, although I never thought to access such a thing. What would be the point? I guess if you wanted to know how many dogs someone had… and the only reason I could think of for needing that kind of information was happening to us. Dogs equal security. Guns equal security. If one intended on taking over a household, it would make sense to know what obstacles were in place. It had a beautiful, stark sort of logic to it. I could admire the fact that somebody had done their homework. I am a professor, after all.

Before the silence could settle back into place and create its own momentum again, Em spoke for the first time since her 'eulogy' to Sadie, torn from her in the opening seconds of this hell. She had stopped quaking, and her voice was strong, no surprise to me, but I could hear the control she was exerting. "You've planned it well. Your information has been good. Guns, Sadie, timing, all organized. That takes intelligence, careful forethought, and a serious commitment of time and resources. There is nothing in the house that is worth that much effort. We don't have a big bank account or investments. There is nothing that would make it worth *this*. But, you know that. If you went to the trouble of checking for guns and dog ownership, you'd also know about our finances. You'd know that ransom makes no sense. Our families don't have money enough to speak about. There is only one thing left. You want one or both of us. Given your warning to my husband a moment ago, I'm guessing that you want *me*. That means that you want me to *do* something. Don't you think that it is about time that you told me what it is?"

I told you Em is smart. I had been working on the homework angle myself. This had to have been in the works for some time. You don't just decide on a whim to gather all sorts of information about folks and waltz in and kidnap them at gunpoint. You don't put a team of four together at a moment's notice, not who have worked together and have established a pecking order. And you don't have all this action with so few words without considerable understanding and foresight. Somebody had thought all of this through and so far seemed to have done a pretty good job of it. As usual, Em was a step or two ahead of me. I'd have gotten there, but she's quick.

Just to point out the obvious, not only was this planned over some time, it also took some money, some expertise and some clout. One can gather a great deal about a person on the web, but not at this level. This kind of information and action took some pull, and *that* meant that it was unlikely that it was the work of these twenty-somethings in our living room. There was somebody and some*thing* serious behind this. Hah! Take *that* Em!

Britt nodded condescendingly, and said, "Very good, Dr. Richardson. May I call you Rita? There are entirely too many Dr. Richardsons around here to keep things straight. Your reputation is clearly well deserved. Correct in every respect. But, no, I don't think that the time has quite arrived. However, I will take a few minutes while the boys are out to explain the rules."

I had lost a great deal of respect for Britt in the last moment or two. First, she had validated our thinking. She did not have to do that. It would have been to her advantage to keep us in the dark for as long as possible. Our deductions were good, of course, but she didn't have to let us know that. There is always uncertainty, and she should have played that out. Secondly, and more importantly, she had called Em "Rita" and if possible, she had made Em even angrier than before. I didn't have to see her eyes to know what color they were.

Okay, Britt-the-bitch, what kind of rules do you play by?

Chapter 7

Britt stood and crossed to the fireplace, directly in front of us. "We, the four of us, are going to move into your home for a short time. While we are here, you will not speak to each other. There will be no communication outside the house. As a matter of fact, while Les and Ray were "exploring" just now, they disconnected all of your phones, and removed all of the cables from your computer. For the time being, you are cut off from the outside world.

"This should not be a big problem for the time that we will be here. It is summer break after all, and it isn't unusual in the least for you two to be off someplace for a week's vacation or out of town to begin a new research project after school is out. To limit any concerns at your offices, we sent an email message to each. For you, Dr. Richardson," as she looked at me, "It says that you will be out of town for a few days and that you'll be checking your email. Actually, *you* won't, but we will. And for you," indicating Em, "the message simply says that you'll be out of the office working on a new research project, and email is the best way to contact you. Actually, we used one of your old messages that said the same thing and simply posted it with the new dates.

"There is no such thing as a normal schedule at the University for the next couple of weeks. Everyone is coming and going as they finish the odds and ends of the term and their summer plans kick in. Nobody will even think twice about you not coming into the office for a few days. We've checked both of your calendars, and they are completely open for the next week. Very accommodating of you. Aren't on-line calendars a wonderful convenience for everyone?"

As she stood in front of us and explained how clever they were, she idly gestured with the gun in her hand. It reminded me of someone at the dinner table, making a point with a fork or a spoon in their hand. It spoke of nonchalance, and a comfort level with the weapon that I, for one, did not find comforting at all. Actually, it was downright maddening and utterly unreal. Here she was standing in our living room, calmly describing how they had surgically removed us from our lives. The damned thing was, she was absolutely correct. It was very unlikely that anyone would notice that we were missing, at least not for a couple of days.

She continued, "We replaced your home phones with an answering machine. You know that annoying woman who tells you, 'You have been connected to an automated answering system, to leave a call back number, dial 5, to leave a message hit pound or wait for the tone'? Oh, we've taken your cell phones, not that they have a connection out here. You know you really ought to switch carriers. Verizon does much better out here, I've found."

Yeah, right, you smug know-it-all bitch! It just so happens that we *like* not having coverage here. Did you ever think that we might not *want* to have folks calling us at home? Did you stop and think that we are just as happy without all that hassle and constant connectivity? Our students can't walk two steps outside of class without sticking a cell-phone in their ear to say something erudite such as, "Like, I dunno. Whazzup? I'm like just getting out of class.

Where, like, are you? Like, yeah..." Unlike them, Em and I delighted in our privacy. Although, at the moment, I *like, totally* would have loved to have been better connected, *like, y' know?*"

All the time she was talking I was concentrating like mad and trying not to look like it. Not a hard task for me, I am told repeatedly by Em. Britt was spewing information like a student who had failed to study for an essay exam. The fact that she was willing to give us such largesse suggested that she was unused to dealing with people who actually used their intelligence, or that she didn't care what we knew. Her association with people like Les hinted at the former, I hoped. The clear planning and the viciousness of their introduction pointed to the latter, not to mention that we had seen their faces and could identify them. While I was happy that we were gaining in the balance of information, they were still way ahead and it worried me. It came to me that at the end of *this* course, it would be 'pass-fail'... for keeps.

Now why would she know, or care about cell coverage out here? It is true that we are in a dead zone for Cinci Bell, but we've seen all kinds of delivery people and contractors of various sorts as they pulled out their phones and used them here with no problems at all. If the four of them had tied up our land line, they'd need their own phones to communicate. That begged the questions of communication with whom and for what purpose. Still, it was potentially useful information.

"When the boys return in a little while, we'll take turns as you get ready for bed. That is, you'll take turns getting ready, and we'll watch. As each of you takes your turn in the bathroom, the other will be with us... for obvious reasons. When you are both ready for bed, you, Rita," pointing the gun vaguely in Em's direction, "will be handcuffed to the bed in the master bedroom. You," meaning me, "will be similarly handcuffed in the room down the hall. We will check in on you occasionally through the night. I do hope you wear pajamas. Otherwise it could be a little embarrassing," she said with a little smile that said that she really didn't care one way or the other if we were embarrassed. "Actually, perhaps we should have you sleep nude. It might help the boys to stay awake and check on you more often."

The thought of Les and especially Ray eyeballing Em handcuffed and naked on the bed did not help my blood pressure at all. I could easily imagine either of them, or for that matter, any of them molesting her and I didn't like the thought one bit. Now that I had the thought, I wouldn't put it past Ray ogling me, either. That was disturbing on a whole different level. Live and let live. I have no problem with that. I hoped they agreed, in more ways than one, but that didn't mean that Ray was my type. Actually, I didn't particularly care for any of them.

"For now, I think we'll leave you your modesty. But, in return, I hope that you'll cooperate with us. Any resistance, any attempt at communication here or to the outside, and we will make things very difficult, very ugly and very painful.

"If you need to use the facilities during the night, please call out and one of us will unlock your handcuffs and

45

permit you to use the bathroom. Don't abuse the privilege. It will be much nicer for everyone if you permit us to be civil about all this.

"Tomorrow morning we'll reverse the process. Again you'll use the facilities to shower and dress, taking turns. When that is done we'll all meet downstairs, have breakfast, and then begin the day's work, Rita.

"Now, the dining arrangements; I understand that you are quite the cook, Professor. Sadly, we will not be partaking of your skills. We are going to have a prolonged picnic while we are here. We'll eat off of paper plates, and we'll have sandwiches and chips and fruit and veggies... all 'finger food'. We'll drink out of plastic cups. No utensils, you see. Nothing sharp or pointed. Nothing to break. Easy to clean up, too.

"I'm sorry, but there will be no hot food. The boys have pulled the circuit breaker out in the garage, so the stove won't work. The microwave has been unplugged and the cord has been cut. Same with the coffee pot and the toaster. You see, it makes it much nicer if you don't have to worry about when to throw some boiling liquid in our faces, or try to burn the house down to attract the fire department. We have removed all the matches and lighters and such.

"Oh, speaking of hot things. Rita, we will leave you the use of your blow dryer. You will want to look presentable. Just remember that while you are doing your hair, we'll have the Professor with us, so be careful, please.

"Back to the dining arrangements. We brought our own food, so we won't have to worry about having enough for everyone. We are, after all, thoughtful house guests. That also means that we won't have to worry about heavy cans, can openers, glass, things that might get added 'just for fun'. Have you ever tried *Dave's Insanity Sauce*? Well, all of those sorts of things are off the table, no pun intended.

"To make things easy on you, when the boys get back, they are going to get out the duct tape and go to work. They are going to seal all of the drawers and cabinets in the kitchen and in the bathrooms. They will tape the freezer shut. Frozen things can be such a bother, don't you think? You *have* heard the story about the woman who killed her husband with a frozen leg of lamb? Your food will be emptied from the refrigerator, and our perishable items will go in there. The wine cooler will be emptied and sealed. Not that Les would know good wine from bad, but you probably *do* have some good bottles in there. Pity, but no help for it; the university already has such a reputation for alcohol abuse.

"And then, of course, Dr. Richardson, we are going to empty the liquor cabinet. You will have to do without your famous *Wild Turkey*. I think that we'll all be better off with clear heads, don't you?

"Now, do you have any questions about the rules?"

Actually, I didn't have any questions at all. Not even one. Britt had covered all of the bases that I could think of and then some. I mean, duct tape? Seriously? Who would have thought of that? Maybe to tape our wrists and our

47

ankles or something, but to cover up the cabinets all over the house? You've got to be kidding me. That was thinking way ahead and at levels that bespoke thoroughness bordering on the manic. I was very impressed... and very scared. "Thorough" meant fewer mistakes and if they didn't make a mistake along the way, this was not going to end well.

Despite my fears, several things came to my mind at that point. I wanted to keep her talking. The more she said, the more we would know about how things stood. And, if she was talking, nobody was being beaten, shot, killed, maimed, raped, tortured, or asked to listen to rap music... the last being the most important of all. I also wanted to hear Zach if at all possible. I wasn't sure how he fit into the team, yet, and I wanted to get a sense of his place in the scheme of things. Third, she *really* pissed me off about the Wild Turkey, and I wasn't just going to sit still for that nonsense. Actually, that was not number three on my list of issues except that I thought I might use it as a way to start influencing things a little bit. If I could encourage them to think that I was a total nincompoop, I might be able to improve the possibilities later.

"I, uh... I have a question."

"Yes, Professor," said Britt.

"Well, I... I am impressed with your planning. I must say, you don't seem to have missed anything. I don't know what to say, or to think. This is all quite beyond me. I can't imagine what you are after, but I certainly don't want any more violence. So, please... I, we... will cooperate however we can. Just, please don't hurt us. Please. We'll do whatever you say. You are in command of the entire situation... Nothing left to chance..."

Britt interrupted, "Professor... Professor! Is there a question in there somewhere? I seem to have missed it if there was."

"I, uh... yes. Of course. I'm not thinking straight, I guess. I mean, I am in some considerable pain. Do you think that I could have a cold wash cloth, and perhaps some ice to put on my head? And, while I appreciate your concern over the effects of alcohol, before you close the bar, do you think that I might have a drink? I think that right now it might help rather than hurt the situation. Please. I could really use it."

I did my best to look as miserable and supplicating as I possibly could. It wasn't hard to do. Frankly, I felt pretty miserable and I really did want a drink. My head was throbbing and I felt a bit nauseated and a lot drained. The adrenalin from the initial shock and pain had worn off and I was shaky to say the least. Who was I kidding? I was a lot nauseous.

I looked at Britt, and her expression was one of disdain, or maybe even disgust. There wasn't any pity; that was certain. Most importantly, though, I did not see any evidence of disbelief. If I had overplayed it, she would not have bought in. She appeared to be thinking about it and hadn't dismissed it out of hand, and that was good.

I was doing my best to accomplish three things; well, four if you count the drink. Most importantly I was trying to begin to lay the groundwork for a role. I wanted them to think that I was a drunken, broken down, wimpy, old fool. I wanted them to think me weak and pliable, and absolutely no threat to them. I had no idea what good that would do me, but I reasoned that it was like Harry Houdini expanding his chest before being strapped into a straight jacket. Whatever "play" or slack I could create, could come in handy. Maybe. Secondly, I wanted to establish a dialogue. So far this had been almost entirely a one-direction experience. They had asked us to be silent and were going to enforce silence between Em and me, presumably to keep us from colluding in any effort to create trouble. Unidirectional communication reinforced their command position, and to the extent that we could create some give and take, we might be able to learn more, or even establish some rapport. Lastly, I was hoping that at some point we might be able to get them to take some symbolic step in our direction. Acceding to an innocuous request for a drink would be such a step, and could lead to other steps down the line.

In essence, I was following the standard opening processes of a sales call or a negotiation. I had "cold called" with my request to move my legs. Now I was "warm calling". Establish ongoing communication, find common ground, build respect and rapport, and ask for some action from the other party to come toward your position. Who knows, maybe I could sell them something later on. Like, letting us live, perhaps.

The fact that Britt had not instantly said, "No!" was an encouraging sign, and to my surprise, after a moment of consideration she actually agreed. "Zach, please pour the Professor a drink. Use one of our plastic cups. I believe that he would like a double Wild Turkey on the rocks, no water. Isn't that correct, doctor?"

"I, that is, yes. Exactly. Thank you," I fumbled in reply.

As I heard rustling noises in the bags and then the pleasant 'plook' of the Wild Turkey cork coming loose, Em joined into the game, just as I had hoped she would. She knew the steps of selling as well as I did, and knew damned well that I was not as wimpy as I was behaving. She would have figured that something was going on and when she saw an opening for her to chime in, she did.

"While you are being so kind as to allow my husband to actually drink *our own* liquor, do you think you could complete the task and arrange for the wet wash cloth and some antiseptic and a baggie of ice, or is that beyond you?" she said sarcastically. "I expect that at least one of you is probably smart enough to string a WHOLE four items together, but then A.D.D. so often accompanies sociopathic behavior. Was it your inability to follow directions in school that caused you to feel so badly about yourself?" said Em with her finest professorial, holier-than-thou disdain.

Now, having been on the receiving end of Em's sharp wit and even sharper tongue on many an occasion, I can speak from experience. She can really dish it out. She has an outstanding vocabulary, an active wit, a creative bent, and when provoked she can be outstandingly hurtful. It's a beautiful thing, if you are not on the receiving end.

She had recognized that she held a certain amount of power in the overall scheme of things. They needed her for something, logically something having to do with her position or skills. If they were willing to go through all of this to acquire access to those skills, it must be pretty important to them. That gave her a measure of power. Recognizing that, Em had obviously figured she could play hard-ass. Good for her! The more she could irritate them and tweak their proverbial noses, the more they would focus on her as being the person with whom they had to contend, and the more they would ignore me. I hoped. Of course, that also made it likely that they would take out their frustrations with Em on me. That part, I wasn't too happy about, but it was about the only approach we had at the moment.

As I saw it, both Em and I had a fine line to walk. She had to irritate them and keep them focused on her antics and bad temper but not go so far that they would retaliate on me in any significant way. By significant, I mean incapacitating and permanent. On the other hand, I had to act innocuous, frightened, and eager to please. If I could play the role of the stereotypical academic-liberal-pacifist, that would be great. At the same time, I'd have to be careful not to cross the line into "chewing the scenery". If I hammed it up too badly, they'd become suspicious.

For that matter, they had a balancing act as well. They needed Em to do something for them. It was something in public, apparently, since they wanted her to do her hair and look "presentable". If they did not impress her sufficiently to control her, she could simply wave her arms and scream bloody murder and that would be the end of it. Might be messy, but it would end there. On the other hand, if they were too brutal, she might get to the point of saying 'to hell with it' and, again it would end there.

Em's jab found its mark and Britt's face clouded over as it had when Les had erred a short while ago. She started to say something, but I quickly added, "Oh! Yes, please. I forgot about antiseptic. That is very important. We have both hydrogen peroxide and poly-bacitracin. Very important to use both, you see. One is for cleansing, and the other provides an ongoing germicidal prophylaxis. We are very careful, you see. We used to use mycitracin, but all of the studies showed that the effects were nowhere near as beneficial as the poly-bacitracin. As a matter of fact..."

"Yes, professor. We'll see to it," Britt interrupted, clearly impressed by my pedantic blithering or by Em's insult, or both.

Undaunted, I continued my puling, "We keep hydrogen peroxide both in the corner cabinet in the kitchen and in the bathroom upstairs. Not only can you use it for cleansing wounds, if you dilute it, it makes an excellent oxygenating mouthwash. But, I'm afraid we only keep the poly-bacitracin upstairs in the top bathroom drawer. Honestly, I have been saying that we should keep another tube here in the kitchen. You know, more accidents occur in the kitchen than almost anywhere in the home?" I am told that I tend to 'lecture' on occasion, and while I am a firm believer in 'life-long learning' some people are just not appreciative of the gift of knowledge.

"That's enough!" Britt said sharply. "I said we'll see to it. Now, do you have any further questions? No? Good. Now, please sit back, both of you and put your feet back up on the coffee table while Zach gets the rest."

Em made a an exaggerated show of complying, and as she did she made a noise that was half "hmph" and half that sort of "ch" sound that you make when you are trying to work up the junk in your throat to spit. It had great tone and modulation and it was supremely derogatory. In one sound it conveyed a complete critique of Britt's ancestry, intelligence, appearance and capabilities, all of which Em obviously found utterly lacking. Nice!

Britt glared at Em and backed away to the corner chair and brought her gun up to the ready position, and I heard the flat rattle of ice cubes in a plastic cup right behind my right ear. I turned my head and there was a red plastic cup, the kind that the students use to play 'beer-pong', in Zach's hand. He was still standing behind the couch and had extended his right arm to full-length. His left hand still held his automatic at the ready, his arm bent, and the gun pointed at the ceiling.

I took the cup with my left hand, slowly. Zach backed away as I said, "Thank you." Now, that was the first thing that had gone right all evening. Zach had never worked in a bar, or if he had, he had lost money for the owner but had gotten great tips. He had poured at least a quadruple, and I intended to make use of every last drop. He might be a dog-killer, but he knew how to pour a drink.

I took a good swallow of the cold, but not yet diluted Wild Turkey and felt it hit bottom with an agreeable 'thud'. Britt glanced over our heads and nodded imperceptibly, then walked around the couch so that she would be behind us. Then we heard Zach pulling out drawers and opening cabinets. He went upstairs and returned a few moments later. We heard him turn on the water at the kitchen sink, and gather some ice cubes from the door dispenser. Then Britt came back around in front of us carrying a plastic grocery sack which she tossed in Em's lap.

"All right, you wanted it. You fix him up. I'm *sure* YOU have the intelligence to handle *that*, or are you like most professors; you can talk for hours in the abstract but can't *do anything*?" she said.

This was good. I'd had another slug of my drink and it was beginning to take hold and back off the pain in the side of my head a tad. Em had clearly hit something sensitive with Britt's ego, so the exchange with Les had been indicative of power issues after all. I was about to have my wound cleaned up. Everybody except Zach was talking with each other, and they had come our direction just a bit. Why, in just a few more minutes I'd be selling them acres of swampland, small bridges, and truckloads of *Sham-Wows*!

Em took out the wet wash cloth and had me turn toward her. As she began daubing at the side of my head, she acidly pointed out, "Yes, of course. We of the academy can do so little. That is, of course, why *you* need *my* assistance for your project and must resort to criminal behavior to obtain it. Your logic is impeccable, *dear*. One really should complete one's education. A mind is a terrible thing to waste, even a simple one."

I *thought* I saw Britt's eyebrows begin to narrow, but at that moment Em managed to press the exact spot on the side of my head where the barrel of Zach's gun had connected. I saw a blinding flash of white, just for an instant, and then the nerves stopped being overloaded and actually connected and the pain hit like an electric shock. I jerked my head to the side and said something clever like, "Ah!"

I was halfway planning on adding to my wimpy image anyway, but damn that hurt! I didn't have to act a part on this one. It brought tears to my eyes.

Britt smirked and said, "Nicely done, nurse Rita."

Em poured a little hydrogen peroxide onto the wash cloth and continued her ministrations. She was a bit more careful around the actual wound this time. She dabbed on a bit of the poly-bacitracin, wiped her hands, and handed me the baggie with ice.

"He could use a paper towel. I've opened the wound and it is bleeding a little, again," she said.

A moment later, Zach provided the towel over my shoulder. "Thank you," I said, ever polite. I folded the paper towel into a layered square and put it over the wound, then held it in place with the baggie of ice. "That is much better. Thank you, Em, and thank you Britt and Zach. You didn't have to do that, I know." So, with my right hand holding the ice pack to my head, I went to drinking with my left hand. Hard to believe, but I have a great deal in common with Michael Jordon. We can both take successful shots with either hand and we both play above the rim. He's taller, though.

Chapter 8

From where I was seated on the living room couch, one can see out the front windows and that provides a view of part of the driveway. A little while later I saw headlights but not the familiar pattern of my Toyota. Apparently the boys were back.

I had wondered how they were going to work it when we saw their car and my Toyota leave earlier, but then I had other things to think about. Now I returned to thinking about the cars.

Oxford is a small town, and we had lived here for about thirty years. In some ways it is very open. It has a large transient population of students, and visitors, and parents, and speakers and performers and you name it. On any given day there would be hundreds of visitors to the campus, maybe thousands. When you add friends of students, spouses of faculty and employees, sports teams, vendors and even those who come to prey upon the innocent, the numbers add up. It is not going to be like the scene in 'Kindergarten Cop' when the kid points and yells, 'Stranger!'

The University has a student population of about sixteen thousand on the Oxford campus. Every year about four thousand graduate and about four thousand matriculate to take their places. Like most universities, there is an eclectic blend of races, colors, nationalities, ages, sizes, shapes, and personal styles. From aborigine to Zambian, and from geek to Goth, we have it all. Britt and Zach and Les and Ray would raise not even one eyebrow.

One or more of them were going to do something in public with Em. I had no clue what that might be, but it was obvious that they had figured on more than one day. The food told me that. They were going to be visible to other people, people who might know Em and therefore they wanted her to appear normal. They would not be able to wave their guns around, so they needed some leverage to keep Em in line. So, 'The role of leverage will be played this evening by John Richardson...'

While the Oxford community is amazingly open and transient, it is like most small towns and extraordinarily close knit and insular. The 'townies', the people who live here and work here year in and year out, are a relatively small number. We all know each other. To misquote the old saying, 'You can't swing a dead cat without hitting someone you know.' Never understood why someone would want to swing a dead cat, but you get the point. We know the merchants, the owners of the restaurants, the service folks. Our kids played little league with their kids, or went to school together. It is like Mayberry where Floyd the barber cuts your hair, and here during the summertime you can get your hair cut and buy fresh produce from his garden all in one stop.

So, I wondered about the car situation. If they drove their car, it wouldn't be long before the neighbors began to wonder about the strange car coming and going out of the Richardson's driveway. Particularly, if the neighbors didn't see either of our cars, they might indeed raise an eyebrow. If they saw one of our cars, they wouldn't think about it at all unless they saw Em in the passenger seat. If

Britt or Zach let Em drive, or even stay in the front of the car, they ran the risk of her accelerating to eighty miles an hour and slamming into a slow moving piece of farm machinery or some such. Or she might even accelerate past the Oxford Police Department and have 'Barney Fife' give chase, complete with his one bullet.

If they put her into the back seat, they could eliminate any risk of her playing demolition derby for dummies, but then they would look odd to anyone who saw Em sitting in the back like 'Miss Daisy'. By driving one of our cars they eliminated all sorts of hassles with parking, and let me tell you, the one thing that will get you noticed around here by the police faster than anything is not having the appropriate parking sticker. Murder, mayhem? Hmph, please. Peanuts. Park your car with the wrong permit and they WILL come after you with "THE CLUB", wheel boots, and pitchforks and tar. This is about money, and the University had ostracized many an alumnus worth millions in order to collect a parking fee of thirty dollars. Hey, a Ford in the hand…

So, either way they were taking a risk. Worry the neighbors, maybe, or take a risk of somebody seeing Em riding around like she is on Cleopatra's barge, eating dates and being fanned by ostrich feathers. If I were in their shoes, I'd put Em into the rear passenger seat of their car. It would look like she was with friends and they preferred to drive, particularly if the two girls were in the back. My bet was that they had taken the hanging tag out of my car and put it onto the mirror of theirs. That would solve the parking problem for them. Even the most Nazi-like of the parking police weren't likely to check the tag number against the license plate.

They had to have dumped my car someplace. Now that was interesting. It emptied a spot in the garage, so their car could remain hidden. But, it isn't all that easy to just abandon a car and have it be ignored for any length of time. The boys had been gone for only about an hour, maybe a little more. That limited the possibilities. They would have had to put the car somewhere where it would not attract attention for several days. Metered locations wouldn't work. University parking lots wouldn't work. If they left it in town, odds were that somebody would see it and recognize it as mine. If it sat for a couple of days, it would be noticed and somebody would probably call to see if I needed a ride or something. As I said, Oxford is a small town. Anyplace in town would be a problem. Student rental housing was notorious for having cars towed.

Unless it were really off the beaten path, the surrounding area wouldn't be safe. At the office we had a running joke with one of my colleagues because his car was seen outside a porno-video place about twelve miles away. This was ten years ago. He was actually getting a VCR fixed, but that didn't keep us from busting his chops about it forever. You had to know the guy, but it really was a VCR deal, I assure you.

Even though we are pretty much out in the boonies you couldn't just park it out on some back road. The township police covered a lot of territory, and the county sheriff's office did, too. An abandoned car would be seen and noted pretty quickly.

61

They had to find a spot where they could park for free, and leave it for several days. It had to be someplace unlikely to be noticed by people who knew me and they couldn't just abandon it to be found by the cops. Shopping mall? That would work, at least in the short run. There were three good sized shopping areas within a thirty minute drive, Hamilton, Colerain, and Harrison. Two of them were reasonably likely to be frequented by friends and neighbors. If I were in charge, I would put it in the Bigg's lot in Harrison. Not many Oxford folks went that way.

Well, that was a nice mental exercise, but it really didn't get me anywhere. If I could figure out a way to deal with the car issue, they probably could, too. They might make a mistake, but somehow I didn't think it would be on something like this. I was looking for weaknesses, but so far I wasn't finding much. They had pretty much shown themselves to be experts to this point.

As I mentioned, my area is business strategy and Em's expertise is in the area of local and regional history, roughly over the past 200 years. They wanted something from her that had to do with that. And... it had to be something that was not available on line. If they could get to it on line, they would be upstairs on the computer right now. So, they were going to have to make a field trip, or trips.

Whatever they wanted also had to be *wrong* somehow. It had to be illegal, immoral or very dangerous. They could have just contacted Em in her office and offered her a research grant or honorarium of some sort. She had done those kinds of things in the past. Local organizations, historical societies, companies, even families had contacted her for her expertise and uncanny ability to ferret out cool stuff. Sometimes they asked her to volunteer her time, sometimes they paid quite well. She kind of balanced it all out and made certain the various animal shelters and protection groups got their share. Anyway, if the bums had made it lucrative enough, Em would have taken it on, if it were an honorable project. Apparently it wasn't.

So, what was public, related to area history, and could require enough work for several days of effort, all in a cause that was seriously bogus, somehow? Damned if I knew. So, I addressed the bottom third of my cup of sour mash bourbon and pondered while I waited for 'the boys' to make their grand return.

Just for the fun of it, I was betting myself that Les would come in first and say something stupid. I expected Ray to follow along quietly behind and say nothing. Put a Coke on it?

Chapter 9

We normally keep the outside flood lights on until we go to bed. The can lights recessed in the eaves and back areas of the house we tended to keep on all night. The controls for most are in the kitchen and Zach had hit all the right buttons and switches, and without even trial and error. Nice. More evidence that we had been the subjects of detailed surveillance. Despite the lack of sight-lines, Britt stood and lowered the shades, shutting off the view from the living room.

That was going to present me with a problem in the morning and I would have to act lively in order to overcome the challenge without attracting attention. Well, there was a way.

We could hear the car in the garage. The door had come up with its usual low, mechanical grumbling. We could hear the motor, and then its silence. The car doors opened and shut, one after the other. Down came the garage door, and then the laundry room door opened and slammed.

"Hi, folks! We're home! Didja miss us?" called Les as he strode into the house and flumped down in the chair opposite Britt, and to our right. Told ya. Somebody owes me a Coke.

"No. You are five minutes late," Britt said sternly. "Was there a problem?" She just wasn't going to give Les any slack at all.

"Hunh? Nah. We cruised a bit until we found an empty spot out in the country someplace. Nobody coming or going and no houses nearby or anything. Dumped the dog in the ditch. Collar and tags are out in the garage. Then I dropped the car at the parking lot at Bigg's. Locked it up and walked around the corner so nobody would see and got into our car and came back. Just like we said. Nobody saw us, and even if they did, I'm leaving the car for a buddy, big deal. Who's gonna even notice? Ten year old car in a shopping center parking lot? Shoulda let the air out of one of the tires so it'd have a reason to stay there. What bullshit."

Ray had unobtrusively glided to a stop and was now leaning on the same spot on the wall that he had inhabited before they left. Britt looked him directly in the face and asked, "Is that right? Exactly right?" Ray nodded and said nothing.

"All right then, *Rita,* I assume that even professors can manage to get ready for bed and brush their teeth without assistance. Nevertheless, we'll keep an eye on you to make sure you don't forget to floss. Remember that Les and Zach will be down here with your husband, okay? Now, get up, slowly and move upstairs."

Em looked at Britt as if she were something gooey that had attached itself to the bottom of her shoe, stood, and shook her head as if to say, "Pathetic." She bent and kissed me, not hard but with great meaning, and turned to head for the stairs.

"How precious!" smirked Britt.

65

Without saying a word, with great tenderness and deliberation, Em dropped her right hand to caress the left side of my face for just an instant. The expression she conveyed to Britt was one of exquisite pity, and the most devastating condemnation I think that I have ever seen. Subtle and brilliant. I told you Em could dish it out.

"Move!" Britt commanded, and Em turned and with great poise climbed the stairs.

It was hard to read Britt's face at that point. She was clearly not happy, but it was hard to say if she was thinking 'on plan' or stressed by the pressures of holding hostages, or angry with Em for being a pain, or rueful of life-paths not taken. Or, she might have had gas. Who knows?

"Um, ah. Excuse me. You are Britt, I gather? May I call you by that name? I, uh... I believe that there is a logistical functionality that must be accomplished, and while I don't mean to suggest that you have failed to consider it, nevertheless it is something to which we should attend." I have often found that proper grammar sets folks' teeth on edge, so I was in full grammatical form.

"As you will have, no doubt, ascertained from your researches, we have two cats. I hope that you will not find it necessary to harm them. They are innocuous creatures, and can do you no harm. Most people think that cats are 'stand-offish' but in reality they are quite loving and warm. I believe that they actually crave our company as demonstrated by the close proximity they choose to maintain whenever..."

"What is it Professor? What do you think we missed?" Britt said, cutting me off.

I really can't tell you why she kept interrupting me. Such poor manners, really.

"Well, I... ah. I was just saying that the cats are free spirits and they come and go as they please. We believe that they should have the ability to go in and out as they desire. I should not want them to surprise you as they appear."

"Okay, great. You've got cats. We know."

"Well, they tend to jump up and if one is not attentive, they can be somewhat, shall we say, abrupt. I would hope that no one is startled, lest someone be hurt inadvertently." Blech. Talking like this was beginning to set *my* teeth on edge.

"Got it. We'll be careful."

"Yes, well. You see, that is not precisely what I was going to say. I mean, that is important to keep under consideration, of course, but that is not the issue to which I referred a moment ago."

"What IS it?" Her tone of exasperation at having to listen to my ongoing drivel was a nice reward.

"In all actuality, I was simply going to point out that someone will have to feed them."

I couldn't believe that she was actually buying the whole professorial vocabulary-speech thing. I was testing it out, but wary that at any moment she could say, "Knock it off, asshole. You aren't that goofy." Still, the stereotypes of professors are widely held, and everybody likes to look down on people, particularly if they are just a little jealous. I'd back off if I needed to, but the more that she thought me to be a total nerd-ball, the better.

I actually think that this time they forgot. Their perfect plans had failed them. Nobody had considered that the two cats would need food. The resulting look I got from Britt was a mix of "Well, duh," and "Oh, shit."

Just call me 'Jesse Owens' at the '36 Olympics. Take that, super beings!

"You'll find dry food in a container in the pantry. We also give them half a can of food in the morning and at night. The cans are self-opening, so you won't need a can-opener or any utensil beyond a plastic spoon."

Now, I could hear the wheels turning in Britt's mind. This was not part of the plan. They had already killed the dog. The cats would either starve or there could be some way to dispose of them, and avoid the hassles. Why deal with it?

"Of course," I said mildly. "Em really loves the cats. She would be very upset if their routine were to be interrupted." Sorry, kids. I had just handed your furry little butts over to the bad guys as co-hostages. Maybe I had just saved your lives. Maybe I had put you on the block ahead of my spot in line. Either way, I'd bet that you would be fed tonight. Small victories.

A little while later it was my turn to get ready for bed. Zach and Les chaperoned me. Em was in the master bedroom. I was in the guest room. They handcuffed me as they had promised, and I had a little play so that I could roll over without too much discomfort.

The last thing I heard before exhaustion and Wild Turkey overwhelmed me was the sound of duct tape being ripped from the roll and somewhere the sound of a cell phone activating, and in Britt's voice a muted, "We're in."

Chapter 10

Mouth… Dryer vent fluff.

Head… Deep, throbbing pain.

Stomach…Acid.

Wugh… Nausea.

Why is my wrist encumbered and sore?

Uhhhhhh… Not good.

I can't say that I normally spring from the embraces of slumber with the lithe grace of the woodland elf, but this was like clawing my way through a poorly constructed graduate thesis. Dear Lord, let it end!

I attempted to roll over and a sharp pain at my wrist accompanied the jerk that kept me from completing the effort. With that literal rude awakening, a few of the brain cells I had not immersed in alcohol last night began grinding out the morning news. I was in the guest room. It was morning, or close enough. I was chained to the bed. There were four armed assailants in my home. One of them had killed our dog. Yeah, and the Reds had probably lost last night, too.

I lay there for a moment, collecting my thoughts and continuing to inventory what I knew, what I thought I knew, and the current conditions.

It was Tuesday. This team of four youngish people had taken over our lives. They wanted Em to do something for them and they were going to take her away for the day, at least. I'd be kept here. That meant that they had to split up. Interesting to see how they divided up the work. They had provisioned for several days. In the short term we were probably safe from serious harm. In the longer term, they were going to kill us. It only made sense. Assault was a felony. Add a gun specification and it became a mandatory sentencing deal. Kidnapping, even if you didn't cross state lines, was a federal offense. I just couldn't see them walking away, saying, "Gee, folks, thanks for the nice visit!"

They had planned all of this extensively and well, so far as I could tell. I mean, I am not an expert on hostage taking and I have had no personal experience, at least up to now. I've heard of the Helsinki syndrome, and I've read news articles and seen a few documentaries on television, but I am not an expert. Still, it seemed to me that their logic had been pretty good and they had made no glaring mistakes, no gaps. I did not count cat nutrition as a major gaff.

I doubted that these four young people had the planning skills, the foresight, and most importantly the resources to conduct the surveillance that it must have taken. That meant that they had at least a backer, and probably a master somewhere. That complicated things.

So much for the predicament. Physically, I felt lousy. I was hung over, and I hadn't slept well. Gee, no kidding. I never could get comfortable with a handcuff on my right wrist and with all that had happened. I doubt that I had actually gotten more than a couple of hours of rest, really. I'd like to say that I fell asleep immediately and was fully refreshed and loaded for bear. I wasn't. I remembered seeing the clock at about three a.m. and again at about four a.m. At the moment, I felt like the rabbit remains the cats sometimes left on the doormat.

I would have continued to lie there and think deep thoughts about how all of this fit together and to cleverly plan to turn the tables on our captors, but I needed to use the bathroom. Wugh...

I started to yell, "Hey, asshole! I need to pee! Where would you like it?" But, I thought better of it and kept in character. I couldn't see any harm in continuing to play the professorial patsy. So, instead, I called out pathetically, "Excuse me? Is there anyone there? I need to use the restroom, please!"

Ray appeared immediately, didn't say a word. He came to the side of the bed and I could see Zach standing in the doorway, gun in hand. As Ray unlocked the handcuff on my wrist, I got a good whiff of him. It was uncanny. He smelled exactly like the blast you get when you open the garbage dumpster on a warm day. I could imagine legions of flies at his command like a poor man's remake of "Willard".

A little later I was seated at the dining room table. I guess I felt marginally better. I'd used the bathroom, showered and dressed. No shave. They had removed my shaving implements, and I assumed Em's were missing as well. I'd had a cup of juice, a somewhat mealy apple, and a half a ham and cheese sandwich, on white. Now, I ask you, what kind of breakfast is that? At a minimum they could have supplied bagels or even whole grain bread, but white bread? Plebian and ultimately, humiliating.

I was pleased to see Marty the cat at his normal spot on the kitchen counter, munching away at his bowl of dry food. I hadn't seen Joe, but he'd probably be around shortly. Someone had found the stash of cat food in the pantry, so at least that was in order. I desperately wanted a cup of coffee, even though I only drink decaf. Wasn't going to happen. Hot liquids, you know.

They had been good to their word. The kitchen cabinets were mummified in duct tape. They had not spared the grey, gooey ligaments in sealing off our stores. I idly surmised that they must have purchased the super economy size, and even at that they must have used more than one roll. As I looked a little more closely, I noted that there were two distinct patterns. In some places the tape was horizontal and perpendicular and mechanically precise in its smooth application. In other sections it appeared that one of the high priests of Imhotep had the palsy and a bad case of hiccups to boot. Ray and Les. Gotta love the boys.

I was waiting for Em to appear. Les was seated at the counter across from the table and a few feet beyond. Ray was, as ever, in a spot to cover both of us, and that placed him in the living room. I don't know if they had eaten. It seemed to me that they were using a lot of energy in double teaming us. At this rate they were going to tire appreciably as time passed. I hoped.

Under normal conditions Em was usually up first and downstairs to feed the animals. After she had showered she'd go down and feed the beasts, make coffee, and organize a brown bag lunch for me. She wasn't much of a breakfast eater. After I came down, I'd go to the end of the driveway and pick up the newspaper with whichever of the animals wanted to go along. For as long as I could remember we had a dog that would carry the paper back. No longer. There was no morning walk, and nobody had picked up the paper this morning.

Finally, the others appeared, Britt first, then Em and then Zach, each one coming down the stairs and reaching the bottom before the next started down. The kitchen clock said 8:30, give or take. Em crossed over to me, kissed me on the side of my face, and seated herself across the table, as directed by Britt's gun hand.

"Would you like some breakfast? Juice, a piece of fruit," asked Britt.

"I'd like some coffee, you stupid skank," growled Em.

One of the reasons that I didn't come down more promptly in the morning was Em's first cup of coffee. I suspect, but can never prove, that she had an entire pot of espresso before I arrived for my decaf every morning. Suffice it to say that Em likes her first cup of joe, a lot.

"My, my. Get up on the wrong side of the bed? Oh, of course, you couldn't. You were cuffed to the *right* side of the bed. Honestly, then, whatever is the matter?" Britt cajoled with a self-satisfied half-smile. "If you are a good girl, perhaps we can arrange for a cup where we are going."

Em just glared.

I didn't expect that Em had spent a good night, either. She was dressed nicely in slacks and a blue golf shirt. Her hair was done as always in a kind of a flip, I think it's called. Never kept track of how hair styles were named. Anyway, it was just above shoulder-length, straight with a nice curve at the bottom, parted at the side, and beautiful. Em worried about it and fussed with it in the mornings, and it always looked good. The only sign that she had a bad night was in the redness around her eyes. The redness made a nice counterpoint to the amber yellow. If Britt made a misstep, Em was going to make her pay, and it wouldn't be civilized.

Britt was dressed in jeans and a t-shirt that said "Ohio University: If it ain't on fire, it's not a party!" on it. Clever. She had on a pair of sneakers, no socks. Her hair was pulled back and held by a scrunchy or whatever they call it. She wore a little make-up, I guess, but it didn't do much to hide the hardness, and a little more had crept in over the night. She looked like a slightly older version of every student I'd ever seen. Maybe a graduate student look... grim, like during exam week. Gotta watch out for stress, it's a killer.

I figured it was about time that I go into my act again, and so cleared my throat and said, "I beg your pardon, but I am certain you are aware that we have medication that must be taken in the morning. Keeping a steady dosage in the bloodstream is clearly to be preferred, and while one's metabolism varies over the course of the day, timing the administration of the prescribed amounts is the optimum..."

I couldn't believe it, but Britt interrupted me again! Absolutely no manners. Hmph!

"Shut up, professor! Get their pills, Les."

I had hoped that they would at least have to untape a drawer, but no. Their intelligence gathering was complete on the medical front as well. Les delivered a few pills to Em and a few to me. Getting old is hell. "Geez, prof, you don't even have anything fun in there. We might have gotten a buzz on or something, but what a bummer." That Les, always a card.

A few minutes later, Britt announced, "All right, let's go Rita. You and Zach and I are going on a day trip. What fun! While we are gone, I want you to remember that Les and Ray will be here with your husband. We will call in during the day. If we miss a call by more than few minutes, they will simply kill him and disappear. If we are not back by the specified time, they will kill him and disappear. If *anything* goes wrong, they will kill him and disappear. Do you understand the situation?"

"Of course," Em replied cooly. "You are going to run us all over Manhattan searching school buildings while you steal the gold from the Reserve Bank, and pretend that you are upset that John pushed your brother off the Nakatome Plaza building. Did you sleep with your brother, too?"

Not up to her normal standards, but then, she hadn't had her coffee yet. Give her time.

"Okay, out."

Britt led the way, followed by Em. Zach, wearing jeans and sneaks and a t-shirt and zip-up, grey hoodie sweatshirt, took up the rear. Just a run-of-the mill graduate student.

As I heard the garage door go up, I stood slowly and asked, "May I use the restroom, please. I try to stay regular and this is my normal time. Right after breakfast. You know, keeping to a schedule is the best method to maintain one's constitution. There are any number of studies on it, you know."

"Yeah, right. Who gives a shit? You do! Ha! Go for it, prof," joked Les.

I stepped into the half-bath next to the entry and watched out the window as the car disappeared up the driveway. As I had conjectured, Zach was driving, Britt was directly behind him and Em was in the right side rear passenger seat. That made sense, they were taking no chances.

I took my time in the bathroom, certainly long enough to make it seem reasonable. Then I flushed, and then took about three times longer than a normal human being at the sink with the hot water running. I doubted that they would notice, but on the off chance, I wanted them to keep thinking that I was thoroughly washing my hands like a good, wimpy intellectual would.

When I came out, Les said, "Okay, Prof. Here's the deal. We're gonna find you a book or something to read, and you're gonna sit on the couch and take it easy for a while. Me and Ray are gonna take turns keeping an eye on you this morning. Then we're gonna have lunch. So, let's go upstairs and you can pick out a book or two and just relax for a bit."

The "library" is upstairs. Actually, it is all over the upstairs because I have a tendency to collect books. Em is happy to use library resources, or to go online or whatever. I like to have my own copy to hold and to pull off the shelf and reread, or to find a reference. The result of years of collecting and keeping books was that we had overburdened the bookshelves in the library room and had spread to shelves in all of the upstairs rooms.

In keeping with my "egghead" persona, I selected the classic On War by Carl von Clausewitz, the Prussian general and military philosopher from the Napoleonic era. I thought the boys would be excited to hear my comments on the application of two-hundred year old principles to modern business practices. Besides which, the old boy had some really sound ideas on marshalling of resources and timing of attack, and I thought that I might brush up.

As we went back to the living room, I passed by the end of the kitchen counter where our mail and newspapers collect. Everybody has a spot like that. All the junk mail and the newspapers and the stuff that you don't want to throw away yet, but aren't ready to read or deal with right now piles up there. After a while, you sort through it and throw 90 percent of it away without even reading it, but it was absolutely necessary for you to let it ripen first. In passing, I grabbed the most recent copy of *Golf Digest* off the corner, in case I got bored with Clausewitz.

I sat on the couch. Les settled into the corner chair, his gun on his lap. Ray went upstairs and did not reappear. I thought it likely that he was going to get some sleep. They had been on watch all night, and they were going to need rest at some point. Again, I'm no expert on abduction, but being on guard is probably hard work if done properly. The price of constant vigilance and all that. So, Les would watch for a while and then he would sleep while Ray kept an eye out, I guessed.

I turned one of the pillows sideways on the couch, put my legs up, stretched out and began to read. I got about five pages into the preface before I fell asleep. Old von Clausewitz would have been proud of how successfully I limited my expenditure of resources.

Chapter 11

I was startled out of a sound sleep by a cell phone ringing. It jolted me awake there on the couch. I opened my eyes to see that Ray had now replaced Les in the corner chair. I was amazed to see that he had the copy of *Golf Digest* in his hands. That was a shocker for sure. He answered the phone by thumbing it into life with his right hand, then held it to his ear.

"Yeah," then he listened for a few seconds.

"No problems," then he listened for a few more seconds.

"Yeah," and he hung up, again with his right thumb, and put the phone into his right pants pocket.

Wow! That Ray, what a talker! He had just infinitely expanded the number of words I had heard from him since the outset.

I glanced at my watch which told me that it was a little after eleven. I closed my eyes again, and resettled myself on the cushions. As I said, I hadn't slept well last night, but the two-hour nap had done me some good. I had some thinking to do, and now was the time. I needed more information than I had, but given Ray's elocutionary ebullience, I figured on collecting from Les. That would have to wait until lunch, it appeared.

I don't think that I had slept through a call, so this was their first check-in. A couple of hours had elapsed. They hadn't exchanged any real information other than to make sure that all systems were operational. "I'm okay, you're okay."

Well, they probably didn't want to get on their cell in a public place and ask, "Do you still have the professor hand-cuffed securely?"

They had left just before nine o'clock and they were headed somewhere public. What opens at nine? They could be driving for hours to get wherever, but why waste the time? If you were going to spend the day doing something and left around nine, it made sense that you'd be going somewhere that opened then. Why get there at 9:45? For that matter, if they were going to go to Columbus or something, why stay here? We could have "camped" someplace closer.

Given that they needed an historian, and one of the best at that, my bet was that they were headed to one of the libraries, or archives or historical collections around Miami. As I thought it, I knew it was true. It just made too much sense. They had young people dressed like students. They were keeping me as insurance to force Em to perform. The timing fit in all kinds of ways. The campus would be almost deserted at this time of the summer. No pesky students milling around. Many of our friends and colleagues would be gone. Offices open at nine a.m.

Of course all of this could be completely off base, and they could be using Em to make porno videos in Millville, or they could be forging betting slips for the trotter races in Lebanon, or they could be cornering the market on antique skee-ball machines in Fairhaven. Somehow I doubted those alternatives. My hypothesis was that they were right on Miami's campus deep into some research that demanded Molly Mae's insights.

81

If I was correct, we'd get another phone call, possibly two during the afternoon. Anyway, that is how I would do it. I'd make the calls at pre-set, but apparently random times to keep me from planning anything. They wouldn't want to call all that often because it meant interrupting what they were doing, or splitting up so one could call while the other watched Em. I think that they would be very, very careful with Em in public. Hell, I always was!

It was interesting that they left Chang and Eng at home to watch me. That had all kinds of implications. Now, as a professor I have spent over thirty years interacting with students and gauging their mental capacities. I confess that I have occasionally been surprised, but for the most part I can judge who will be the players and who will sit on the sidelines, who will catch on quickly, and who will not.

It was pretty clear from last night that Britt was the boss, and that Zach was number two. Les and Ray were not in the same league. They were not leaders, they were extras. They were shock troops. They were go-fers, and there was a certain resemblance with Ray's teeth.

Now, I could think of four reasons why you would leave the two nincompoops in one spot while you took the two stars to another spot. Reason number one: you needed the brain power of the two stars in whatever was going on at their location, and the cannon fodder couldn't help. Reason number two: like hockey, you kept your lines together because they played off of each other's strengths that way. Reason number three: you needed smart people for one task and you did not need smart people for another task. Reason number four: the fans had stuffed the ballot box and you had to play somebody from every team for P.R. purposes.

When you really looked at it, reasons one, two and three all fit together. Reason number four was just a slam on Bud Selig, and his answer would have been to have people running all over the house, taking turns every fifteen minutes and we'd all walk away with nothing decided when we ran out of players. Okay, so it was NOT number four.

Whatever Em was doing at their direction was complicated. Couldn't be anything simple or they would have done it themselves. They needed serious smarts and were willing to go deep into the criminal code to get there. They needed people who could watch over Em and make certain she was doing her job. That meant they needed to be of the right age and image, they needed to be capable, they needed to be smart, and they needed to be seriously bent. Other than the right age and image thing, it sounded like Bernie Madoff.

So, Britt and Zach had to go with Em They figured that the Bobbsy Twins could handle the old addle-pated professor. That pissed me off, but on the other hand, I kind of liked the challenge. The best part of it was that they had put the "second line" into the game against some serious opposition – me. At least I hoped that I could play. We were going to see, no doubt.

The vaguest outlines of a plan were taking shape in my mind. I had lots to think about and many factors to consider and validate. There were far too many assumptions and woefully incomplete data with which to contend, but I was beginning to see a pattern. With a modicum of contrary statistical tendencies and operating at broad confidence intervals a nominal outcome might be attained. In other words, we had a chance, but we'd have to get lucky.

Chapter 12

Sometime short of one p.m. Les reappeared. I had spent the rest of the morning lounging on the couch, reading von Clausewitz and thinking about what I needed to do. It was simple, really. I needed to find a way to overpower two thugs, "Thing One and Thing Two", who were infinitely better at this line of work than I. Second, I needed to overpower a second set of thugs who were holding my wife hostage at gunpoint, and who were in a different location. As the great sage, Bullwinkle Moose of cartoon fame said, "Nothing up my sleeve..."

I'd heard the shower upstairs a few minutes ago, and now Les reappeared, freshly scrubbed. He looked all bright and pink and cherubic. He fairly glowed with good humor and bonhomie.

"That's a great shower you got there, Doc! Lotsa pressure and lotsa hot water. There just isn't anything as great as shower head, but you gotta have a ton of hot water."

That set him into a fit of chuckles. What a sweet, misunderstood kid. Gosh.

I sat up on the couch and put down von Clausewitz.

"Huh-hem. If we are going to be in close quarters over some indeterminate time, may I suggest that it is appropriate that we have some means of acknowledging one another? I do not mean to be forward, but it is an annoying inconvenience having no means of communicating directly. May I propose that we arrive at some accommodation as to address?"

Don'tcha just love the English language? If I really practiced this, I could become a politician.

Les looked at me, completely dumbstruck, his mouth agape. Ray, as always, was completely blank.

"I mean, may I call each of you by some name? It would make communication much more efficient."

"Hunh? Oh, sure. I'm Les. That's Ray. Our last name is Smith. Les Jacob Jingleheimer Smith and Ray Nickodemus Smith. We're identical twins. I'm older. That's why he is so quiet. They named the cough drops after us."

It became instantly clear that Les was a writer for Dave Letterman as his day job. I was in stitches. It was also clear that he had not come up with this on the spur of the moment, and I concluded that my hockey analogy was not that far off. These two bozos had worked together for a while.

"Ha, ha! That is very clever. Smith Brothers. I'm surprised that you know about them. I would have thought that they were more my generation than yours. Very good. Of course, I preferred Luden's. Far more efficacious, don't you think.?"

Have you ever seen a dog who doesn't quite understand you? He kind of sits there and turns his head to the side and looks at you and gives this impression of cluelessness. Then he turns his head to the other side and kind of hopes that there is something else, like maybe a biscuit? Well, picture Les, turning his off-kilter cherubic countenance from one angle to the other and you have the picture perfectly.

"Well, do I call you Mr. Les, or is Les acceptable to you? I wish that I could say that I am pleased to meet you, but under the circumstances, I am sure you understand. Nevertheless, I am gratified to have a means of communication with you and I am truly appreciative that you have acquiesced in my request."

Les gave his best impression of Fido with ear mites. I could almost see him shake his head. I wonder if he could scratch behind his ear with his off-hind foot.

Like the tar-baby, Ray didn't say nuthin' and I hoped that I, not he, was the fox, and I lay low.

"Well, now that we have that settled," I said cheerfully, "Shall we see to lunch? I think that it is past time, and I am certain that you are hungry. May I be of service in preparing the meal? I have been sitting here on the couch all morning and I could use some physical activity, you know? I do most of the cooking here. Without boasting, I confess that I am something of a gourmet. You have not provided me with a great expanse of culinary options, but I can endeavor to make our meals a modicum more pleasant, if you will permit me?"

Ray just sat in the corner chair, his gun and *Golf Digest* in his lap.

Les was trying hard to figure out a snappy come back, and finally volleyed with, "Knock yourself out. I don't see why we should wait on you, and there's nothing you can do to screw things up. Go for it. You can be our mom. Yeah, Doctor Mom."

If I'd had even an inkling that I could produce such offspring, I'd have had my tubes tied and I'd have done sitz-baths in boiling radiator flush every hour on the hour. Nevertheless, I thanked them sweetly, and went into the kitchen to make sandwiches.

"One thing that I don't quite comprehend fully. I am quite happy with the current state of affairs, you know, but I am confused on one point." I actually was wondering about this and wanted to understand the situation. "Why have you not kept me handcuffed, or even shackled completely? While I am certain that I could pose no possible physical threat to you, it seems to be an unnecessary risk to allow me to remain comparatively free. I am, after all, not a person of small stature."

I was watching Ray as I made these mawkish remarks. For an instant, I thought I saw a glimmer of a smile cross his face. Perhaps it was wishful thinking on my part. It evaporated as quickly as it came, and Les, as usual, stepped into the silence.

"It's real simple, Doc. If we kept you cuffed or taped up, then every time you needed to use the john or go to bed or dress or anything, we'd have to let you loose. That would mean that one of us would have to get right up close to you, and sooner or later you might try something. This way we can keep you at arm's length. It also keeps you in better condition, so the missus will be happier. She might not like it if you were taped into a bed upstairs, all covered in your own shit. Might make her less willing to do her bit. We can always go that way if she doesn't cooperate, or if you try to pull something, but for now it is just easier for everyone. Besides, whaddya gonna do, take on both of us? Don't think so. Not Doctor Mom."

Well, I'm not sure I agreed with their assessment of the situation, but I wasn't going to argue the point. I was happy to have the use of my hands and feet, at least during the day. They could have shown a little more respect for me as a potential threat, though. It was a bit embarrassing to be taken so lightly.

"Yes, I see your point. Most logical. You certainly seem to have thought of everything. Do you have a preference for American or Swiss on your sandwich?"

After lunch, I cleaned up by collecting the paper plates and plastic cups and putting them in the trash. I carefully sealed all the meat and cheese packages, and closed up the bread with the twist tie. I put them all in the refrigerator and wiped down the counters. Just call me Doctor Mom.

"Les, do you think we might turn on the television? I think that it might help to pass the time. I don't normally watch television during the day, of course. I am always in the office. For that matter, I don't watch a great deal of television at all. There is so little that is of sufficient quality to hold one's attention, don't you agree? Nevertheless, do you think we might see what is on?"

"Sure, I got nothing against it. But, you are gonna sit or lie down on the floor with your back against that little couch in there. I don't want to have to watch you for any sudden moves."

So, we turned on the TV. I surfed the channels fairly quickly and settled on the Golf Channel, where they were showing a classic rerun of Nicklaus' 1986 Masters Championship. I settled on the floor with a cushion behind my head and began to watch.

"You've got to be kidding," grumped Les. "Golf? OLD golf? Look, we could watch MTV, we could watch Walker, Texas Ranger, we could watch the comedy channel. "Deal or No Deal". We could watch "Golden Girls"... anything but this... You gotta be kidding!"

Ray said nothing, but came into the den and positioned himself in the easy chair where he could watch me and the television screen, silently and intently. Les gave up and went into the other room, saying, "Jesus. Golf. Totally, fucking boring. What a bunch of homos."

The phone rang again at about 2:20, with the same kind of conversation. This time Les answered. "Yeah... It's cool... Yep, Ray and the Doc are 'bonding'... (chuckle). Okay."

At 5:05 the phone rang again, and again Les answered. "Okay, see ya." About twenty minutes later I could hear the garage door go up, and a few moments later Em came in, followed by Britt and Zach.

Em looked tired, but none the worse for wear. Britt and Zach looked about the same, like they had spent a long day at work and were ready to knock it off for the evening. I expect that they were tired. They had probably not slept well last night, and they had been in public with Em, exposed all day. That kind of focus would use up a lot of energy.

Em and I looked at each other and in the one instant gave a series of those long-married, silent signals that no one else would ever pick up.

"You okay?"

"Yeah, you?"

"Yup. Any idea what this is all about?"

"Not really, but I'm working on it."

"Yeah, me too."

"Hang in there."

"Don't do anything stupid."

"I love you... a lot."

"Yeah, me too."

Doesn't matter who "said" what... we both said it all in just a look.

Britt walked over to me and with a sadistic smile rapped me with her knuckles, hard, right on the spot Zach had hammered the night before, driving me to my knees. She broke the silence, "Something to remember, Rita. Behave yourself. Now, get upstairs. You've got an hour to rest up. Then we'll all get cleaned up and have dinner." She and

Zach followed Em up the stairs, and I heard doors close, and then silence for about an hour.

Dinner was uneventful. I mean, how exciting can a ham sandwich be? That was followed by a couple of hours in front of the television watching the Reds stupidly blow a lead and fail to bring in about 47 runners in scoring position. Gotta love 'em. Could be worse, they could be the Cubs.

Oh, I did my level best to get Britt to relent on the "no alcohol" rule. I asked sweetly, then used "logic", and then finally resorted to pouting. Yeah, I would have liked a drink, but mostly it was intended to make them think even less of me, if possible. So far they seemed to be buying into my "potted pedagogue" role pretty well. I hoped.

Bedtime was a repeat of the night before. We took turns getting ready for bed. Like good little doobies we laid back and were handcuffed. Only difference was we slept better, or at least I did.

Chapter 13

Wednesday. Same breakfast routine as Tuesday. I was up early with "Alphonse and Gaston" and seated at the dining room table. Maybe I was just hoping, but they were beginning to look a bit haggard. Ray didn't show it much, just a bit of red around the eyes, and he didn't seem to be quite as alert to everything going on around him. He seemed to focus on one thing and then another, rather than shifting his focus constantly and quickly to make certain he caught it all. It was kind of like he was reading and only catching the key words, not the entire meaning.

Les for once was quiet. He had no great quips, puns, or gaiety. Apparently he and Ray were the night watch and they didn't get a whole lot of sleep.

After a while Britt came downstairs, followed by Em, then Zach. I looked at my watch. 8:32. I liked that. There seemed to be a pattern, and they were sticking to it, even the order in which they came down the stairs. I mean, it made sense. Put Em between them, and have Zach in the rear where he could control the action. Still, it was good that they were consistent. No surprises for anyone.

Em came over and kissed me and gave my shoulder a squeeze. After she sat beside me at the table, I leaned over and kissed her back.

Britt just couldn't resist. It was like those underwater shots you see in infomercials for fishing lures. The bait comes by and the humongous bass just can't help itself and lunges at the bait.

"How sweet, the Cleavers at the breakfast table."

Em went off like a cherry-bomb in a clogged toilet.

"You lousy excuse for a yeast infection! You wouldn't know an honest emotion from a gerbil crawling up your ass. Tell me, when your family was taking turns abusing you, did they have to PAY the pimp, or did they just take your incestuous offspring and sell them? For that matter, how in hell did your mother slip up and allow your existence? Couldn't she find a coat hanger?"

I'm telling you... coffee. Coffee is the key.

"Now, sweetheart," I jumped in. "There is no call for that kind of aggressive outburst! I think that you should apologize. There is nothing to be gained from a confrontational attitude. It is a sort of violence really, and that never solves anything. Incivility can cause deep seated psychological trauma that can result in long-term resentment and even damage to one's self-esteem. I'm sure that you didn't mean to be so abrupt. Really, I think that an apology is in order. You are aware of my deeply held beliefs that we must all deal with our differences with respect and tolerance in the spirit of establishing a healthy community. Of course..."

At first Em looked at me like I was crazy. She knows damned well that I couldn't give a flying rat-butt about "healthy community" or hurting somebody's feelings. As for violence never solving anything, tell it to the American buffalo or the carrier pigeon or the defenders at the Alamo, or Custer's 7th Cavalry. Not to mention that I had never in

94

over twenty years of marriage called her "sweetheart"…
ever. It took her a split second and then she got it. And
here it came…

"What!? Apologize? To THESE people? You must be
fucking out of your mind! Are you taking THEIR side?
You cannot be serious! You think that your pacifist ideals
are going to help here? You and your alcoholic, liberal
crap. Apologize! I can't believe you! Aaargh!"

She launched herself from the table and stalked into the
living room. Atta girl!

Britt was getting that "bass" look again, so I intervened
once again and addressed her directly.

"I am terribly sorry. Please, allow me to apologize for my
wife. That outburst was completely inappropriate. I'm
sure that we are all under a certain amount of stress, and
that under such conditions studies have conclusively shown
that special care must be taken to consider one's words
much more carefully in order to communicate effectively.
Miller and Brock's seminal treatise in 1987 concluded
that…"

"Shut up, Professor! Your wife is going to find out how
unpleasant things can be if she doesn't watch it," snapped
Britt, interrupting me yet again. It was getting so a guy
couldn't pontificate in his own home. Hmph, I say.

This morning Britt was wearing a pair of low-cut shorts and
a different tee-shirt. The shorts were black and revealed
what would have, under other circumstances, been a very
attractive pair of legs ending in a pair of nice sandals. The

matching shirt proclaimed in red letters, "You Can't Spell S U C K without U C!" Of course, being a loyal Miamian, I agreed with the sentiment. Today her hair was pulled back with a comb of some sort. Like yesterday, she'd fit right in as a grad student without a second glance, except maybe at her legs.

Zach had stood back, amused by the whole exchange. He was dressed in exactly the same clothes as yesterday, and that fit, too. Sloppy male grad student. Perfect. The only difference was that today he had a worn ball-cap with a Cleveland Browns logo on the front. Good God, man! Have you no sense of decency?

Em was dressed in a pair of khaki slacks and a pink Polo golf shirt. Same hair style as always. No socks. TopSider-like shoes, but they weren't the actual brand. Em wouldn't be caught dead in the official yuppie footwear.

Zach shrugged and said, "Well if you girls are ready, let's get going." Britt picked up a backpack, and strode manfully for the door. Em walked by me with her nose in the air, pointedly ignoring me. Zach watched them both walk toward the garage, and shook his head, smiling.

As soon as the door had closed, I stood and headed for the bathroom. "I'm afraid my stomach is a little upset by all of this. Most unpleasant."

Again, I watched as the car disappeared up the driveway. Zach in the driver's seat, Britt directly behind him, and Em in the back seat on the right side. Patterns. Habits.

I flushed and then waited a while, and then flushed again. Nervous stomach, you see? Actually, that was an interesting thought.

When I came out, Zach was already seated in the corner chair in the living room. Les was on the other side of the room and was yawning.

"You know, Doc-Mom, it doesn't pay to piss Britt off. I wouldn't want to be in your wife's shoes when Britt decides that she's had enough. You might want to get her to cool it. Gotta say, though. That bit about the gerbil... that was pretty good. I gotta remember that one."

Now, in Les's case I wasn't quite sure whether he was referring to it as an insult or as a sexual proclivity. Nevertheless, I responded, "Well, as I said, I see no reason for incivility. Diplomacy and understanding are the cornerstones of coexistence, and I feel very strongly that such principles are to be followed, especially in trying circumstances. I am sure you concur. As you saw, I tried to impress that upon my wife. If we are permitted, I shall talk to her most sternly about the matter."

I hoped to God that we would be allowed to talk at some point. It would make it much more difficult to break away from them if we couldn't work together. But, then, that was the point, wasn't it?

Chapter 14

Les went upstairs and I settled back on the couch. This morning I spent about an hour doing the crossword puzzle, Cryptoquote, and Sudoku. They had brought the newspaper back with them when they returned last night. I was a little off my game. I had to actually use several of the vertical clues on the crossword. Well, under the circumstances...

I asked Ray if he had finished looking at the Golf Digest, and he nodded yes. He tossed it over to me, and as he did another glimmer of an idea began to form. I said, "There are a whole bunch of back issues in the bathroom. There are a couple in the magazine rack, and probably two years' worth in the cabinet under the sink. Would you like one?"

You know, it's amazing. You never know who you'll meet on the golf course. I've travelled all over the world and I've played golf wherever I've gone. Em doesn't play, so I've been a single at dozens of golfing venues. Sometimes I've played alone. Most often, I am matched with someone. You never know who your playing partner will be, and they come from all walks of life.

I've played with pros and I've played with duffers. I've played with CEOs and I've played with the unemployed. I've played with the famous and with the unknown. Once, I was playing in Ixtapa, Mexico. I was paired with a businessman from St. Louis, and we came walking up to the 17th tee where another twosome was waiting. They invited us to join them as there was a foursome in the fairway in front of them. One of the men was wearing a

University of Pennsylvania hat. Now, I happen to be an alumnus, so I asked about the hat. He replied, "Oh, I'm the President."

Several years ago, I had the opportunity to play Carnoustie, one of the sites for the Open Championship in Britain. Again, I was a single and they had placed me with a playing partner. As we walked to the first tee, Raymond Floyd and his family walked up. Since they were a foursome and we were a two, they encouraged us to go ahead. Frankly I'd have rather played behind them so I could watch. Teeing off in front of Ray Floyd was a little daunting, but I managed to put it in the fairway; not very far out, but in the short grass.

Or, there was the time that I got matched up on a little public course in Florida. My playing partners were these two older black gentlemen dressed like Art Carney and Jackie Gleason. They played together every week, and they had so many bets going at one time that I couldn't keep track. At one point, I think that there were actually SEVEN presses going on, not to mention greenies, sandies, snakes, gotchas and more. Furthermore, they never stopped talking! That is not true. They were perfectly still while I was playing, but they were jawing constantly through each other's games. On about the fourth hole, one of the guys had a long, twisting putt of about 40 feet for par. So, he pulls out his "special putting ball" which has markings like a miniature eight ball and proceeds to drain the putt. For the next four or five holes the other guy complained that the ball was illegal and wanted me to make a ruling. At the end of it all, it came down to one putt on

99

the eighteenth green for all the money. This time the other guy made a long twisting putt over hill and dale. As we walked to the clubhouse I observed a begrudging 30 cents change hands. What a hoot!

In all the rounds that I have played with strangers over all the years, I've only had one bad experience. They had put four singles together and we were playing the old Dunes course in Las Vegas. On about the twelfth hole, one of the guys hit a ball into the water. He teed up another and did the same thing. He got so angry that he told the rest of us to go fuck ourselves, and he drove off to another hole to play on his own. Weird.

Anyway, you never know who is a golfer or who you'll meet on the course.

To my surprise, Ray nodded in the affirmative. Well, one would never have to worry about Ray talking in one's backswing.

We spent the rest of the morning reading about golf. I occasionally tried to engage Ray in conversation about golf, but with no success beyond an occasional, noncommittal grunt. About 10:30 the phone rang.

"Yeah. Okay," and he hung up.

Wow! It was like a filibuster, only in reverse. Ray would never be at a loss for words. He never used any.

A little while later Les came back downstairs and the guard changed. Les took one look at the stack of Golf Digest back issues and almost visibly shuddered. I continued to read and to think about gaining more "slack". After a while, he got up and went to a window and looked out for a moment, then crossed the room to look out the back. Then he went back to the chair. Then he asked, "Hey, Doc. You got anything to read other than this golf junk?"

It was pretty obvious. Poor Les was bored. Ray was content to sit and read about golf, or for that matter, to sit quietly and simply keep his watch. I could picture him silently waiting for prey to come to him, just like a spider or a snake, waiting until the time was right to strike and kill. Les had no patience. He was probably ADD or close to it, and he just couldn't sit still. That probably accounted for his clownishness as well. He needed the action and attention. Another key slipped into place.

"Well, of course. We have an excellent library here at home consisting of nearly two thousand volumes, if I am not mistaken. Of course a portion of the collection consists of rather technical works on policy and strategy, organizational structure, competitive environmental analysis and the like. And then, my wife's work spans a broad front of historical, genealogical and demographic issues. Did you have something specific in mind?"

I expect that what Les wanted was the complete collection of "Girls Gone Wild – the Magazine", or "Penthouse Letters", or the all-time classic, "Shaved Sniz". Barring that, I suspected that whatever passed for comic books these days would be a winner. On that subject, I am morally certain that the popular shift from D.C. comics to Marvel was the beginning of the downfall of American civilization, but I digress.

101

"Uh, you got any magazines, I mean besides this golf crud?"

Bingo! If we'd had a bunch of old Playboy magazines, a box of Kleenex, and a jar of Vaseline, I could have distracted Les 'til doomsday. Sadly, my subscription to "Lesbian Lust" had expired recently. Damned shame, I say.

"I see. Well, I'm afraid that our selection is somewhat limited. You understand, I am sure, that my wife and I have a great deal of reading to do just to keep up with our respective professions. We each subscribe to various periodicals, journals really, that publish the latest research in our fields. That leaves us little time to partake of the popular press. However, we do receive the "Birder's World" if that might be of interest?"

Les's expression became even more crestfallen than it had been when he was looking at the "golf crud".

"Oh, and that reminds me. I appreciate the solicitude you and the others have afforded the feline members of the household. While you had not contemplated feeding them in your planning, I believe that you will agree that it has not been a burden. I would therefore hope that you would extend the same consideration to the avian population as well."

Les was back to playing Fido again.

"What the hell are you talking about, Doc? You can say less with more words than anybody I ever met."

"Please pardon me. I am told that I occasionally overstep in matters oratorical. I mean that I should like to feed the birds. There is a bird feeder in the back yard. It is empty and needs to be refilled. It is important to provide a continuous food supply year-round. We normally replenish the feed every morning and, well, yesterday we failed to do so."

Strictly speaking that was not completely true. It is a good idea to keep the feeders stocked all year in order to encourage the birds to make it part of their routine. It was not true that we filled it every day. Okay, so I lied.

"Yeah, great. Bird feeders. Jesus! Are you shitting me, Doc? I mean golf and now this? What a bunch of crap. Total wuss. Don't you have a subscription to Sports Illustrated or something worth looking at?"

I put on my most hurt expression, and replied in a subdued tone, "Yes, well… I was never good at the more physical sports as a child, and I was often left alone. I discovered that solitary pursuits such as golf and bird watching provided intellectual stimulation and physical exercise outdoors. While those activities may not seem exciting to you, they have been a haven to me."

Blech! Ptooey! It was like talking with a mouthful of cat fur. If I got any wimpier I'd have to ask to pay him Tuesday for a hamburger today.

He seemed oddly taken aback by my "hurt feelings". Maybe I was right and he WAS just a poor misguided youth. He'd happily shoot me, but he didn't want me to feel bad about it.

"Well, sorry, Doc. I mean, I just can't take that stuff. It's okay for you if you want. To each his own. Live and let live. Whatever. We'll see about feeding the birds when Ray comes back down, later. But I gotta find something to keep me occupied while you're just sitting there. Look, go into the den. I'm gonna turn on the TV. You can read in there."

A few minutes later Les was happily mesmerized in front of Sports Center while I continued to read. I looked up to observe the segment on how the Reds had managed to pull defeat from the jaws of victory once again last night, but went back to reading. Les was enthralled.

Around 12:30 Ray reappeared, and as I had yesterday, I got up to make lunch. Ray sat at the kitchen counter and watched, but without much interest. We ate in front of the TV. Very homey, but television stifles conversation and is the downfall of family togetherness, especially at meals. I suspected that if this continued we would not be a tight family unit over the long haul.

Chapter 15

After lunch I pressed on the bird feeding issue.

"Excuse me, Les. I don't wish to interrupt your television viewing. The three stooges are quite amusing, I agree. I once read an entire research thread that described the bases of their humor, and traced it from the early days of vaudeville, and actually plotted many of their now famous antics across a multivariate construct showing relationships with the theory of humor and specific demographics and sociological strata. Fascinating conclusions regarding the universality of slapstick. Nevertheless, might we take up the issue of replenishing the bird feed at this time?"

I added a wheedling conclusion, much like a child whose parent had given the proverbial "We'll see," response. "You said that we'd take care of it when Ray came down."

Les said, "Yeah, what the hell. I need a break anyway. Ray, the Doc here wants to fill up the bird feeder because the poor little birdies are going hungry out there and he's all worried and stuff. You got any problem with Doc-Mom feeding the birds? I mean, I don't think he's a flight risk, right! Ha ha, ha ha ha, ha! If he tried anything one of us could wing him! Ha ha, ha ha ha. After all, we are kinda cooped up in here. Hee hee, ha ha, ha ha. Oh, man this is good!"

Ray's expression didn't change, nor did he respond to Les's question or comic routine.

Les continued, "The back yard is fenced. Nobody can see back there anyway. If we go out, one of us can stay with him and the other can keep watch from the deck. So what's gonna happen? If it makes Doc-Mom happy, I'm in favor. I mean we're buddies right? Birds of a feather! Ha ha ha. You know, Doc, I used to have a girlfriend who liked a cockatoo! Ha ha hah... But she wasn't big on swallows... HAH HAH ha ha, haaaahhhh. Oh, man! You shoulda brought up the birds before, Doc. This is great!

"So, okay. Where's the birdseed? In the garage, right? Awright, we'll all stretch our legs a little and go feed the little birdies. Doc, you happy? Okay, let's go."

I had never expected that they would actually let me feed the birds. I was just trying to play some games, see what I could get away with, and test the limits. I'd expected one or the other of them to say, "Screw that. Who cares about birds? Siddown and shuddup." At the best I thought that maybe I could get one of them to do it so that they were split up for a moment or two. And even if it didn't work, I thought that perhaps I could prove once again that I was no threat to them at all. Who ever heard of a violent bird watcher?

This was outstanding! We were going out to the garage, a place fraught with possibilities. There were tools, gas cans, solvents, extension cords, ropes, a chain saw... They hadn't had the time to clean it out or "sanitize" it. I couldn't wait to get out there! So, I stalled. "Um, if you will permit me, I need to use the restroom first." I went into the bathroom and took a leak, and washed my hands for far longer than normal, and then just stood there for another moment. By the time I came back out Les was already "antsy". Perfect.

"Come on, Doc! Geez, you are worse than a woman. Let's go!"

Les led the way and Ray brought up the rear. We went through the laundry room and out into the garage. It was still there! Yay! Funny, I'd been in the house for almost two days and under guard the entire time, and it was like going on an adventure to a foreign land.

I went over to the corner where we kept the bird seed. I had built a wooden frame for the three garbage cans that we filled with seed. The wooden frame had a hinged lid of ½ inch plywood and a hasp that was closed with a spring clip all for security from marauding raccoons. As I picked up the bucket and opened the lid, I said, "Ray, you might want to take a look at my golf clubs. Right there in front of the car. Titleist, with foam-core shafts in the irons. Nothing real fancy, but, well, on a professor's salary one cannot always aspire to the penultimate." As I was dipping seed out of the end can, I noticed that he did look, for just an instant.

So, we fed the birds. I lugged the bucket of seed out to the feeder, extra-large as I mentioned. Filled it up, spilled some on purpose just outside the fence for the ground feeders and the deer, and then walked back to the house. Les kept me company all the way while Ray watched from the deck. I supposed that he was the better shot at that distance.

On the way back into the house, I dumped the bucket back in the corner where it belonged, and observed closely to see if the garage and its contents had remained intact. To the

107

best I could determine, they had left things completely untouched. As I said, "fraught with possibilities" and my seedling ideas began to grow.

A little while after we got back into the house there was another phone check. Les watched television, I took a nap on the couch in the living room, and Ray read Golf Digest and kept an eye on me.

Chapter 16

Just after 5:00 o'clock Les's cell phone rang again. "Yeah, cool... Okay... Nope... Yeah."

I was afraid to take the risk, but I didn't see any way around it. I had to see how Britt and Zach and Em were arranged in the car on their return. Logic told me that they would be set in the same fashion as they had been on the way out each morning, but I didn't want to take that chance at all. I had to know.

I didn't want them to think that every time the car went up or down the driveway that I was going into the bathroom. I didn't want them to see a pattern to it. I thought about alternatives and finally decided on the library upstairs. It had windows that overlooked the driveway, and I could get a clear view if the shades had not been pulled down completely. They hadn't bothered since the door had been shut and nobody had been in there, but I wasn't sure. So, bathroom and have them catch on potentially, or library and hope for open shades?

At about 5:20 Ray made up my mind for me by finishing the Golf Digest he had been reading. He had pretty well gone through the few issues that I had brought from the bathroom before, cover to cover. So, I stood up and asked, "You seem to have finished with those, shall I procure another few issues for you? Please, allow me." With that I went into the bathroom and pulled out a stack from under the sink and then stood there pretending to go through them while waiting for the car to arrive. Within a minute I was rewarded by the car coming down the driveway, and they were in their standard positions. Thank God for logic and professional behavior.

Dinner was another culinary triumph. This time we had sliced turkey and pepper jack sandwiches. Yum. I became even more petulant about wanting a drink, and pouted. I did everything but throw myself on the floor and kick and scream. All for naught. Oh, well. It served its purpose. Britt thought even less of me.

Em followed up on our morning "spat" and figuratively kicked me in the shins by talking about my "precious booze" and how only an alcoholic would sell out and take their side for a drink. After dinner we went to our respective "corners" and stayed apart until bedtime.

About 10:30 Britt said, "Okay, that's enough for today. Bedtime. I'm sure we could all use a good night's rest. And, Rita definitely needs her beauty sleep!"

Em was about to launch into another attack, but I caught her eye and signaled her not to. Instead, I stood and went over to her and gave her a kiss and hugged her for a moment. As her head was turned against my chest she whispered one word so only I could hear, "Tomorrow."

She wearily moved toward the stairs but looked back when I called out, "Good night, dear. Please don't be cross with me." I nodded almost imperceptibly and she caught it.

After I had prepared for bed and had been tucked in, cuffs and all, I listened to the noises of the household. I could hear the peepers and the frogs outside as they serenaded the pond. The air conditioning cycled on and off. After a little while all the water sounds from the bathrooms and the flushings all ceased. The air conditioning fan stopped, and just for a second I could just barely hear Britt's voice. She paused after each comment, as if she were waiting for someone to respond. Ah, a phone conversation, thus proving my surmises about a silent partner. "We're getting close... Maybe tomorrow, but Friday for sure... Of course not... We'll handle it."

Em knew. She would be better able to judge than Britt. Whatever they were looking for, whether they had found it or not, they would have finished their task tomorrow or the next day. That meant that they'd finish with us as well. Em told me "tomorrow". It would have to be. I lay in bed for a long time thinking about possibilities and finally fell asleep.

Chapter 17

Thursday morning was a dreary, overcast day. As we had been the previous two mornings, Les and Ray and I were already downstairs and breakfasted before the others showed. As always when they appeared, Britt was first followed by Em with Zach as "tail-end Charlie". I was comforted by their adherence to the proper method. They were nothing if not consistent.

There was nothing remarkable about breakfast. Em looked tired, and she didn't say anything while the others ate. Zach looked pretty much the same, and was wearing pretty much the same as he had the previous two days. Britt looked somehow tougher, harder. She had the grim look of an athlete who was bearing down and who was going to finish the event come hell or high water. There was no doubt that the stress was taking its toll on us all. Keeping watch is not easy. It takes energy. Keeping things looking normal in public would wear on them too. It was my fervent hope that their boss was putting pressure on from his, or her, end as well.

Today Britt was wearing blue jeans and a grey tee shirt complete with "The" Ohio State University buckeye logo on the front. She had a black windbreaker that zipped up the front. Graduate student chic. Em was wearing a pair of navy blue slacks and a light-blue button-down shirt. And, God love her, she had her hair looking great. She could be in the trenches in WWI and getting ready to go over the top in the middle of an artillery barrage, and she'd have her hair looking nice. Vanity, thy name is Em, at least when it comes to hair. I wondered if this would be the last time I saw her.

As they stirred around and prepared to leave, I stood behind Em's chair at the dining room table, and bent down to kiss her at the crook of her neck. I whispered my one word response to her warning from last night, "Stall," and then added in a loud and clear voice, "Please do everything that you can to assist them, today. I know that we have all been discomfited by the arrangements and conditions, but that is no reason to be difficult or confrontational. I am sure that you agree with me that they have treated us well, under the circumstances. Your assistance, delivered in a positive manner will undoubtedly result in their continued beneficence."

Em stood and looked at me as if I had crawled out from under a rock.

Britt picked up her windbreaker and looked at me as if I had crawled out from under a rock.

Zach looked through me like I didn't exist.

I didn't bother to go to the bathroom to watch them leave.

The rest of the morning was a repeat of the day before. Les slept first. I napped. Les returned and Ray slept. I did puzzles and read while Les watched television. Les fielded the check-up call. After a few minutes, I stood and went to the window.

"Les? You might wish to see this. It might provide you with a greater understanding regarding the need to keep the bird feeder filled."

There were at least five deer that I could see surrounding the bird feeder. One had jumped the fence and was standing in the back yard. Two small deer were licking the ground for spilled seed while another was off to one side and the fifth appeared to be standing guard a couple of paces back into the woods.

"Geez, Doc! Why didn't you tell me you were feeding the deer? Look at that, will ya? Man, I could get one of them easy from here. Shit, if I had my bow, I could nail that one in the yard. Wouldn't make a sound. Damn it!"

Les continued to stare out the window and curse his luck at being unable to kill deer, and finally turned away. "So, do you ever hunt deer, Doc? Nah, what am I saying? You, kill deer? Hah! Fuckin' Bambiland is more like it. I know, you just like to watch them. Geez, Doc, you are some wuss. What a waste. All those deer and nobody to kill 'em and eat 'em. Pitiful."

I mustered up as much righteous indignation as I could load into my voice and posture, and retorted, "We were not allowed to have guns in our house when I was growing up. My parents did not believe in guns or violence."

Please forgive me, Mom and Dad. The role demands that I spew this garbage.

"Oh, yeah? Then how come you had all those evil weapons we found upstairs then?" asked Les.

"Oh, those? Those belong to my wife."

Les burst into laughter. "Oh, that's perfect! Omigod! Perfect!"

"Well, yes. Uh, well… Do you think that we could replenish the birdseed again today? As soon as Ray comes down? We normally deal with this in the early morning to accommodate the birds' early energy needs from the overnight fast. You can see that it is nearly gone."

"Sure, Doc. That'll be just peachy. Peachy. Wife's guns! Wait'll Ray hears that."

Peachy, indeed. One more grain of my plan slid nicely into place.

Chapter 18

When Ray came back downstairs I was careful to be seated in the den reading Golf Digest while Les watched mindless drivel on the television. I had worked my way through the past issues that Ray had been reading and selected the one that most suited my cause. It was an article on the keys to putting and how to groove your stroke.

As Ray came into the den I began to mutter about what I was reading. "Absurd! This is complete hogwash. Why, the physics alone dictate that such an approach cannot be consistently successful. I am appalled. How could a Professional Golfer's Association touring professional allow his name to be associated with such rot? Preposterous, I say!" The tone and volume of my criticism escalated as I went.

"Ray! You have been reading these issues of Golf Digest, have you not? Of course you have. Now, have you seen this article, ostensibly by Jim Furyk, regarding the proper techniques of the putting stroke? I contend that it was not written by Mr. Furyk at all, but rather by some unprincipled hack who knows nothing of the game. Nothing, I say! I am outraged! This is nothing less than academic dishonesty. I fully intend to write to the editors and to Mr. Furyk about this! I shall contact the commissioner!" As I loudly made the last statement I abruptly stood from my chair and gestured with the offending magazine.

Les reached for his gun and jumped up from the couch, "Whoa, Doc! Just sit back! You don't want to be making sudden moves like that!"

"But their entire contention is patently incorrect! Totally false I tell you! It is unconscionable. Look here, Ray, surely you will agree that they have completely overstepped the bounds of propriety. As someone who appreciates the game of golf, you must agree with me on this! They are contending that the putting stroke is in many ways simply a regular golf swing in miniature! They take great pains to illustrate that the toe of the putter must open in the backswing, come back to perpendicular with the desired line as the ball is struck, and then continue to close in the follow-through. They actually advocate this approach! They compare the putting stroke to the swinging of a door!"

"Yeah, right... Whatever. Just don't jump around like that, Doc," warned Les, as he settled back on the couch, shaking his head.

"Their argument is devoid of logic. The swinging arc of a door is repeatable only because it is fixed at its axis of rotation, the hinges of course. Since those hinges are immovable, that permits the door to return to the perpendicular at precisely the same point in each event. Clearly, the human axis of rotation is heir to all forms of variance. Posture, balance, uneven terrain, weather, all will play a role to introduce variance into the system. It will simply be impossible to maintain a consistent result as the angle of intersection of the putter blade and the sphere of the golf ball must change minutely."

Ray continued to stand at the edge of the carpet, and while he wasn't applauding or nodding his approval, he was listening intently.

117

"Thus, you see, consistently initiating the roll of the golf ball along the proper geometric line will be compromised. By comparison, I should point out to you that the correct putting stroke is that of a pendulum. By approximating the linear momentum of a pendulum, one can reduce the variance producing factors. I point out to you the success of the "belly" putter on tour. I also introduce as evidence the United States Golf Association tests of golf balls and how they come off the face of clubs. While they were testing the variance reducing properties of various putter club-face materials, and not the golf stroke, the important point is that they used a pendulum-like device to limit the variance! You see? The logic is inescapable!"

If this had been a debate, I'd have won. I could see that Ray was buying it. Not that I cared a purple patoot whether he agreed or not. I only cared that he was listening.

"Now the only question remaining is whether the human form can approximate the motion of a pendulum with less variance than it can a swinging door. That is obviously true, given the number of muscle groups required in one action versus the other. I rest my case."

Ray was unmoved, or at least showed no sign that he wished to either take the other side or endorse my views. I didn't have time to find out, as Les, clearly exasperated by my diatribe, rose and said, "Okay, Doc. Your golf lecture can wait. You want to feed the birds again? Now's the time. My show's over and I want to see the next Sports Center, so let's get a move on, hunh? Ray, me and Doc are gonna feed the birds again, like yesterday. Okay?"

"Well, I, uh… Of, course," I stammered.

"You know, Doc," Les continued, "I been thinkin'. I kinda like birds after all. I mean, I been looking at boobies my whole life! Ha, ha, ha, ha-ha. And, last time I was at the beach I saw some rosy-bottomed beach walkers! HAH, ha-ha, haaaah!"

Gotta love that Les. Always trying, and completely undeterred that nobody else liked his jokes… ever.

As we went into the garage, I continued to obsess about the putting article. "I cannot believe that with the research and ergonomics facilities available to the PGA and the USGA and to the equipment manufacturers that anyone could be so utterly absurd as to propose anything other than a pendulum motion for putting. Inexcusable."

Les was only half paying attention as I went over to the bird seed bins. I grabbed the bucket, and removed the lid to the garbage can and placed it upright on the workbench. I dipped the bucket into the can, filled it with seed, and under cover of the upright lid, I slipped a small bottle out of its rack with my left hand and put it into my pocket.

Bucket in my right hand, I started for the back door when Les said, "Doc! Whaddya think you're doing," and began coming toward me. I froze in my tracks. I'm glad that I had taken my blood pressure medicine at breakfast, but I doubt it was helping. My God! If one of them had picked up on my sleight of hand, the whole deal was done. All of my efforts of the past two days were wasted. I had no more ideas.

119

Les pushed by me, "You gotta put the lid back, Doc. Geez... Unless you want deer in the garage? Hey, maybe that's a good idea! Then we could whack 'em with a shovel." He put the lid back on the can and closed the plywood lid on the frame. Then he led the way out to the back yard. Sweating profusely, I staggered after him.

There are a few moments in your life when your bowels literally turn to water. When your fear overcomes your bodily functions. Close. Very close.

I repeated the steps to fill the feeder, spread some for the deer and squirrels, and cleared my throat several times. I didn't trust myself to be able to speak in a normal voice, but I had to. Next step coming up.

Back in the garage, I replaced the bucket and as I followed Les back into the house, I called back to Ray, "If you would bring my putter into the house, I shall show you the proof of my argument. This is easily demonstrated. Conclusive evidence, I should say... And grab a sleeve of balls as well."

Chapter 19

Les waved me into the den and vaguely pointed toward the chair with his gun. His show had just begun and he flumped down on the far end of the couch.

If Ray did not rise to the occasion and deliver the putter, I was going to have to find some other way to beg, or cajole, or carp or somehow manage to get it into my hands. Everything I had been doing up to this point had been directed at creating a certain image. I had been playing possum, and if it didn't work, I'd have to find some other way. The key was in my pocket, without which nothing else would work. Inwardly I sighed deeply and gave thanks to all that is good and right in the world that at least that part of my plan had succeeded.

And with that, Ray appeared, and glory be! He had the putter and a sleeve of balls in his left hand. Of course, that was balanced by the gun in his right hand, but let's not be overly critical. I was beginning to think very kindly of Ray. True, he appeared to be inbred, weasel-like, and smelled like the inside of the elephant house at the zoo, but I was willing to give him the benefit of the doubt; perhaps he actually walked when he played golf. Maybe.

"Excellent! Thank you, Ray. I am certain that you will see my point immediately. However, as the demonstration will take some time, I suggest that we postpone it until after the lunch hour. I shall be happy to prepare lunch whenever you wish."

As I sat in the reclining chair, I had my left hand in my pocket and was busily prying off the cap of the vial and emptying the pills. The arm of the chair made it impossible for Ray to see what I was doing and Les was on my right, and engrossed in the "Network Battle of the Bimbos" or some such intellectual pursuit. I began to crush the pills against each other, grinding as best I could to obtain a fine powder.

Les mumbled, "Yeah, sure. Goferit, Doc. One of these days you are going to make somebody a wonderful wife. Heh, heh, hah."

I dutifully rose and went into the kitchen and began to lay out the lunch preparations. Today in honor of the occasion I pulled a package of salami, jack cheese, and a plastic squeeze bottle of mayonnaise. Spartan fare, but sufficient. I carefully laid out the bread on three plastic plates, placed a slice of salami on one piece of bread and then a piece of cheese on top. Ray sat across from me at the counter and idly observed.

I rinsed my hands at the sink, and dried them on a paper towel, and went back to the plates on the counter in front of Ray. Picking up one of them in my right hand, I went to the edge of the den and innocently asked Les, "Mustard or mayonnaise or both on your salami?" I put my hand in my left pocket.

"Whatever… Nah, mustard!"

"As you wish. I turned back to Ray and gestured with the plate with a slight bow and flourish. "And for you?"

"Both."

Wow. Another oration by Ray.

I made a small show of looking for the mustard on the counter, and not seeing it, mumbled, "Dumb of me," and went to the refrigerator, still holding the plate with the open faced sandwich on it. I opened the door to the fridge and, shielded by the door, sprinkled as much of the white powder as I had been able to pinch between my fingers on top of the white cheese. I turned from the fridge, closed the door with the sandwich and plate hand, holding the mustard bottle in my left. Putting the plate on the island stove about six feet from Ray, I twisted open the top and squeezed a slalom of mustard down the bread, then closed the sandwich and presented it to him.

I put the other two sandwiches together and then washed my hands again. I grabbed a bag of chips and drew water from the dispenser on the outside of the fridge. We dined in silence, accompanied only by the sounds of Les's bimbo show. It was now about 1:30.

A short while later, the afternoon call came. "Yep. Sure, whadja think? Nope. Okay."

I had no idea how long it would take the chemical to work, or for that matter the potency or the size of the dose I had administered. Most of the commercial products available over the counter suggested that the medication be taken at bed time so as to operate effectively overnight, but I knew that those had to be tiny doses as compared to what I had used.

123

Oh... Phenol-phthalein. We used to have a hot-tub on the back deck, although over the years we found that we didn't use it, and finally had it taken out. The chemical is used in testing water for ph, or acidity/alkalinity. You can use test strips, but harking back to my old life-guard days as a high schooler, I preferred the old fashioned method, so I had bought a pool test kit. You put a sample of the water in a little bottle, add a pill, shake it for a minute to dissolve the pill and check the color of the water against a chart. Simple.

By the way, until recently when they found out that there was a link to cancer, phenol-phthalein was the active ingredient in Ex-Lax. Now the way that I figure it, the little mice would have crapped themselves to death long before they developed cancer, but I'm not in charge. I was betting that Ray the rat was going to have a challenging afternoon, but not because of sudden onset of cancer.

And now it was all about timing, and luck... and execution. Em had to stall until the end of day, execution in both senses of the word.

Chapter 20

It took a while to clean up after lunch, and then I sat on the couch with a piece of paper and a pen, seemingly engrossed in creating the "grand experiment". In reality, I was watching Ray for reactions. Thankfully, for now I saw none.

The "golf lesson" took quite a while. It took us over an hour to set up. First we had to find a yardstick and tape it, duct-tape of course, to the baseboard on one side of living room. Then we had to create our own version of the stimp-meter, a device that allows the measurement of the speed of a green. Eventually we simply used an open text-book from upstairs and rolled balls down the inside of the open book. We aimed our device at the 18 inch mark on the yardstick marked where each ball actually hit. We repeated the process a number of times with excellent results. The floor "broke" a little to the left, but the degree of consistency was very good.

We put a piece of tape on the floor to be the marker for the spot from which to putt. We also put a long piece of tape "down the line" of the putt, both before and after the point of impact. The reason for this was to show the line relative to the club head. In that way we could judge by careful observation whether the putter was going inside the line on the way back, back to the line at the point of impact, and back inside the line on the follow-through, as it would in a "gate-like" motion. Alternatively, we could see whether the putter-head stayed on the line as it would in a pendulum motion.

I was, as you might suspect, the architect of all of this and a great stickler for the scientific method. I even required that we write down our hypotheses, the first being that the amount of variance would be statistically greater with the gate swing than with the pendulum motion.

Hypothesis number two was that 'gate" results would deteriorate over time as fatigue overcame practice and muscle memory.

Hypothesis number three was that "pendulum" results would not deteriorate over time, but actually improve.

With pen and paper, and a plastic ruler from the upstairs office, we began the trials. First, Ray "gate" putted while I wrote down results. We agreed that he would have to putt for at least a half an hour. Then we changed to "pendulum" putting. I had to spend some time describing the motion to Ray, and then explaining how he had to get his eyes directly over the ball. That led us to using a piece of string as a plumb line to show how much he had been inside the ball in his normal putting. For that part of the "lesson" I should have charged him a whole lot of money. His putting would improve dramatically by getting his eyes over the ball.

Les even joined us and was watching from the corner chair. His interest stemmed from the fact that I had bet him $100 that each of my hypotheses were correct. He wasn't interested enough to help with the measurements, or the actual putting, but he was interested enough to make snide comments about the sexual orientation of anyone who played golf. What a guy!

A little after 4:00 o'clock Ray finished making his fiftieth putt with the pendulum swing. I dutifully measured and marked down the results on my pad. There was still no indication from Ray that he was feeling anything out of the ordinary. I requested a calculator from the upstairs office and some time to examine the data, and therefore called a break in the putting.

After about 45 minutes I asked if they would allow me to test a couple of things with the experiment, and without any fuss, picked up the putter and began to putt myself. Neither of the boys even thought twice about it.

After about five minutes things really started to move, literally and figuratively. Ray nodded to Les and said, "Break," and disappeared quickly into the bathroom and closed the door. A few minutes later, Les's phone rang. "Yeah... Good... Okay..."

My heart was pounding. Les's gun was in his lap and he was as alert as he ever was, but I had to move now and move quickly. The clock was running. The others would be home soon and if I had read Em's warning correctly, they were about through with us. It had to be now.

I took my normal stance and took several practice swings using the pendulum stroke and after two or three passes, "accidentally" hit the ball off the toe of the putter on the backswing, sending the ball under Les's chair and into the corner.

"Oh, good heavens! How silly of me! I cannot believe that I did that!"

"Geez, Doc. You really like this shit when you suck at it so bad? Where'd it go?" As he asked, he turned his head to look over his shoulder, and it was my turn to tee off. After all, I was away.

I took one big stride across the room and smashed the tip of the putter into Les's left temple.

Chapter 21

Les was slumped in the chair, half his head splattered over the head rest and the wall beyond. Ray was barricaded in the bathroom, oozing fluids from all sorts of holes, mostly from bullets, I hoped. And I had no time to think about it. I had to move!

I charged up the stairs taking them two at a time and began to search for their luggage. I had three rounds left and Zach and Britt still to deal with. I wasn't happy about those numbers. Ray was still downstairs barricaded in the bathroom, but I had no intention of checking to see how he was doing. I hoped that there would be additional clips, or at least loose ammunition in their baggage, but there just wasn't any. I guess that they figured that with four of them and only Em and me in close quarters, they would only need the natural loads. Forty rounds and only the two of us versus the four of them? Made sense, really. Loose ammo was a potential risk, why take it?

For the record, all of that nonsense that you read about the hero shooting the bad guy and then because he is such a sensitive guy, he goes into the bushes and throws up? Nonsense. Utter nonsense. If I'd had another clip, I'd have happily sat there in my living room shooting Les and/or Ray to mince meat. I was shaking with adrenaline, true. But, those bastards had kidnapped me and my wife, had shot my dog, and were still likely to kill us in about fifteen minutes. Screw 'em. Where's the chainsaw when you need it?

I'd been thinking about this since the first night. Planning, weighing possibilities, hoping for a chance. Two of them were gone, well one for sure and the other pretty durned likely. I wouldn't carve a notch in my gun for Ray yet. I had about fifteen minutes to set an ambush for the remaining two. That wasn't going to be easy. The "boys" hadn't been the "A" team. I couldn't kid myself about that. I could take some small measure of satisfaction that so far some of my plans had worked, but Zach and Britt were an entirely different matter.

It posed a difficult problem. Whenever they moved anywhere they had Britt in front, Em in the middle and Zach bringing up the rear. Inside the house, up or down the stairs, coming or going, always the same. I could take out Britt with a surprise attack, but Zach would instantly shoot Em, and I had every expectation that Zach would be good at it. If I waited until Britt and Em passed, I might take Zach out, but that left Britt and Em would be between us. Again not good.

I had to assume that their arrangements in the car would remain consistent. Zach was in the driver's seat. Britt was directly behind him, and Em was on the passenger side in the back. If I waited until they pulled into the garage and threw open the door, I'd have to shoot through the car and Em in order to hit them. Even if I'd had a full clip, the geometry of that approach was just plain impossible. Even if I got lucky and hit Zach, I'd have to go right through Em to get to Britt.

The configuration of our garage made me think about it, though. We have a three car garage. Mine was the right-hand spot, closest to the door. Em got the middle spot, and the left-hand spot is where we park the tractor. Since they had dumped my car, when they pulled in, they'd be close to the laundry-room door, so the idea of throwing open the door and banging away made sense if you wanted proximity. I wondered if I could leave some sort of clue for Em, like a homemade sign that said "DUCK!" or something. Nice idea, but I didn't think that if Em saw it and acted as instructed that Britt and Zach would just blissfully sit there while I took pot shots.

So, conclusion number one: nothing could look different in the garage as they pulled in. Conclusion number two: I couldn't rely on Em seeing some subtle clue or acting on her own in this. I had to do it on my own. That led to conclusion number three: whatever action I took had to be utterly unexpected and hit both of them so fast that they couldn't react.

I thought for a long time about hiding out in Em's car. It was sitting in the center spot, and if I sat in the front passenger seat I'd be about four feet from Zach when they pulled in and stopped. That gave the idea a lot of merit. I could throw open the passenger side door and I'd have an angled shot at Britt in the back seat of their car, and then I could go after Zach. If possible, it would be better to eliminate Britt first since she was right next to Em. To get to Em Zach would have to pick up his gun and turn to shoot over the seat into the back, and that split second could make all the difference.

I really liked that plan and had worked it over and over in my mind. It had some problems, sure. I'd be shooting at

131

an angle to get to Britt. I could resolve that by putting myself in the back seat of Em's car, but then I'd be shooting directly on a line toward Em. By shooting at an angle, I reduced the likelihood that I'd hit Em, but I also increased the likelihood that I would miss Britt, or that my shots would be deflected by the car window or frame or whatever. Who knows what kind of deflection a bullet takes when hitting glass or a car door at an angle? The FBI ballistics experts probably do. Sharpshooters in the military probably do. CIA assassins absolutely do. I don't, nor did I sleep in a Holiday Inn Express last night.

The great advantage of that plan was that it put me within just a few feet of each of them. I am not a bad shot, but I am also not a great shot. Standing in a range or out back by the pond, I could shoot pretty well, and usually hit what I was aiming at. But under these circumstances, shooting at live human beings who are armed and moving, and worrying about hitting my wife, and having to do it NOWNOWNOW... I wanted the distances and angles to be as easy as possible. Ever see a professional golfer miss a two-foot putt under pressure?

I had thought about sitting in the car with the ignition turned so that I had power to the windows. I could wait for Zach to get out of the car and I couldn't miss. As Zach got out of the car, I could roll down the window and not have to open the door. How quiet is your power window? I'd still have to go for Britt first. Too many things could go wrong. Window noise. Window takes time to roll down. Britt sees the window moving. Zach sees the window moving. Zach is out of the car and free to duck and return fire. The biggest problem with both versions of the car as a site from which to attack was that Zach would have time to kill me, and I was the only armed good guy. Once he took care of me he could kill Em at his leisure. Nope.

I had considered a variant on the plan that would have me hiding outside the garage. When they pulled in, I would enter the garage behind them, staying low. Pop up beside Britt's window, a quick shot or two, and then Zach. I liked this one, too. Biggest risk was that Zach would see movement in one of the side mirrors. If he caught even a glimpse, game over.

So, my first thought was to hide in the front seat of Em's car. It made sense. It had surprise and maximized my chances. The problem was I couldn't use plan "A", not with only three shots. I just couldn't risk taking two of them with only three shots. I could, perhaps, hit them with all three, but could I count on not only hitting them, but either killing them or incapacitating them to the point that they could not act against Em or me? Doubtful, really doubtful. I had to find another way.

I thought a lot about diversions. I could siphon gas out of the car, or diesel out of the tractor. For that matter the jerry cans that we used might still be full. There was paint thinner in the garage, unless they cleaned that up. We had fertilizer in the barn and ammonia... Given time, I could blow up the whole damned house. I could use sound and set off the stereo at about 130 decibels using the remote. There were lots of options for startling them with a diversion. But, thinking it all through during the wee hours of the night, I just couldn't risk any of that. Not with two of them. True, they might be shocked, but could I count on both of them being sufficiently non-plussed to give me time enough to do my bit? Again, doubtful.

So, I held onto plan "A" and hoped that I could put it into play. And I worked on plan "B" and "C" and on through the alphabet.

With only three rounds and no more ammunition, I was forced to shift to plan "B" and I started to sweat. I had no more time to worry or fret over it. It was time to act.

Chapter 22

I grabbed the bedspread off the bed in the guest bedroom and from the closet a canvas duffel bag that I used for overnight trips. I also picked up two twenty-pound dumbbells and moving as fast as I could, I took it all out into the garage. Three more trips and I had two twenty-five pounders, two thirty pounders, and two thirty-five pounders. Four minutes gone!

Each time I came down the stairs I listened as I passed the alcove leading to the bathroom where I fervently hoped that Ray had long since gone to his just rewards. I tried not to make noise as I passed and paused and moved abruptly. If he were alive and listening, I didn't want to give him a target. He could shoot through walls and doors just like I could, probably better.

At the side of the garage there was an old, left over piece of ¾ inch plywood, about two feet by four feet. I grabbed that and the eight foot step ladder. I made one last trip into the house for the duct tape and to listen and snagged Sadie's old backyard tie-out on the way back into the garage. I took one of the heavy duty extension cords from the garage storage and picked out the old heavy duty u-shaped bicycle lock and a flat-head screwdriver and a jar of grease. Six minutes gone!

I set up the ladder under the attic access in the garage and pushed the trap door open and shoved it to the side. The plywood went up first and I placed it across the joists to the side of the opening in the garage ceiling. As quickly as I could, I carried the rest up the ladder and placed it carefully on the side of the plywood platform. One last look around the garage, and as an afterthought I pulled the hand sledge hammer from the rack and took it up with me. I settled on the plywood and pulled the ladder up behind me. Ten minutes gone!

Now, I can't tell you why there is an attic in the garage. When we built the house, I suppose that we wanted to have extra storage space. I don't remember. I can tell you for a certainty that we never put anything up there. The trap was just a piece of plywood, and there wasn't a set of pull-down stairs or anything. There wasn't any lighting. Just joists and insulation. Thinking about it, I can't even tell you why we wanted a ceiling in the garage. It's there, but I couldn't tell you why. Now, I was thankful for our foresight.

When I had made the first trip for birdseed the day before, I had noted the location of the trap door. It was directly between the two cars and its front edge was just about over where the roof of the cars began. In the regular sitting positions for anyone in a car in the right hand garage space, the trap door should be out of sight. When I dropped my first load in the garage, I stooped and tested the lines of sight as best I could. It was close.

I hurriedly continued my preparations with the trap open to provide light for my work. And just under four minutes later, I was done. I carefully replaced the trap and tried to calm my breathing as I waited for Britt and Zach and Em to return.

Chapter 23

When you are scared, frightened to death, time does funny things. It seemed like an eternity and an instant all at the same time. I was doing my best to keep my breathing under control, but I don't think that it was working. My heart was beating a mile a minute. God! Had I thought of everything? Had I left any signs? Most important of all, was Ray out of commission? What else could I have done? Could they see if the trap came open? Too late now. Breathe.

I flinched when the garage door opener came to life. I hadn't thought how loud it would be. Of course it was mounted into the ceiling of the garage about six feet from where I was kneeling on my plywood platform, and it was using the garage ceiling like the sounding board of a giant bass fiddle.

I heard the car roll into its space and stop. I slid the screwdriver into the edge between the trap and the frame, levered the door out of its seat and slid it back out of the way. Zach turned off the car's ignition. The car door opened and Zach slid out of the driver's seat and stood up. When he reached his full height the top of his head was about two feet from the trap door opening. Now!

With my left hand I reached down and slid the loop over his head and pulled tight. At the same time I pushed the duffle attached to the other end of the wire over the edge. Two hundred twenty pounds slammed down five feet and smashed taut. The thin, vinyl-covered wire of Sadie's old tie-out buried itself in Zach's neck and jerked his body off the floor.

Holding onto a joist with my left hand, I leaned out and down and from a distance of about four feet put three shots through the driver side passenger window into Britt's face and chest as fast as I could pull the trigger.

Mostly I missed.

In the split second that it took for Zach's body to rocket upward toward the ceiling and for me to lean downward, Britt reacted. As I shot, she ducked to her right and down. Of the three shots, only one connected and hit her in her left shoulder. She came back upright and swung the gun in her right hand to return fire. As her gun came in line with me I caught a shadow of movement and saw the flash of the gun accompanied by the most hideous scream I have ever heard.

It doesn't pay to piss Em off, nor to ignore her. She had been preparing to take matters into her own capable hands as they returned home. She knew as well as I that things had to come to a conclusion today, and she could do the math as well. Four armed assailants and two hostages was infinitely worse than two on one. She had been prepared to act while in the garage, and did.

When Britt turned back toward me, Em took aim and with all her strength drove a couple of inches of a Bic Round Stic pen into Britt's right eye!

At the time I had other issues. I had hoped that the momentum of the weights snapping the wire loop shut would have been enough to break Zach's neck and crush his windpipe. Whether it did or didn't, Zach was frantically clawing at the cable and the framing of the trap door. His head was just below the opening and one of his hands found a grip. Sometimes hunches come in handy. I crushed his hand with the sledge hammer.

Another shot exploded from the car, and then another. From my vantage point in the rafters I could see that Em and Britt were struggling over the gun. Britt still held it, but Em had a death grip on her arm and wrist and shots were spraying all over. Both of them were screaming obscenities at the top of their lungs. Two more shots came in rapid succession.

I hadn't figured on the way this was playing out. When someone is hanged, they are supposed to die. When you shoot someone they are supposed to die. At least they should have the common decency to be incapacitated! Zach was still jerking and grabbing and swinging back and forth like a demon. Em was in trouble, and Britt, though wounded, was putting up a damned good fight.

I couldn't get down out of the trap door without giving Zach a chance to grab me. Our combined weight would pull him down and relieve the relentless stranglehold of the noose. The thought crossed my mind from my life-saving days at the pool; the last thing you want to do is to get into the water with a drowning person. They'll grab you and take you down with them. That didn't seem to be such a good idea. Or was it?

The second it came to me I knew it was right. Holding the hammer, I swung around, dropped my feet over the edge and grabbed Zach! I slid off the edge and we slammed down. As my feet hit the floor I pushed him away. He tried desperately to grab with his good hand, but he couldn't hold on and the sack of weights pulled him back to the ceiling. I fell backward and bashed the back of my head against Em's car and then scrambled to help her.

While all of this was going on, shots continued to explode from the back seat. I lost count of how many. Just as I regained my feet Britt's door opened and she started out. I roared in rage and raised the hammer to destroy this bloody bitch who had killed my wife, only to watch as she rolled forward out of the car and onto the floor of the garage, a scant inch of a Bic pen protruding from her right eye.

Stunned, I stood unbelieving at the bloody body at my feet, and then Em's feet appeared and she slid out of the back seat. "You had any doubts?"

It wasn't a "death rattle" but more like flatulence and I turned to see that Zach had finally quit moving.

Em and I looked at each other for a long moment.

"Your hair's a mess," I said.

We held each other in the silence, for a long time.

Chapter 24

Em and I stood in our garage holding each other, our hearts hammering and our ears ringing. For some time we simply stood there, her head on my chest, one bloody body at our feet and another hanging from the rafters. Neither intruded on our rush of relief at having survived, together. Finally, the long moments passed, and still holding on we parted enough to look at each other.

Em was a mess. Her face was splattered in blood. Her shirt and pants were alternately soaked and splattered in a grotesque imitation of modern art. The pattern was studded with pebbles of broken glass from the car window. A couple of leaves that had found their way into the garage over the winter were stuck on her shirt, and of course, there was the inevitable dog and cat hair and just plain dirt. Tears were running down her face, streaking the blood. Her lip was beginning to swell, and her nose was running and bleeding. She never looked so beautiful to me as at that moment.

"Are you all right," I tried to ask. Didn't come out quite like that. It was mostly unintelligible. Oddly, my throat wasn't quite working and the tears in my eyes were quickly wiped on my sleeve. That sufficed for the moment.

Em took a deep breath and paused for a second to take stock.

"Yeah. No permanent damage, I don't think." For Em to actually use a double negative was not a good sign, and I intended to remind her of it at some appropriate time in the future.

"How about you?" she asked.

The adrenaline was still pumping, and I could have been wounded multiple times and not even known it… I think. I have never been shot or blown up or bayoneted, so I really don't know, but it felt that way. I had banged my knee in my rapid descent from the trap door, and I had a burn across the side of my face and neck, I guess from Zach's fingernails as he tried to claw his way free of his noose. Other than those minor inconveniences, I seemed to be undamaged. With all of the shots blasting away from Britt's gun, it could easily have been very different.

"I'm a little banged up, but I'm okay. Nothing that a half a bottle of Wild Turkey and a whole bunch of ice won't fix."

Em just nodded, and managed to say, "Good," and swallowed hard.

We stepped back and took stock.

Britt-the-bitch was lying on the garage floor between the two cars. She was mostly on her right side facing the driveway. Like Em, she was painted with blood. I had managed to hit her with one shot in her left shoulder and there was a hole in the back of her shirt and a lot of blood. I guess it went all the way through given the apparent crater where her shoulder blade should have been. She was facing away from me and I couldn't see her face. Her gun had slid, or bounced on the concrete and was under the far side of the car, under the muffler. She wasn't moving, thank God.

I thought about making sure, much the same as I had with Les, one more carefully placed bullet in the brain. "Em, stay here while I get her gun. I want to make SURE she is dead. I don't trust her."

But, Em, turned around and viciously kicked the back of Britt's head as hard as she could. "I don't think that will be necessary," she grunted through clenched teeth. The kick had moved the body about two feet and as it came to rest I could see the last inch or so of the Bic pen sticking out of Britt's bloody eye-socket. Em turned back to me, her eyes blazing yellow. "Trust, but verify."

I told you. When Em's eyes are that color, take cover!

At which point I nearly jumped out of my skin as Zach moaned and jerked! I spun around and gaped in horror as the human piñata danced and twisted. I flinched into a crouch, ready to fight again as another round of adrenaline shot into my already jangled nervous system. I needn't have bothered. Zach's body was simply becoming accustomed to the idea that it was dead. On those very sad occasions in the past when we had finally been forced to euthanize one of our pets, we had seen the same. His arms and legs were completely limp, save the occasional twitch. When our pets had twitched, I fervently believed that they were gamboling in the Elysian fields. I hoped that Zach was losing his race with the hounds of hell.

He hung there with his head smashed up against the side of the trapdoor opening. His face was an appalling liver color. I am reminded of the unpleasant hue of an antique mauve couch in need of cleaning. Sadie's tie-out had done its job.

As I uncoiled from being startled, however, I noticed that blood was dripping from his leg, slowly creating a pattern on the smooth concrete floor beneath him. As his body turned slightly, I could see that low on the right side of his back was a hole. Blood had worked its way down from there, soaking the back of his pants and right shoe and finally making its way to the floor. I'm not sure, but I think that he inadvertently had saved my life.

As Britt was blasting away and I was taking the Zach down elevator, I think that she shot him! He was between me and the backseat of the car at that point, and he took the bullet that could have been mine had I simply jumped down.

Honor among thieves and all that. "Britt-the-bitch" to the last.

Chapter 25

I turned back to Em. The moment for relief and victory celebration was over. We were alive, but we still were in a world of hurt.

"Okay, Em, here's the deal. Les's dead. The chubby one. I'm absolutely sure. I put a bullet through the side of his head from about five feet. I do NOT know about the other one, Ray. I THINK he's probably dead, too, but I can't be certain and there is no way to find out without taking a totally stupid risk. I put six shots through the closed door to the entry bathroom while he was on the pot. I don't know how I could have missed, but who the hell knows about stuff like this? Anyway, I haven't heard a sound from in there, and I put up a sort of barricade, but this isn't over yet, okay?

Thing is, we've been out here at recess with Bonnie and Clyde and he could be anywhere in the house by now. We wouldn't have heard a thing. Hell, I STILL can't hear a thing. If he were going to move, it would make sense that he would do it when these two got home. If he could do anything, he'd hear the shots and yelling from out here and do it. Since the shooting is over and we haven't seen him, and he hasn't heard his team come into the house calling on him, he would have to figure that things are screwed up. So, we can't just walk in – yet. We're going to have to do this in stages, and we are going to assume that Ray is in the house somewhere, waiting and plotting on how to come out of there and kill us both.

Em scrubbed her hands up and down the front of her pants, listening intently to me, and again nodded. "Okay, I got it. You can tell me the rest later. First things first. Where is Zach's gun? I'll get the bitch's from under the car," she said, stepping over the body and ducking down behind the car. "Got it! I'll cover the door while you look." I always loved that about Em. When it came down to fish or cut bait, she'd nail the fish every time. Of course, to be fair, I had to bait the hooks because she didn't like worm goo, but still.

Every time I had seen Britt and Zach escorting Em, they moved in tandem, one in front and one behind. Zach had gotten out of the car first, of course. That way he could watch Em as Britt got out and into position. He always had his gun out, usually in his right hand, and I'll bet it was ready to fire.

He had opened the car door, turned and put his feet on the ground, and then leaned forward to get his center of gravity over his feet and then stood. I had been counting on exactly that sequence as I thought throughout the prior nights. When you are getting out of the driver's seat of a car, you HAVE to bend forward and look down in order to stand up. That was the only reason that I could open a great, gaping hole in the ceiling unnoticed. The front edge of the roof of the car blocked the view while he was in the driver's seat, and he was looking at the floor as he got out.

When the wire snapped shut around his neck and he was jerked off his feet, he lost the gun. Honestly, I had hoped that the weight and the loop of wire would have been enough to literally tear his head off, but that did not happen. Pity. I had worried a lot about him being able to hold onto the gun and get a few shots off at me. If I had seen the gun in his hand as I leaned down out of the attic space, I'd have used one of my remaining shots to blow his brains out. Didn't happen. So, he had dropped the gun as he had been yanked to the ceiling. It could be anywhere toward the front of the car.

I found his gun under the front of Em's car, which made sense. He got yanked up and forward by the cable, so it would have gone that direction unless it bounced like one of my golf shots heading to its "laughin' place" in the woods. On my hands and knees, I located it in front of the left tire, and carefully picked it up expecting it to be cocked and ready to shoot. As I reached to pick it up, I caught a glimpse of an ejected shell casing under the front of their car. Odd. I held the gun up and smelled it. Yep, it had been fired. I guess you shouldn't be surprised if you drop a loaded, cocked gun on a concrete floor and it goes off. To tell the truth, until just now I had no idea whether his gun had fired or not. Things were going pretty fast right at that point. Now I wondered if the bastard didn't shoot himself! I kinda liked that better than being shot in the back by his partner. Sadie got him all on her own!

I ejected the clip, and other than the one shot it appeared to be full. I didn't want to take time to empty out the rounds to count, but the weight seemed about right and I couldn't imagine Zach walking around with a half-loaded weapon. I seated the clip again, made sure a round was chambered and the gun was ready to fire.

"Okay, Em, I've got his gun. I'll watch the door. How many rounds do you have left?"

"Five."

"Are you sure?"

"Of course," she replied, giving me one of those spousal "looks."

"How do you know?"

"Because I counted the shots." With that, Em deftly ejected the clip from Britt's weapon, thumbed the rounds into her hand, replaced them into the clip and slapped it back from whence it came. Did I mention that Em is a better shot with a hand gun than I am? I'm better with a long gun, or at least I like to think that I am. But there was no doubt about her superiority with a hand gun. "Yep, five."

"My God! She only shot FIVE times? It felt like World War Three in here! Wait a second! Whaddayou MEAN, you counted! Jesus!"

Again she gave me the "look" which said that OF COURSE she counted and she couldn't believe that, a) I had doubted her, and b) I hadn't counted the shots myself.

"Yeah? Well, I bet you don't know which putting stroke is the most consistently effective!" I retorted. I was pleased to see that she was entirely nonplussed by this statement and thereby I regained some small portion of my manly dignity.

Chapter 26

With the door to the laundry room closed, and with both of us armed and paying attention, nobody was coming through without getting shot. The door was hinged to open into the laundry room, so there would be no surprise bursting into the garage. The overhead garage doors were closed. For the moment we were safe, but we needed a plan.

"You got a clue on what this is all about?" I asked.

"Yes, but now is not the time to go into it. I'll tell you later. We can't leave until we finish this!" she said. "You agree?"

"Well, personally, I'd love to just get the hell outta Dodge. Look, do we absolutely HAVE to get back into the house? It'd be safer to just cut and run."

Em looked thoughtful for a second, then reluctantly shook her head. "It's going to make it a lot easier later if we can. We could get by if we left now, but there would be a lot of stuff that we'd have to replace. There'd be a lot of people we'd have to deal with. Bank. Pharmacy. Clothes. Phones. That would mean a lot of explaining. Most importantly, we can't just abandon Marty and Joe! If we leave here, we lose control of this thing we're in. Oh, and finally, it is OUR DAMN HOUSE!"

I took a deep breath and let out a heavy sigh. Can't argue with logic. "So, how the hell are we going to get in?" I asked.

Now if you think about it, we were more or less safe in the garage. One of us could cover the laundry room door. The controls for the overhead doors were in the garage, except for the remotes and they were in the cars. The only other door opened into the garage and provided access to the back deck and back yard, and the all-important bird feeder, of course. It was kept locked from the inside of the garage. Nobody could get to us without putting himself at the wrong end of a shooting gallery. "Bummer of a birthmark, Hal."

That was the good news.

The bad news was that we were bottled up, too. We had no idea if Ray was out there, or where he might be. If we burst into the laundry room, we would be the targets. If we went out the back door, he could just as easily be standing at the back wall of the house on either side of the door, almost within arm's reach. We wouldn't be able to see him. He could be out front, waiting for us to open an overhead door. It was kind of like a giant game of "whack-a-mole" and we were the moles, only getting "whacked" didn't win a bunch of coupons for carnie junk and bad pizza.

Frontal assault into the laundry room just made no sense at all. The laundry room was narrow and he would have cover and we wouldn't. There was no way for one of us to cover the other. Just impossible. Now, with body armor, breaching charges, flash-bang grenades, poisonous gas, REAL grenades, okay! Squad of SEALS would be nice, too.

The back-yard door was tempting. The advantage of going out the back was that once free of the garage, one could belly-crawl all the way around the back and side of the house without being seen from inside. The raised deck provided enough cover that it would be possible to get all the way to the northwest windows. From there one could see if the alcove barricade was still in place. Em had her purse with her. She had a small mirror in her purse, I was sure. If not, I could tear the vanity visor out of the passenger side of the car and use it. Duct tape it to the end of a rake handle, and it would make a dandy periscope. Of course, while one of us was trying to see around corners, the other would have to be at full alert for Ray to pop up and take a shot or two. The second the back door opened, he would know for sure where we were. Better than a frontal, laundry assault, but still awfully risky.

The third option was out the front via the overhead doors. We could start one of the cars and open all three doors at the same time. Keep ducked down in the front seat so as not to be seen, and simply floor it in reverse straight out and up the driveway. The car would be moving fast and it would offer some protection. Once we got a hundred yards up the driveway, we wouldn't have to worry about anything other than an unbelievably crazy-lucky shot. Once there we could stop and take a look. If we didn't like what we saw, we could just keep going. There was a lot to commend this choice.

Of course, when the doors started going up and the car started, Ray would know what was happening and where we were. The time that it took for the doors to clear could give him time to get into position at the front of the house.

There were other options, too. We could simply wait. We had time, at least for now. If he had been hit, perhaps he would bleed to death. Ultimately, though, we'd have to move and the same options came into play.

At that moment, Zach's corpse made a rude noise and brought my attention back to the trap door and again I looked to the heavens for inspiration.

A short, whispered conversation with Em and we went to work. Well, I went to work. Em kept careful watch. We had a huge advantage now. We outnumbered him and could cover each other as we acted. If Ray were still alive, he'd be alone. We would have to be precise to avoid exposure, while pushing him into the open.

First, I rummaged through the drawers of the workbench, and found a suitable piece of hardware, a ¼ inch by 3 inch lag bolt, which I screwed into the outside of the frame at the laundry room door. Careful to stand to the side of the door and to make as little noise as possible, I used a roll of braided picture-hanging wire and tightly fastened the doorknob to the screw. Nobody was coming out that door without blowing a big hole or taking it off the hinges.

Getting back up into the attic posed a small challenge, since I had used Zach as a dumbwaiter and had left the ladder above. The roof of their car and a couple of spare lengths of 2X6 slanted up into the trap and I was in business. I used my electric power saw to cut through the roof at the back side of the house. A little noisy, but Em kept watch. There are no windows that overlook the garage roof. Ray would have to stand in the middle of the back yard to see me, and that would give Em a clear field of fire from the back door, if needed.

With the addition of about fifty feet of string, an old golf shoe, Em's cosmetics mirror and Zach's gun, we were set to go. James Taylor had it right!

Chapter 27

In the final event we agreed on a combination. As Em watched the back I levered myself up onto the roof. Then, I slid down to where I could use her mirror over the edge to see if Ray had hidden himself along the back wall of the house. All clear. I signaled Em by pulling the string that I had tied to my golf shoe, then clambered over the roof to the front.

I again used the mirror to check for Ray. There was no sign of him, but there was also an alcove that was out of my view where he could be hiding close by the garage. I signaled Em by jiggling the shoe. She hit the buttons on the remotes, started the car, and ducked down in the front seat to wait for my final signal.

We figured that when he heard the car start and the doors go up, he'd have to move to stop us. He wouldn't know who was in the car, and he couldn't afford to let us go. He'd have to show – if he could. If he were in the house, he'd have to go out a window or the front door. If he were outside, he'd have to show himself to get a shot at the car, and I'd be waiting. If he didn't show, Em was good to back out and we'd proceed with the next steps.

After a few seconds, there was still no sign of him, and I signaled one last time by dropping the shoe altogether. Em instantly put the car into reverse, having waited until then to maximize the guesswork as to which car was going to move. She stomped on the gas, keeping the wheels straight, and shot out of the garage, accelerating up the driveway. Actually, the driveway bends and she was onto the grass, but what the heck.

I kept watch as she stopped about three or four hundred feet out in the yard. Still no reaction from the house. I waved and crawled to the corner of the roof closest to the tractor, and checked using the mirror to check all down the front and side of the house. Satisfied, I put the safety on Zach's gun, and dropped to the grass at the end of the house. An eternity later, heart pounding all the way, I had wormed my way around the back. You know, a sixty-year-old body is not very well conditioned for belly-crawling. Adrenaline will only take you so far. My back hurt. My elbows and knees hurt. My neck stung. My head still hurt. And the whole, interminable way I was listening hard for the creak of wood decking, the opening of a window, the turn of a door latch, or worse, the startling, explosive shock of a bullet. I fully expected at any instant to have Ray loom above me with a feral grin of victory.

I almost lost it when Marty the cat jumped down from his perch on the railing and hit the deck with his usual ka-thud! Next I knew, he was "helping" me on my way by stropping on my face and doing circles around me. Marty is usually quiet. Good thing it wasn't Joe. He'd have been "talking" all the way. I tried to impress upon Marty that this was a secret mission and that he should set up a diversion someplace else. He rolled on the grass directly in my path and twitched his ears as a bug flew by. Finally, insulted by my lack of attention, he haughtily strode back the way I had come, jumped up on the deck and began to wash to repair his dignity.

At the front corner of the house I peered out from between the bushes and could see Em in her car. I waved, but she gave no warning signal. Good! That meant she hadn't seen anything. No movement. Finally, I was in position to see through the northwest window whether the barricade had been moved. The shade was down, but our windows crank open and the handles block the shades from completely closing. There is always a very small opening just above the sill.

I could see directly across the living room and entry to the alcove barricade. The front entry tile was splattered with glass. My pickle jar alarm had gone off! The door to the bathroom was open half-way. One of the stools had fallen, and lay partly out into the entry. Ray appeared to be lying in the alcove his gun extended in front of him. He didn't seem to be moving, but what did that mean?

In position, now Em could move. I waved her in with a "come hither" sign, and continued to watch the inside of the house. Instead of going back to the garage, she drove at an angle across the front lawn to the front door and left the car parked facing the front corner of the house, just a few feet from the bathroom. She exited the car from the passenger side, and positioned herself behind the right rear tire, gun ready, for all the world like a police officer in a movie.

With Em in position, I was free to move. She could see the bathroom window and the windows at either side of the front door. I went through the fence at the corner of the house, pushed myself upright and tried to straighten. I made it to Neanderthal status by stages.   Maybe Quasimodo.

I pantomimed to Em that Ray was in the alcove, prone, and directed her to watch from her post at the front door. Then I joined her behind the car, although I was at the front passenger side fender. There was no movement, no sound. I looked at my watch. Just approaching six o'clock. In all, the entire bizarre battle had taken only 45 minutes from the stroke of my putter to now. An eternity in miniature.

"I don't ever want to do that again," I rasped. "Okay. Come here. See the edge of the alcove through the front door windows?   I'm going to keep this gun. I'll need the extra ammo. I'm going back to the garage and in the through laundry room.   If you see movement, start shooting."

Em looked at me as if I had three heads and said, "Then what, Sherlock? You are going to have to show yourself in order to get to him. And, when you come around that corner you will be right my line of fire. Not good! Why not just go back to the window by the fireplace and shoot from there?"

It was my turn to deliver "the look".

"I have no intention of offering him a shot at all. Nor do I intend to put myself in your line of fire. You might find the temptation too much to handle. From across the living room, whichever of us was there would absolutely be in his line of fire and silhouetted against the outside light. Not to mention that it is a longish shot, we would be upright, and he would be dark and lying down."

"Look, just trust me on this one. We've done okay so far. I promise, I'll be careful and I won't be at risk. When you hear my first shot, be ready if he comes out... and stay behind the car!" I kissed the least messy spot on her hair that I could find and crouch-ran, well, crouch-gimped back to the garage.

I checked the gun in my hand, made sure I had a round chambered, and took a deep breath. I unwound the wire that had secured the laundry room door, and slowly and quietly turned the knob and eased it open with my left hand, gun in my right, pointed toward the far door. If Ray came out, I'd hear the crash of the furniture, then Em's shots, but I fully intended to be ready. I eased the door back and left it not totally closed. Silence is good.

The laundry room connected to a short hallway. On the left the hallway opened into the kitchen. To the right were bookshelves underneath the stairs that rose from the entry as they came toward me. There was storage under the stairs, on the other side of which was Ray and the alcove. But between me and the stairs was the pantry, and just inside the pantry, lined up exactly with the alcove was the freezer.

As quietly as I could, I eased open the door to the pantry, stepped inside, and closed the door. The freezer was almost exactly the width of the alcove. There was just about two inches on either side. I knew where Ray was, and some folks just don't learn from experience. Standing behind the freezer, I extended the gun into the gap, carefully aimed and put six shots through the wall as fast as I could pull the trigger!

My reward was a crash of furniture, a scream of rage, and then four shots in return. I could feel the impact as they whanged into the metal back of the freezer and the frozen food inside. Then, another shot, and then more slowly, another. And then, from farther away, the sound deadened by walls and distance, three more shots almost together. After a few more seconds there was one final shot, again louder and closer.

"Hon? It's over," Em called out.

For the first time since I opened the door in front of me three days ago, I let down and relaxed.

I walked around the stairs to the entry. As I shuffled around Ray's body I didn't stop to count the holes. There was a lot of blood in the bathroom, so I'd wounded him right from the start. Is that where the term "pot shot" came from? I doubted it. I'd probably hit him again just now from the pantry. He had rolled over and shot back at me all the while scooting on his back into the entry. That's when Em had gone to work. I think she hit him twice. Then finally, she had made sure, just as I had with Les. I like the way that woman thinks.

Em stood shakily just outside the shattered front window. I unlocked the door and stepped outside. Again Em and I held each other. The relief was overwhelming. We had

159

survived. We were alive! Miraculously, we had no major injuries. And there were four dead people in our home.

Chapter 28

We sat on the front lawn, reluctant to go back into the house. I guess having multiple decomposing bodies strewn about is not much of an interior decorating coup. It just doesn't say "welcome" somehow.

This was the first time that we'd really had to talk together, and it seemed like a good idea to just sit and "review the bidding". They had kept us apart to make us easier to manage, and to keep us from working together to create an escape plan. How'd that work out for you, eh? When you have been married as long as Em and I have, and when you have complete faith in your spouse, conversation is overrated. Still, now was the time to catch up.

"I'd say that we have four or five hours before we have to make the next move, but what we do at that point will define things from here on out. Does that make sense?" I asked.

"How do you figure?"

"I was in the front bedroom, so I was closer, and could probably hear better than you could. Did you hear the phone calls?"

"I thought that I heard something on the first night, but I wasn't really sure."

"After they put us to bed, Britt-the-bitch checked in. She was reporting to somebody. The time was a little different each night, of course, but it was pretty obvious that she was letting somebody else know what was going on," I said.

Em sat back against the side of the car, and with a disgusted look, wiped a sticky hand on the grass. "Yeah, that makes sense. I didn't really believe that they were the brains behind all of this. They just didn't know as much as I would have expected. Not to mention that they would have to have some serious resources, assuredly beyond their reach."

"She always called 'him'. I don't know why I say 'him' - I just have an image of a male. At any rate, it makes sense that she'd call out. A – I didn't hear a ring-tone, and B – even on 'vibrate', you wouldn't want to have an incoming call at the wrong time. Anyway, I don't think that whoever is on the other end will expect a call until bedtime. So, we have a little lee-way."

Em looked at me and said, "I love you. A lot."

"Well, I love you, too. But the next time you decide to work with some folks on a new project, you might be a little more selective in your choice of colleagues, though. You seriously should think about some interviews, maybe have a committee do a background check, have them pee into a cup or something?"

"Hey, YOU let them into the house!"

"Yeah, well, at least I don't use double-negatives." Let her chew on that for a while.

We lapsed into silence and each retreated into our own thoughts. It was amazing how normal it all seemed. The front of the house looked like it always does, if you don't count smashed glass at the side of the front door and the

162

bullet holes in the siding outside the bathroom. I hadn't noticed them until now. It seems that a 9 mm bullet takes some serious stopping. I'll never speak ill of frozen food again.

It was so quiet! Despite the ringing in my ears, I could hear the breeze in the trees. A dog barked from way off. A cardinal was calling from somewhere near the bird feeder. An airliner slid by on its way to the Cincinnati airport in northern Kentucky. All of those people gliding by, blissfully unaware of the troubles below. Hell, they were probably full of righteous indignation about not having enough peanuts or some such.

Marty pranced over and joined us and bonked and stropped for attention. Joe emerged from the bushes in front of the house and flumped down doing his king lion act, supremely powerful over all he surveyed. No big deal. Nothing had happened in their world.

I looked at Em "Whaddya wanna do now? We probably ought to get moving."

She looked down at her hands, now having accumulated a few bits of dried grass and leaf particles to go with the sticky, drying blood. She rocked forward, and pushed herself to her feet. Putting the car keys into the ignition, she said, "First things, first. I'm going to put the car in the garage and close the overhead door. Then I'm going to take a shower. You feed Marty and Joe. And, lock 'em in. We don't want to have to hunt for them later."

First things first sounded like a very good idea. "Gotcha. But first I'm going to pour myself a quadruple Wild Turkey and wash off my putter."

Chapter 29

While Em went upstairs to shower, I un-taped the liquor cabinet. I grabbed a favorite old purple plastic cup that had been given to me as a specialty advertising piece at a career fair years ago. None of the lettering was still visible, but I loved that stupid cup. First I filled it with ice and then with bourbon. I rattled it for a moment and then set it down on the kitchen counter so I could extricate a stool from its most honorable position atop the remains of the barricade. I half-sat, and took a deep pull from the now icy elixir.

There is a certain yin and yang of drinking Wild Turkey. It is a veritable symphony of extremes. It is sharp enough to take your breath away, and yet it is smooth like a fine wine. It has an icy solidity to it as the first swallow plummets down your throat, and then a warm, suffusing glow as it hits bottom. It is sweet and tart. It is complex from the tannins in the oak barrels in which it is aged, and it is simple in its direct statement of strength. It is a depressant, but it brightens one's outlook. It is both old enough to have developed character, and it is still young enough to be trouble. Damn! That first swallow was good!

After a few vacuous moments and another pull at my drink, I went out to the garage. I turned on the lights and began searching through Britt's things. She had a bag, of course, and I simply tossed that into an empty cardboard box. Then I went through her pockets. Not the most pleasant experience, but under the circumstances, I'd rather go through hers than have her go through mine. For all of that, I came up with bupkis. To be expected, of course. That is why women carry bags, but I wanted to be thorough. I wanted information, badly.

Zach was a bit more of a problem. It was awkward trying to reach into his pockets to pry things loose. He swung, and twisted and for every intent and purpose did his best to keep me from despoiling him. It was almost like he was continuing to fight. Nevertheless, I finally won, but I cheated. I pulled an Exacto knife from the tool cabinet, and slit his pockets open. The take; a wallet, complete with credit cards, driver's license, various insurance and other identification, a set of car keys, a cell-phone (off), one hundred, thirty-seven dollars in mixed bills none higher than a twenty, forty-three cents in change, a handkerchief (relatively clean, though bloody), and a mostly empty tube of Carmex. I suppose that I could have cut him down, but screw him! Let him swing.

I added the take to the cardboard box and taking out a couple of old painting tarps, went back inside. Another pull from my purple cup, and I repeated the process with our other two guests. My putter had fallen down beside the chair. I guess that the shock of the 9mm slug slamming through his skull had dislodged it. I picked it up and true to my word, took it to the kitchen sink and scrubbed the blood and gore off of it, with soap and lots of hot water. I dried it with a handful of paper towels. Always take good care of your tools.

I spread one tarp at Les's feet and rolled him out of the chair. He landed on the tarp with a liquid, flatulent sound. The movement had extruded the contents of his bowels with some force, and, despite his jeans, I was now

166

absolutely certain that I was going to need a new favorite chair. I opened a couple of windows, and it helped a bit. Ray wasn't nearly as putrid as Les was. I guess that made sense given the dose of phenylpthalein he'd been dealing with. He'd been pretty much emptied out before he died.

One by one, I wrestled the two bodies onto the tarps, and dragged them separately out into the garage. It was a lot of work. You don't realize how uncooperative two hundred plus pounds of limp meat can be. They don't bend helpfully to get around corners. They catch on changes in surface. They get slotchwise with a perverse "attitude" all their own. They pull back, and try to slide off the end opposite from you. Still, the tarps helped as I slid them across the tile of the entry, and the linoleum of the laundry room. Finally, I had both of them in the garage. I pulled Britt's body over to join them, leaving a gooey smear. There is one helluva lot of blood in a human body and she had left a crimson puddle about twice the size of her body on the garage floor. Zach's mess had lost its Rorschach style and had filled out in its own sizable pool, complete with tributary following a contour of the cement under the car. I cut him down with a pair of bolt cutters, added his body to the makeshift morgue and covered it all with one of the tarps.

I could have waited for Em, but I wanted to get the mess out of the house and onto the sealed concrete of the garage floor as soon as I could. First, I have no idea how long it takes for rigor mortis to set in. Once that happened, moving the bodies from inside would probably be more difficult. Second, I figured that the mess would get worse over time. Third, Em and I were going to have to have a "council of war" over the next few hours and I just didn't think that it would be conducive to our thought processes to have two dead bodies twitching and oozing and making wretched noises a few feet away. Granted, it would make me feel like I was in classroom full of students, but nevertheless.

By the time I had "taken out the trash" I was pretty much a wreck myself. I was covered with various bodily fluids, soft tissues, grass, dirt, dog and cat hair, grit, muck, the remains of dead bugs, and petroleum products that had leaked from the bottoms of our cars. I also hurt like hell from my knee to my throbbing head to my now overly-taxed back.

My favorite purple cup was still on the kitchen counter, and as I took another long pull, I finally heard the shower shut off. If Em had used all the hot water, there was going to be hell to pay!

Chapter 30

Half an hour later we were seated at the dining room table, picking at our sandwiches and discussing the events that had just transpired.

"So, how was your day, honey?"

"Oh, nothing special. How about yours?"

"I just killed a guy with my putter."

"Really? Did he step on your line?"

"Nope, talked during my backswing. What did you do today?"

"Lost my pen."

"No! Not the red one that you use to mark papers!"

"Yep, the very one."

"Tragic. I'm so sorry. Can you find a replacement, do you think?"

"I'll keep an eye out."

"You know, the strangest thing happened to me this afternoon. This guy called at home and immediately hung up on me."

"How rude. Better than just dropping in, though."

"Well, no noose is good noose."

Actually, the conversation went nothing like that. It would be cool if it had, but our discussion was much more somber and far more practical. Em had put on a pair of jeans and a smoke-blue "Your Dog Don't Know Sit" t-shirt. Of course she had taken time to dry and style her hair, and she looked great. True, her lip was swollen and she had a couple of bruises that were beginning to show like storm clouds, but I'd never seen her look better. She was sipping from a glass, half-filled from a newly-opened bottle of Sunny Slope cabernet sauvignon. Seemed like a good idea to break out the best for the occasion.

I had on a pair of jeans and an old, blue fishing shirt that had been washed so many times that it was nearly see-through. The sleeves were rolled up past my elbows.

"Awright, I think I know the answer, but I want to go over this carefully, together. This is going to affect the rest of our lives, and in ways that we probably can't imagine. We have to get this right. Absolutely right. We won't get any second chances. So, here goes... Question one; do we call the police <u>right now</u>?" I asked.

Em stared off into space for a time. "If we don't, we'll be looking over our shoulders for the rest of our lives. We'll never know if the next knock at the door will be the police. Every time the phone rings, or a car comes down the drive, it'll set our teeth on edge. That's a helluva way to live, hon!

"These *people* came after us. They came into our home and shot Sadie! They assaulted you, and kidnapped both of us at gunpoint! No jury in the world would convict us. If there ever were a case of self-defense and people afraid for their lives, this is it!

"And don't I recall hearing about Ohio passing some form of 'Castle' law a couple of years ago; basically a 'hold-harmless' clause for people who defend themselves in their own homes? As I remember it, right after it passed there was a test case when some guy shot and killed two people who came into his house. He wasn't even charged. The new law basically assumes that if there is an intruder in your home, you are justified in using whatever force you deem appropriate. It used to be that you had to, what was the word... 'retreat' even in your own home. And even then, you could only use appropriate force, whatever the hell that means. Can you imagine? I'm five-two and I weigh one-hundred and ten pounds, and some guy comes into my house in the middle of the night and I am supposed to keep it 'fair'? Bullshit.

"I had a conversation with one of the Oxford cops years ago. He told me that if I had to defend myself in my own home that I should shoot the bastard, and if I had to, I should drag the body over the threshold and put a kitchen knife in his hand. Well, hon, here we are, and nobody can deny that we were the victims. Bring out the kitchenware!" Em was on a pretty good rant, and her eyes were glinting toward the yellow end of the spectrum. She had some good points.

"Well, in a normal household invasion, you might be right. But for the sake of argument, let me paint a slightly different picture for you.

171

"First, while you were out and about, did other folks see you and Britt and Zach together? I assume so, since that was obviously the purpose of keeping me here."

"Of course."

"Okay, did you try to escape? Did you look frazzled? Did you attempt to leave a note? Did you write S-O-S in lipstick on the bathroom mirror? In short, did you give any observer any reason to think that you were in distress?"

"No, of course not. If I had, I'd have been risking that they would hurt or kill you. That was the whole point of keeping you here while I was out."

"So, if someone were to testify, they would have to say that you appeared to be your everyday, smiley, regular self... not somebody who was in the midst of being kidnapped. Right?"

"I suppose."

"Now, while you and I know differently, Britt and Zach would appear to be run of the mill students to anybody who saw them, maybe graduate students. They weren't exposing fangs, or waving guns around. So, to an outsider it looked pretty much like regular daily activity, yes?"

"Yes, probably so," Em said. "Where are you going with this?"

"Bear with me."

"Now, poor Les was minding his own business, sitting in an easy chair in the living room when he had his skull bashed in with a golf club! He never even fired a shot. He was just a member of the gallery, watching as Ray and I practiced our putting on the carpet. I think that the forensics would bear all this out; angle of attack for the blunt instrument to the head, no gunpowder residue, etc."

"But he was in our house!" Em objected.

"Yes, but who's to say that we didn't invite him. Who practices putting with intruders?

"To continue, poor Ray is sitting on the pot blowing his brains out, so to speak, because he had been poisoned with a massive dose of phenylpthalein. And while seated behind a closed door, he is the subject of a vicious gun attack! To this point he has been a model citizen, practicing golf, reading golf magazines and being a good houseguest. Who kidnaps people and then reads golf magazines and practices putting? C'mon! He hasn't fired a gun. No residue, not until later.

"Oh. Then Les gets a bullet to the head from about five feet. Sporting, that, don't you think?"

"This is all twisted! Nobody would believe that you and I are monsters who would just lure people into our home and murder them! That is just too fantastic!" Em exploded.

"Oh really? Can't you just see the interview? 'They were such a quiet couple...' Or some of our wacko colleagues? 'I always thought that Richardson was some sort of psychotic sadist. He IS in the BUSINESS school, you know...'

173

"So the kids come home after school, and in an intricate surprise attack, Zach almost gets his head torn off when he gets yanked off his feet as he gets out of the car. After Sadie, Zach never fired a shot, except the accident in the garage. No forensic evidence that says that he ever threatened us at all. Maybe his prints on his gun, but that doesn't say that we were in danger. For that matter, that is true for all of them."

"But wouldn't the fact that they all had guns, and oh, by the way, of the same make and model, prove that there was something going on?" Em asked.

"Who knows? Maybe the 'Browning Automatic Club' was in town and they were working with you on the history of weapons in Butler County. I don't know. Of course it looks odd, but is it reason enough for us to have killed all four of them?

"Anyway, before I was so rudely interrupted... so, Zach is garroted in bizarre fashion, never having done anything threatening. And, at this point I open fire on Britt in the backseat of the car. She returns fire. So far, she is the only one of the four who can be shown to have done anything at all to put us in danger. Please note, she could just as easily have been responding to the horrific sight of her boy friend being hanged! You could make a good argument that SHE was acting in self-defense!"

"Jesus! What a mess!" groaned Em

"Oh, it gets better. First, if we had been kidnapped, and I was being held hostage at home, when I eliminated the threat here, why didn't I call the police right then and there? Bring in the SWAT team and the Marines and the cavalry right then? Doesn't that make more sense than the crazy trap that I tried? Most folks would think so.

"Second, when you and I were in the garage and had freed ourselves from this horrific ordeal, why didn't we just take off? We were free to leave! We proved it by your departure in the car at that point. Poor, poopy Ray was on the floor of the foyer, wounded, in pain, bleeding. All we had to do was leave. But, no! We created a carefully constructed cross-fire and please note, because this is the key to the whole thing – WE WENT BACK IN TO FINISH HIM OFF! Again, the forensics would show that you were outside. Only at that point did Ray do anything that put us in danger, and again it's pretty clear that he would have been in fear of his life, ergo self-defense for him, too.

"Frankly, you and I make Bonnie and Clyde look like Shirley Temple and Richard Simmons. We are bloodthirsty ghouls. Now, do you still want to go to the police?" I asked.

Em got up from the table and walked to the kitchen sink. She looked out the window at the pond and the woods beyond. "Yeah, maybe. What about all the duct tape? Doesn't that prove something?"

"We're getting ready to fumigate."

"Damnit! Do you have an answer for everything?"

175

"No.   But I sure as hell hope that WE will, because otherwise we are either going to jail for a long time, or we are going to die.   And THAT'S why we are taking our time on this discussion, and why we are going to argue this out from every perspective that we can.

"Look, I'm not sure, either.   There are some very good arguments for going to the police, too.   As you said a few minutes ago, I am not looking forward to playing 'Telltale Heart' for the rest of our lives.

"We have also been your basic pillars of the community for the past thirty years.   We both have doctorates for God's sake.   Lots and lots of folks know us and respect us.   They will never believe that we have just been playing a role for all those years and that deep down inside we have been secretly preying upon visitors to our home.

"If we tell the whole, unvarnished truth the facts will support what we say.   We can show what we did and how we did it.   The forensics will bear it all out.   From a legal standpoint, we'll probably have to go to trial, but we will almost certainly beat it.   A good lawyer and our own testimony will make people believe that this was the only way out for us.

"One of the biggest things going for us is motive.   What possible reason could we have for ruthlessly murdering four young people?   It just doesn't make sense.   I'm beginning to lean back in your direction. Maybe calling the cops is the best thing after all."

Em turned back toward me and began to look distinctly uncomfortable. I almost didn't hear her one word reply, "Treasure!"

Chapter 31

"Excuse me?" I gasped.

Em straightened and sighed. "Treasure. This whole thing is about treasure. Somebody thinks they have the key to a treasure trove and they want it badly enough to do whatever it takes to get it."

I literally busted out laughing. "You have got to be kidding! Like buried treasure? That's hilarious! I can see it now. The year, 1657. The Spanish galleon Oro de Isabella, laden with gold plundered from the New World, is on its way back to Hispania. For days the ship has been blanketed in fog. The fog lifts and for the first time el Capitan can use his sextant to sight the sun. The first mate stands by anxiously, and finally asks, 'Where are we Capitan?' El Capitan replies, 'Well, Francisco, as close as I can make it we are in McGonigle, Ohio!' This is a riot! What total bullshit!"

"Shut up, hon. You don't know what you are talking about," Em admonished.

"Hunh? What do you mean? You can't be serious?"

"Yes. I'm serious. Serious enough that we have four dead bodies in our garage. Serious enough that I've spent three days combing records and maps. Serious enough to think that we have enough to go on to investigate further. And serious enough that I've been obscuring information from our abductors however I could, and as you asked."

"Oh my God," I groaned. "Holy Kafarley!" I have no idea who Kafarley is or was, but it seemed as good an oath as any. "Well, on the one hand, that is really cool. On the other hand, we now have a motive. Well, maybe, depending on the size of the treasure. Please, tell me that it is just a little treasure and that nobody in his right mind would hurt someone over it. Please!"

Em looked grim and professorial. "Actually, that is part of the mystery. Nobody actually knows what the treasure is, just that it existed. Until all of this I had pretty much thought of it as a quaint story that probably developed out of local gossip. But now, I'm reasonably convinced. I think that there is something out there waiting to be discovered, and right now you and I have the best shot at doing the discovering."

"Well, yeah, maybe. IF we can stay alive and out of jail. And IF there ever was a treasure. And IF somebody didn't dig it up two days after it was hidden, or stumble over it while digging a privy or something."

"You're right. All of those things come into play, but I have reason to believe that the treasure actually existed, and that we could still find it. And, it is obvious that someone else believes in it enough to assault, kidnap, and even kill for it. Don't forget that there is somebody out there behind all this, and they probably have information that we don't," Em reminded me. "I'll go a step further. I think that our only way out of this mess is to find it. It is the only leverage we have."

Em continued, "There are two newspaper accounts of the story, one in the June 22, 1893 edition of the *Hamilton Telegraph*, and the other a day later in the June 23, 1893 edition of the *Oxford News*. The stories have a few inconsistencies, but agree on a number of pertinent facts. About two weeks prior to the news stories, a stranger showed up on a local farm and asked the farmer if he could look around the place. He had some kind of paper, a letter, I now know with directions to a buried item. The local farmer permitted the man to investigate and he soon came to a large stone, estimated to weigh several tons. The stone was covered with Indian markings, supposedly. One account described the markings as having been chiseled over a lengthy period of time and said that the rock was a 'marvel' in that it was perfectly round. Both articles agreed that the stranger scratched the top of the rock with a cross and was never seen again. One of the articles conjectured that the stone might cover the entrance to a large cave in which a treasure might be found. The other story spoke of a treasure buried on the property by a wealthy owner years before. Of course the farmer on the property at the time vowed to keep watch over the rock until he could excavate and discover what it might hide.

"So, you see? This part of the story is all perfectly true, or at least as true as newspaper articles of the day might make it, which leaves quite a bit of leeway. Newspapers of the time weren't too worried about faithfulness to the truth. They often exaggerated and hyped stories, and were often full of gossip and opinion and out and out fabrication."

"You mean like the communists at the *New York Times* and the *Washington Post* today," I deadpanned.

"Well, sort of, only not so sinister. These were small, local papers operated by the owner who was probably also the editor, the chief reporter, the sales person, and the printer all in one. At any rate, both papers had the story, and the discrepancies themselves suggest that the story was making the rounds. One had the farmer named 'Baker' and the other 'Bakin'. One had only the top of the rock visible and the other had it almost entirely uncovered by spring rains. These were weekly newspapers, and yet both articles appeared on nearly the same day. That suggests to me that both newspapers picked up on a story that was being talked about by the locals. So, they investigated some, but didn't get all the facts exactly one hundred percent correct.

"One interesting point is that neither newspaper did a follow-up story. I looked through the archives for both for a year after these articles and there were no additional updates. What does that say to you?" Em asked.

"Well, I'd say that the farmer didn't find squat, because if he had, there would have been banner headlines, fireworks, parades, you name it. And, that just proves my point. There wasn't any treasure in the first place, just a highly decorated rock. Probably the Indian markings said something like, 'Deer Place H.S. Class of 1743' or 'For a good time try Little Flower' or some other Indian graffiti."

"You are an idiot, you know that?" Em laughed. "What it proves is that the rock itself did not mark the location of the treasure, at least not directly. It was probably a reference

181

point of some sort. Let's get serious. If you had a map that pointed the way to a buried treasure, would you walk up in broad daylight and say, 'Howdy! Mind if I look for a treasure on your property?' That's crazy! It would result in exactly what happened, which doesn't get the stranger anywhere at all. The farmer brags about this rock and tells the story to his friends and family and the grapevine begins to do its thing and voila, you have a story in the newspapers! Everybody is talking about the treasure on the Baker farm! Until Baker and his family and friends can dig it up, he's probably sitting out at night with a shotgun, keeping watch."

"So let me get this straight. Somewhere around here there is a rock that was some kind of a marker that would help to locate a treasure that consists of nobody knows what?" I asked.

"Yes, that's about right," Em replied.

"And that gives us a motive for killing four people?"

"Actually, it does. Some of the materials that we took out of the archives had to be signed out. They would show in general what we were doing. These people turn up dead and it looks like we found the key clue and decided to hog it all for ourselves. A prosecutor could make a pretty good argument."

"Peachy! I concede the point. But, as riveting as all of this is, I don't think that the treasure will have moved in the last couple of hours, and we still have to figure out what the hell to do with the house of horrors in the garage. Do we call the cops or don't we?"

Em returned to the dining room table and poured herself another half-glass of cabernet. I liked that. It showed that her mind was still working and that her attention to detail was not to be overwhelmed. Never fill a wine glass more than half-full.

"There is one more thing to consider," she began. "The children in the garage didn't come up with this on their own. Neither of my two had any real background or training or knowledge of historical research. And, your two were clueless. The phone calls iced it. There is somebody else out there, behind all of this."

"Agreed. From the beginning they had information about us that they should not have had. Not that it is hard to find information on people these days from the web and all. But, still, there was planning and reconnaissance and money that had to be managed. I don't think that the four could have done all that."

"What that means is that this other person..."

"Or persons!"

"Or persons... were willing to commit mayhem to get what they wanted. They are not going to just shrug their shoulders and say, 'Oh, drat. We give up. Better luck next time.' They want the treasure! But we'd have to be looking over our shoulders forever! They could kidnap one of us any time they wanted. It's not like we are going to be

183

part of a witness protection program. They're hidden and we are out in the open."

"The good news is that whoever they are, they aren't going to go to the cops, either. If they blow the whistle, they are going to have a lot of explaining to do. 'Oh sure, I hired these four to kidnap the Richardsons.' Even if they were to make an anonymous call, how does that help them? If we're the subject of a huge police investigation at this point, it would totally screw up their efforts for a long while.

"And so," I continued. "We don't want to go to the police, because we'd probably end up in prison. We leave the mastermind, or minds, out there to try again with us or with somebody else. We become vulnerable to whatever they want to do because we have no idea when or from what angle they might come after us. They don't want to go to the police because they need help to find the loot, and they can't stand exposure. Make sense?"

"Yes, I'm afraid so."

"I'd say we've answered our first pressing question. No police."

Chapter 32

We cleaned up the "dishes" which consisted of putting the paper plates and paper napkins into the trash. I put the leftovers into the refrigerator and Em wiped down the table, carefully sweeping the crumbs into her hand and then into the sink. We freshened our drinks and tried to make ourselves comfortable in the den.

"You ready to move on to the next?" I asked.

She shook her head wistfully, and replied, "No… but I guess we had better. Which do you want to tackle first?"

"Mr. Big."

"Yes. That's the most pressing, timewise."

"And, I don't think it is going to take a long discussion to figure this out. It's pretty much a no-brainer."

"Maybe, but let's lay it out anyway. I don't think that we have a whole lot of room for mistakes, and I for one am pretty well smushed."

"Yeah, me too. But this is the last thing that we have to do tonight. At least it is if you agree with my thinking," I said.

"I'm going to refer to the behind the scenes person or persons as 'Mr. Big' just for convenience." I pronounced it 'Meester Beeg' in a Peter Lorre voice. Rocky and Bullwinkle would have been proud, although I could just as easily have used 'Feerless Leader'.

"We know that Mr. Big is after the Baker treasure," I began.

"And that he has first-hand knowledge of at least a part of the mystery," Em interjected.

"Hunh? You lost me."

"They had a copy of the stranger's letter. It's in Britt's backpack, and there's more."

"Really!? Well, that makes it even more straightforward. So, Mr. Big has a massive interest in the Baker treasure. He has historical information and artifacts to support his search. But, he runs into a dead-end. He's stumped," I said.

Em picked it up. "Of course. That is why he needed me. It wouldn't have taken much to find my background and credentials on the web. He needed my help, but there's something fishy going on because he couldn't just ask me to join his hunt. He had to force me by holding you hostage!"

"That meant that he needed to have a team, and if you think about it, a team of at least four. Somebody had to watch me to keep the pressure on you while you were out doing whatever the hell you have been doing for the past three days. You'd have to have at least two so that things like bathroom breaks and sleeping would be covered. With you they'd need a female to escort you to the powder room, and somebody to drive, although they might have gotten away with just one if they thought you were sufficiently afraid for me.

"So where do you come up with four people willing to commit kidnapping and assault, and probably murder? I'm guessing that you don't just casually ask a few friends. More than that, if you are going to trust these people to do what you want from a distance, there would have to be some serious controls in place. Let's put it another way. How are you going to show four people where to find a treasure without solid assurance that they won't run off with it? Not going to happen.

Em paced a bit and said, "He'd need some pretty twisted people, and some very solid indication that they would be willing to take on a seriously illegal project. My bet is that they have criminal records or at least criminal pasts! If Mr. Big had something to hold over their heads, it would be helpful. And... if he added a nice paycheck, he'd be in business."

"Good, that makes sense. They do their homework, find out as much information as they can about us, and put together a plan. They timed it, they orchestrated it, and then they put it into action. It would have taken some time, and some money, and some brains. And THAT leads us right back to: Mr. Big does not want to involve the police. He wants the treasure!

"In a few minutes we are going to call him and play 'Deal or No Deal'!"

Chapter 33

We gathered the cell phones that I had removed from our four "guests". Four brand-new phones, all of the same make and model, neither very expensive nor el-cheapos. Nothing surprising. One by one we turned them on and began to compare the numbers in the call logs. Obviously, the four cell phone numbers appeared. Our number was in there, although they had never called the home number to my knowledge. And lo and behold, there on Britt's phone was the check-in number. It corresponded to the call in times over the last couple of nights. I guess they were confident that we would never have access to the phones or they would have erased them. It was nearly time.

Em and I sat across from each other at the dining room table, and nodded to each other. I accessed the number, and put the phone in "speaker" mode, and we waited for an answer at the other end. "Mr. Big" picked up on the second ring.

It would have been nice if he had answered, "This is Mr. Burfington Tweed-Whittle IV, at 1492 Columbus Acres, how may I be of service?" Can't have everything. All he said was, "Report."

Fine. Be that way.

Em opened. "Since it was about time, we thought that we would pay our respects. Britt and Zach are indisposed at the moment, and we knew you'd want to hear all about our day so we took the liberty of making the call for them. Let me introduce myself. I'm Dr. Rita Richardson, but of course you knew that."

"I'm here, too… Dr. John Richardson. We're on speaker."

Silence from "Mr. Big."

Em continued, "We have a proposition to put before you. We suggest that you don't hang up, and that you listen very carefully. You may want to take notes, because this will be a bit complex and it must be handled exactly. Are you ready?"

More silence.

"Let me put it this way. You WON'T get your treasure if you don't step up right now. So, nod your head if you agree," I added helpfully.

"Put Britt or Zach on," Mr. Big rasped. Oh, by the way, it was a he and his voice was Midwest and reasonably masculine and deep. I'll attribute the rasp to being taken unawares.

"That is not going to happen," said Em.

"What have you done?" he asked.

"You will not ever know, nor do you wish to know," I replied.

"What do you mean?"

"Which part of STAY THE HELL OUT OF IT don't you understand? You pushed some damned big buttons, buster, and it didn't quite work out the way you planned. You lost. We won. Get over it. Have you got that through your thick, pompous skull?" To a certain degree I was enjoying this. Em just rolled her eyes at me.

Silence, again.

"And that brings us to point number one. Do you have something to write with?"

"A moment," he gulped. "Now."

I continued, "No connection will ever be made between your four employees and us. No searches will ever be done. No effort will be made to find them. Should ANY investigation ever arise that would connect them to us, it all goes bad. Do you understand?"

"How do you mean, 'goes bad'?" he asked.

"We will have a complete description of everything that has occurred since Monday night, including our sworn statements, photos, all of the notes and copies of research materials, one of the weapons, and one of the cell phones, all in a package in a bank safety deposit box by tomorrow morning. You will not know which bank. We will have a duplicate key and a letter of instruction with an attorney. You will not know who the attorney is. The instructions will have him access the box and do what is necessary if we should be harmed, arrested, or implicated in any, shall we say, incident? We include in that any form of accident. Does that spell it out for you?" Em explained.

"That is sufficiently clear."

"Good. Point number two. You will provide all of the documents, prior research, artifacts, and anything else you think might help in the search. You will send them to me in a package to be delivered to my office as soon as possible. I shall expect it no later than the beginning of next week," Em demanded.

"There is only a little that you have not already seen or surmised, I am sure. But how am I to be assured that you will not simply solve the puzzle and disappear with the results?" asked Mr. Big.

My turn. "Don't you get it, pal? Do you remember Britt and Zach and our little relationship over the past couple of days? You got any kind of clue about how that all ended up? We are in this now, whether you like it or whether we like it! The only way for us to get out is to get you what you want and for us all to part company. I believe the U.S. and the U.S.S.R. called it 'M.A.D', mutually assured destruction, a.k.a. nuclear holocost. You mess with us and you lose what you want. We mess with you and we are in deep trouble. NOW do you see it?"

"Yes, that could work," he said after a moment.

Em added, "Point three. You will keep this number available to us. We will call you. You will not call us."

"All right."

"I will find the answers. I will finish the project and recover the treasure. When I have done so, there will come a time when we will have to meet in order to give you physical possession of the treasure. There will be a

191

commensurate fee for our participation at that time. When we have completed that final transaction, we will part company and never see each other or communicate ever again."

"How much is this fee?"

"I am sure that you will find it quite reasonable," Em concluded.

"I must say that I am surprised at this turn of events," Mr. Big said. "First, I thought that my colleagues were sufficiently professional in their skills that we would not have come to this. Your abilities have surpassed my expectations in that regard. Second, I am surprised at your confidence in locating the treasure. I had expected more difficulty, even from you. Third, and most surprising, I find your willingness to participate in the financial rewards of this enterprise to be, ah, shall we say refreshing? Hmm, interesting. It seems that we have common ground upon which to progress. All right. I agree. You shall have your package on Monday."

"You'll be getting yours shortly," I said drily, and closed the phone.

Em looked at me and said, "Well, that went well," as she turned off the digital recorder.

Confident that nothing further was going to happen that night, we went upstairs and went to bed, without handcuffs, without taking turns, and fell asleep in our own bed, in each other's arms.

Chapter 34

In the morning, our next big issue was to deal with the mess in the garage. Of course, after we followed up on our announced plan from the night before. We took everything to the office and made copies. We added a flashdrive with the pictures and the recording from the night before. We dictated our version of the events and put it all into a sealed envelope, and by a little after ten o'clock on Friday morning we had stopped by a bank in a nearby town and arranged for the safety deposit box. A little later we dropped off a letter of instructions to our lawyer, actually an old friend of the family and a local judge who was highly respected in the community.

With the insurance in place, we had to move on to the next and most unpleasant task. What to do with the bodies?

As with the discussion over going directly to the police, there were a great number of issues to consider and, we covered them in some detail. The two basic proposals boiled down to either burying them on the property someplace, or simply driving them in their car to a spot that would not be associated with us and just walking away. Both had their advantages, and their problems.

To start, burying the bodies was not a big problem. As I mentioned, we have an old John Deere tractor, a fairly large one. It has a number of attachments and we had kept it in pretty good repair over the years. We had used it to dig holes, pull out stumps, put in drain pipe and pull out old stuff that had decayed in the back fields. We had even buried Em's old horse on the property. It really does not

193

take all that much to dig a hole, put a body, or four bodies into it, and cover it back up. You can get fancy and put lime on the bodies and help the process along, but even that is not necessary. The horse's grave is covered with a small garden and a beautiful maple tree to commemorate the spot. Never had a single issue with it, except that it was a somber reminder of a faithful friend.

Nobody was going to get all exercised about us digging a hole in our back field. Nobody would even see us. And if they did, all we would have to say is that we were burying Sadie, and in a way that would be true. The real thing about bodies is that if nobody is looking, nobody is likely to find anything.

The downside was that it left evidence of foul play on our property where it would be associated with us without any doubt if anything were ever to bring the grave to light.

Piling the bodies into the trunk of their car and simply driving it to a bad part of town also had its appeal. If we took it out into the country someplace there would be some major uproar. One does not find four bodies in abandoned cars out in the countryside around here anyway. There would be massive concerns, investigations, hoopla, political posturing, you name it.

However, not too far from here there is a war zone in a section of Cincinnati. Its record of mayhem, murder, drug shootings, arson, and general mischief is well known to the point of cliché. It would be nothing to strip the bodies, put them into the trunk, take the car to a location in that zone and simply leave the keys in it and walk away. Wipe the guns down and leave them, and they'd probably show up in a shooting sometime soon, muddying the waters even more. Knowing the folks who stalk this area, they might even dispose of the bodies for us. They get a free car and three free guns out of the deal. What's not to like? If I thought that it would help, I'd have filled it up with gas just to be nice, but screw 'em, have you seen the price of gas these days?.

The downside was that we might be seen dumping the car. One never knows who is watching, and Em and I would stick out from a socio-economic and/or racial and/or ethnic status where we would be dumping the car, you might say. We'd also have to have a means of leaving and that would give some witness an opportunity to identify our car and so forth.

The bodies would be discovered and that would bring some sort of investigation for certain. If we just buried them in the backyard, there might never be an investigation. However, if the bodies were in the war zone, then how hard would police look for a non-obvious answer when they had the zone to blame and four dead miscreants on their hands? Our only real concern was that the police would publish pictures of the dead and that someone would recognize Britt or Zach as having been with Em over the past few days. We reasoned that it would take some time for that to happen, making it hard on memories. Also, how likely would morgue or mug shots be to look like two students helping the professor? We'd just have to chance it.

In the final analysis, we had to accept the combined risks of someone seeing us and the possibilities of immediate police

195

attention to four bodies in a car. The quiet burial on the back part of our property would have been nice, but we had this small problem of their car sitting in our garage, not to mention the long-term presence of evidence.

We dealt with it by driving Em's car to Hamilton and paying for a "rent-a-wreck" for the weekend from a place on Route 4. It was an old beater, and completely non-descript, perfect for our needs. We wiped down the "fab four's" car, inside and out, with a cleaning solution, anyplace that we could have conceivably touched it, and Saturday morning just before dawn we pulled up and parked the gang's car on a street in Over-the-Rhine. I got out and walked back to the rental car and got in and we left. Em wore a hat. I wore a hat and jacket. We had taped over parts of the license plates to give a different number. We were in and out of the area in a matter of minutes. We left and drove south across the river into Kentucky and then back around through the back roads of Indiana and Ohio to get home.

We got off the interstate in Harrison, and drove slowly through the shopping centers. Sure enough, in the third big shopping area, the one with Bigg's and Home Depot, there was my old Toyota Avalon. It could have been Colerain/Northgate, or it could have been Hamilton, but my bet was on Harrison all along. The timing and the logic just made sense.

When we got home, we found a bonus in the trunk. Our collection of guns, knives, and other assorted confiscated items were happily home again.

The next few days were busy, but not a great deal more than a regular "home improvement" weekend would be.

We washed walls and floors. We washed them again with bleach. We measured and bought glass and re-glazed the front windows to the side of the door. We filled holes with plaster and sanded and repainted. I got up on the roof and replaced the plywood and then replaced the tarpaper and then re-shingled. We replaced vinyl siding with the leftovers we had kept all these years 'just in case'.

There was only one place where we needed to replace the carpeting entirely. In the bathroom and hallway where Ray had died, there was a lot of blood and water and we had to take up the carpet and get rid of it. As with most folks, though, we had a couple of good sized pieces left over from when we had the carpet replaced a year ago, and it was enough to do the job and more.

By Sunday evening, we were tired but we had nearly put the house back into "ante-bellum" status. The holes in the walls had been patched. The place had been cleaned. The carpet had been replaced. We had to put in a new tank for the back of the commode in the bathroom. As noted previously, a 9 millimeter slug will penetrate a great deal. We even replaced some of the front siding.

One of the biggest hassles was the damned adhesive on the duct tape. It had a tendency to come off on the cabinets, and that created a mess. Turpentine worked as a solvent, but then we had to wash the cabinets and air out the house. At least the cabinets were Formica-covered so we didn't have to repaint as well.

197

When we sat down to dinner on Sunday night, we needed only to replace my favorite chair in the corner. I had taken the old one and broken it into pieces and burned it in a 55 gallon drum that we use for trash burning on occasion. Damn near broke my heart to see that chair go. The new one was on order.

The freezer in the pantry was a goner as well. Multiple gunshots will do that to the best of appliances, I guess. We pulled out all of the contents and inspected them for wounds and saved what we could by putting it into ice chests and cramming the kitchen freezer full. Some we allowed to thaw and cooked on the grill as we often do on a Sunday. The new freezer was on order, too. Needed defrosting anyway.

Oh, and we bought a new jar of pickles.

Chapter 35

While all of the repairs and reconstruction were underway, Em and I took time during breaks and over meals to exchange our stories about the prior few days. She had a pretty good idea what I had been up to, although she hadn't known the details about either the phenylpthalein or the scientific investigation of putting principles.

Em had been busy, too, as she explained.

Em's Story

When we got into the car on the first morning, I had no idea where we were headed, or what it was all about. You and I both had a pretty good idea that they wanted me to do something for them and that it had to do with some historical event and that it was illicit as hell, but even that was an assumption on our part. It turned out to be correct, but I didn't know that as we left the house.

We didn't go very far, just to the community park. We pulled into one of the parking areas and the bitch, Britt, handed me a folder. She had her gun out in her hand, resting in her lap and pointing in my direction. Zach just sat in the front seat and watched us in the mirror.

"First you need to understand. We are going to be doing some research. More correctly, you are going to be doing some research. That may lead in any number of directions, we just don't know. If we did, we wouldn't need you. There are probably going to be times when we are going to be in public. If you didn't know it already, your husband is our insurance that you will behave yourself. If you do anything to cause problems, he will pay for it. His well-being and your own depend on your cooperation and your success. No tricks, no heroics. Just do your job. Do you understand me?" Britt said.

"Yes, you bitch. I understand."

"Good. Read what's in the folder, Rita."

There were two pieces of paper in the folder, copies of the news stories in the Oxford and Hamilton newspapers. Like you, I busted out laughing when I read the story and realized what it said.

"You've got to be kidding! THIS is what all this is about? That is about the dumbest thing that I have ever heard!" I couldn't help laughing out loud as I said it.

"Good Lord, this rumor has been around since forever. Everybody knows the story, or at least everybody who is interested in local history knows the story. I think that I first heard it when I was a grad student. Idiotic! God, as frightening as the concept is, you really ARE as stupid as I thought you were."

Britt's eyes flashed and she jabbed me hard in the ribs with her gun.

"Rita, you have to be presentable in public, but that doesn't mean that I can't hurt you where it won't show. And, remember, your husband isn't going out in public at all… Now, read!" she growled.

As imbecilic as I thought this was likely to be, it was clear that THEY were serious no matter what I thought. So, I sat back and carefully read over the two articles. As I read, the story began to come back to me. Sometime in the first week or so of June, 1893, a man had showed up at a local farm and asked if he could look around. The farmer agreed and the man pulled out a map or directions of some sort. He paced out distances and soon arrived at a large rock, supposedly covered with Native American markings. He scratched an "X" on the top of the rock and left. The farmer swore that he would dig up the rock and find whatever treasure there was. There were two theories about the treasure. One was that it consisted of a cache of indigenous artifacts or gold and jewels, and the other the hoard of an eccentric old man named Hetrick who lived on the property years before. No treasure was ever found, or at least, not that anyone ever let on.

"All right, I have read the articles. Now what?" I asked after a few moments.

"Now you are going to locate the property for us," the bitch replied. "You tell us what you need to do and where you need to go to make that happen, and Zach and I will take you wherever you want."

I thought for a moment, and then asked, "Does it matter to you if we work in public or in private as much as you can, or do you care?"

At this she glanced at Zach and quickly replied, "Private is good, public as necessary."

That was interesting. I interpreted that glance to mean that one or the other or both of them had reasons to remain out of sight.

"Okay, then. Let's start at my office. We should be able to find something there. If not, we can move on."

We parked at the Cook Field lot and walked up the Circle and were in my office by about 9:30. We saw almost no one. The departmental office was open, but few of the faculty members were around. That was no surprise. We closed the door to my office and settled in. I had a pretty good idea that we would be able to find the property fairly easily, but you never know. History is full of surprises.

The *Oxford News* article noted that the visitor had gone to the "old John Wright" farm. The first thing that I did was to pull down the Rerick Brothers 1888 Atlas and checked the 1888 Butler County Farm Index. There were four Wrights noted, two of whom were in the Oxford Township. Only one was on the west side of town, and that property did not match the rest of the story. "Chas" Wright owned a small property of what appeared to be about fifteen acres between Contreras Road and the railroad right of way. The fact that no John Wright Farm was listed did not surprise me, but I wanted to start with the closest date to 1893 that I could find and then work my way back as needed.

Next, I checked the 1875 L. H. Everts Atlas of Butler County. There, in Oxford Township map section 29, plat 3, was the J. Wright farm, consisting of 100 acres. It was bounded on the north by Fairfield Road, and on the west by Riggs Road.

"Oh, for heaven's sake!" I exclaimed.

"What is it?" Britt asked.

"Well, I've driven by this property probably twice a day for the past fifteen years. It's only about a mile from the house. And, given the topography of the land and the location of the house noted on the township map, I can even tell you approximately where the rock would have to be," I explained.

"But before we go off half-cocked here, let me look at one more thing."

I pulled out the John Crane map of the Oxford Township from 1855 to get a sense of how long the property had belonged to Mr. Wright, and to see if there were further details about the property or the surrounding area. Crane was a Hamilton surveyor who took pride in his work and showed some topographical detail that did not appear on later maps. I was rewarded by the discovery that in 1855 the property had belonged to Daniel Fields, and two water courses ran westward from the property, draining to Indian Creek a short distance away.

"Look here," I said, as the three of us hunched over the map on my office table.

"If any erosion were taking place, as the newspaper article suggested, then it would pretty much have to be along one of these runs, or gulleys. As I said, I drive by this property every day. The northern branch is still there, and other than that one run-off the place is completely flat. Either the rock would have been in that gulley or it would have been a few paces to the south.   Given the description in the newspapers, I would start with the northern run," I suggested.

The two of them looked at each other with stunned expressions, as if to say, "It can't be this easy, could it?"

Well, actually – no, it probably couldn't be.

Chapter 36

"There is something that you might want to know, though, before you get too excited," I told them.

"The property is still farm land today, so that's good news. It isn't in the middle of a sub-division or guarded night and day, so that's good for you and your treasure hunt. However, the current owner of the property might not be too excited about your messing around there. Worse, it is likely that the rock won't be there any longer."

"Why wouldn't it be?" asked Britt. "Why would anyone go to the trouble of moving a large boulder from a gulley?"

"Well, you are probably right. In 1893, the farmer, Mr. Baker, would have had his hands full. He would have been using horses, more than likely. A rock of that size would have been a struggle for a team to move. If he moved the rock to dig underneath, as he said he would, he probably wouldn't want to drag it very far. I'd guess that he would use levers and a team of plow horses and a chain. He'd simply slide or roll the rock a few feet downhill, in this case, west and dig around to see if anything was underneath.

"But," I continued, "That's not the issue. Your problem is Pearl Harbor," I chuckled.

The look on their faces was priceless. Like the stricken look of the unprepared upon seeing the first question on the final exam.

"You see, the Wright farm is now part of the Miami University Airport property! During World War II Miami largely became a naval training facility. As part of the war effort to develop pilots the air field was constructed in 1942, although as I recall, it was not officially dedicated until 1943. So, east of Riggs Road and north of Brookville Road, they would have excavated and graded that entire portion of Section 29, you name it. We can look in the University Archives to see if there are plans or photos of the construction, but my guess is that they wouldn't want a big rock sitting around."

Britt and Zach sat down, somewhat deflated from what had a moment ago looked so promising, and so easy.

I continued, "We're just getting started. It's nice that we found a Wright farm west of Oxford, but who is to say that was THE Wright farm? Wright is a common name, and we may find another location or even several. If you spend any time with these old maps at all you begin to see the same family names in different spots. The families moved around, and different family members grew up and started their own households nearby. Offspring inherited, so the last name stays, but a new first name appears. I didn't see anything that jumped out at me at first glance, but I need to spend some time with the maps and the census data.

"What do you mean?" Britt asked, truculently. "The articles both say that it was the old Wright farm west of Oxford. What more do you want? You wouldn't be trying to stall us, would you Rita? The sooner that we can get to the site, the sooner this is going to be over for you and your husband, you understand?"

"Yes, I understand. Further, I begin to grasp the limits of your intellectual capacity. But, if you noticed, and are able to actually recall something that you have read recently, the newspaper articles differed in their spelling of the farmer's name. One had him as 'Baker' while the other named him 'Bakin'. That's just one example. It is typical of historical records. Names were often misspelled, or even phonetically spelled, changing from one record to the next. We could just as easily be talking about the 'W-R-I-T-E' Farm, or the 'R-I-T-T-E' Farm, or the 'W-H-I-T-E Farm' or any number of other possibilities. Even today, newspaper articles are full of inaccuracies and misspellings. It gets worse the farther back you go.

"The obvious location on the airfield property is a good possibility, so if you want to assume that is the spot, by all means, go for it; your choice. But, don't gripe at me later when we've wasted a whole bunch of time hiking around in the wrong spot and have to crawl back to the office to start over.

"Let me try to explain this so that even you can understand it. Jesus! Amateurs! The LAST thing that you do is to go out into the field… THE VERY LAST THING. You put in the imagination and the hard reasoning and the grinding research in the office and the library and in the archives up front. Did you ever see *Raiders of the Lost* Ark? Remember the part where Indy and Sallah start dancing saying, 'They're digging in the wrong place!' Am I getting through to you? If you want to hire an army of Egyptian diggers or a fleet of bulldozers, cool by me. I really couldn't give a rat's patoot. But you're the ones who want to keep it private.

"There is an old saying in this business. 'An inch is as good as a mile.' You miss by even a little and you find nothing. We still have work to do before we go traipsing around with shovels," I concluded. I wound down my rant on the difficulties of historical research and Britt's expression continued to sour. Zach was as imperturbable as ever.

"All right, Rita. We'll do it your way, but watch your mouth. You are starting to piss me off, and if YOU can remember a fact or two, you might keep in mind that I can have your dear old lush husband pay for your bullshit," Britt reminded me, and the temperature in the room dropped measurably.

I glared at her and turned my attention back to the 1875 map.

As you know, I love the old maps. They are fascinating. I can spend hours poring over them, particularly examining the movements of families and the name shifts, and how properties were divided among families. After some time, magnifying glass in hand, I made a few additional observations and noted them on a legal pad.

Watching somebody else research something is horribly boring and aggravating. You essentially have no idea what is going on. The person doing the research is actively engaged. Their mind is working, and they are moving from one item to the next, going back and checking, and making notes. If they are really annoying, they nod to themselves and mutter. All the while, the person watching is clueless. They have an interest, but they are frozen out. It is even worse than having a conversation while a third party listens but can't take part. At least in that situation they can hear what is being said.

Britt was not a patient bystander.

"What are you writing? What have you found?" she spat out.

I looked at her over the top of my glasses. "First, the 'Chas. Wright' property closer to town had been owned by J. Wright in 1875. Chas. may have been the son or brother or even father of J. The census data will probably tell us, and keeping the town location would make sense if Charles had an occupation other than farmer," I explained.

"Second, there were no other 'Wrights' or close matches. So far so good for the airfield property as an option.

"Third, about a mile west of the Wright farm there were two properties in the Indian Creek valley, straddling Contreras Road. The two properties were owned by 'Jno. and P. Bake'. In 1888 the Wright farm had passed to the ownership of H. D. Hinckley, but was being farmed by Mr. Baker or Bakin. It would not be unusual for an absentee owner to have someone local farm a property, so I wondered if the tenant might actually be part of the Bake family."

Now that I thought of it, I wondered to myself about the actions of Mr. Baker/Bakin. If the property were owned by

209

H. D. Hinckley, then anything under the rock would have belonged to him, not a tenant farmer. Odd, I thought, that Baker was going to guard the rock night and day until he could excavate. I didn't say anything, but wouldn't the first thing a tenant would do be to tell the owner what was going on?

"Similarly, I found a farm owned by V. Baker just northeast of town, off Bonham Road. Again, this could be a connection to the tenant farmer, or it could be nothing. At this point I don't know what is important and what isn't. I'm covering the bases. We may need to look at the census data, I don't know."

I set aside the 1875 map and turned my attention to the 1855 map and began a careful examination. Twenty years prior, the 'airfield' Wright farm had belonged to Daniel Fields, but as I carefully inspected the map a familiar name caught my eye, but not where I had expected. John Wright had owned two parcels totaling one hundred acres on the opposite side of Oxford Township, in section 24, on the very easternmost edge.

"Hmph," I grunted. "As I warned you. Here is John Wright again, but this time on the eastern side of town in 1855. Is it possible that the news accounts got the name right, but the direction wrong? And, this older property is almost adjacent to what became the Baker property. That connection raises questions for me. Both names are common enough, but the ongoing link suggests something, perhaps a marriage between neighbors? I don't know. Now, we'll have to look at the census data for certain.

"I don't know that I don't like this location even better as a potential site. For one thing it's right on Harker's Run. That means that there would have been more erosion than on the western site. In addition, the news articles mentioned the 'old Wright farm' and this certainly predates the other location. And, one more thing; as I recall there were no Native American archeological sites known in section 29. Indian Creek was full of sites, but in Reilly Township, considerably south. There was nothing up on the high ground where the airfield is. But, there were all sorts of mounds and such on Four Mile Creek and Harker's Run.

"Oh, and look here," I drew their attention to the map. "Here and here, south and southwest of Oxford there is a Joseph White farm and a John White farm. I'm not as excited about these spots as I am about either of the Wright locations, but who knows? As I said earlier, history is an inexact science."

Britt looked increasingly unhappy. She had an expression like someone who has just found out the hard way that the cat barfed in their shoe overnight. Zach, on the other hand, appeared unperturbed. He stretched, glanced at his watch and said, "About lunch time. I'll fly."

"Yeah, I guess so. Rita, we'll take a potty break. You first," Britt instructed.

I think that she wanted me to check out the hallway to make certain that we were alone, not that it would have mattered. None of my colleagues would have thought for a second about a couple of twenty-somethings being in my

211

office with me. Just another day at the office, but I suppose that there was no use in creating confrontations. But then it struck me. If they were seen clearly, they could be described later. But, that would only matter if they intended to harm us once they got what they wanted. Not a nice thought.

Chapter 37

I was actually pretty pleased with what I had accomplished that first morning. From a standing start I had identified two good prospects in the Wright farmsteads and two alternatives. I had a tenuous connection with a "Baker" and I had a fairly good idea on how to follow up with other resources. As we waited for Zach to come back with lunch, I jotted down a few questions and sources to follow up later.

He arrived a few minutes later with three Subway subs, assorted chips and diet drinks. He also had a copy of what appeared to be the latest issue of *Sports Illustrated.*

"Next time, go to Jimmy-John's. Their subs are much better," I griped, and Zach amiably nodded his assent.

After lunch I pulled out the Richard Brown *Archaeological Map of Butler Co., Ohio.* My memory had been good. There were many mounds noted along Indian Creek, but all of them in Reilly Township, well south of the 1875 Wright farm. However, just about opposite the 1855 Wright farm, on the west side of Harker's Run there was a known mound. Close, very close. For good measure I looked at the White farms as well, and there was also a known site near the Joseph White farm. From what I could see, it would be just on the east side of U.S. 27 just south of Collins Run, more or less across from what is now the cemetery.

By now I had just about exhausted my hard-copy office resources. The old atlases and maps and histories of the region were things I had collected over the years. These are some of the tools of my trade, but also I like having the actual old books and manuscripts in my hands. There is something about holding the same book or the same map or letter that felt the hands of the author. When you hold a flint scraper in your hand, you can feel the presence of the artisan who created it a thousand years before, and the human who used it to prepare a hide. Call it what you will, but there is a spirit in such things, and sometimes I can connect with it and 'feel' its story.

"Well, we've come to a situation," I said. Britt continued to 'grump' in the chair by my work table, and Zach looked up from his magazine reading.

"There's nothing more I can do here in the office, unless you're willing to let me boot up my computer. We have several choices. You can let me do my work here on my office computer, we can go to the Smith Historical Library uptown and I can work on their computer and use their records, we can put out a want-ad for Egyptian diggers, or we can have a good laugh and call it quits. Take your pick," I told them.

"You knew it was going to come to this. I mean, you're lucky that I had the maps in hard copy. Most people just get on-line and do their research there. But, from this point if you want to accomplish anything, we are going to need a computer."

Britt scowled at me and asked, "What are you looking for? It'd be nice if I had some idea what you are doing and that you aren't just playing games."

"Well," I replied, "The first thing that I want to do is to get on-line and play 'Frogger' for a while, and then I thought I'd email all my friends in law enforcement, what else? Goddamnit! First I want to get on Google-Earth and take a look at what the different sites look like today. Are they open fields, shopping malls, residential areas, who knows? We'll get some idea of the terrain and whether we can just walk up and look around, or if we will have to come up with some other approach. I'd think that just MIGHT be interesting to the two of you.

"If that doesn't tell me what I want to know, then I am going to look up the appropriate real estate information and try to find out who owns the properties now.

"Beyond that, I intend to look up the census data on the Wright family to verify that they actually lived where we THINK they did from the maps. We might also find out if there is some connection to the Bakers. And finally, and most importantly, I hope to get a handle on Mr. Hetric or Hetrick, the guy who supposedly buried the treasure in the first place.

"Does THAT make sense to you, or do you figure on calling up NASA and having them task a satellite with ground-penetrating radar to overfly Oxford? WHY do you feel the need to keep questioning my professional skills? If YOU could do this, then why didn't you without bothering my husband and me? Let me do what I know how to do, already!"

Britt smirked in reply, "Of course, dear. We figured you'd have to get on-line at some point, but be careful. I'll be looking over your shoulder so let's stay away from emails, Skype, and other embarrassing problem areas, eh?"

Zach went back to his sports.

I booted up my office computer and pulled up Google-Earth. I have a 'pin' for our home and started there, since it is just a little south of the airport. The satellite view clearly showed the dense copse of trees on the northwest corner of the property, and knowing that the drainage was there, I could pick out the direction of the watershed westward toward Indian Creek. It was remarkable how similar the land was to the 1855 map drawn by John Crane.

"Look here," I pointed at the circle of trees with the mouse from an eye-altitude of about ten thousand feet. "You can see two places where water flows off the property. Given the location of the house and the newspaper article saying they walked north, I'd focus on this area."

I zoomed in to an altitude of about two thousand feet and could clearly see the trees and the surrounding area under cultivation. Sadly, there was no boulder, and no marker saying 'Historical Native American Rock'.

Moving to the east and north, I found a photo marker on Bonham Road and 'flew' to that spot. The overhead view was nothing but forest.

"Amazing! You are in luck, again! This is part of the Miami University Nature Conservancy. The whole area that we would be interested in is a nature preserve. We can hike all over it and nobody will take any notice at all, unless we litter or something. I'd think that we could literally wade up Harker's Run on a boulder hunt," I said.

"There's a parking area just off Bonham and an access trail right about at the edge of what would have been the Wright property. Interesting."

I printed off hard copies of the overhead views for use later and moved on to the U.S. Census Data from ancestry.com. This site has U.S. Census Data going back to the early 1800s and is searchable by name, location, date and more. It even provides an assist by searching similar names. So, for example, my search for Wright in Oxford Township in the 1850 Census would likely have brought up the two White families as well. The search engine works pretty well, and once you have found a name, the site permits you to examine a scanned copy of the original census document, and it was the copies of the originals that I wanted to see.

The census takers back then literally went from house to house and interviewed the people living there. They wrote down the information the residents gave them in their book, including the name, male or female, age, relationship to head of household, occupation, and place of birth. In some years the value of real estate and other property were estimated. Other data were collected as checked boxes, including parents of foreign birth, marriage within the year, attendance at school during the year, literacy, and so forth.

Different census takers had different styles and approaches. Their spelling of names and places differed, as did their attention to detail. I suspect that the residents' memories wavered over ages and birthplaces as well.

The first thing that I wanted to see was whether the maps were consistent with the census records, in other words, did John Wright live where the maps say he did, and was it the same family on two different farms in different time periods.

I started with the 1880 Census because by 1888 the Wright farm west of town was owned by H. D. Hinckley. John Wright appeared in the 1880 census along with his daughter Emma and son Frank. John was age 69 at the time. Comparing the 1880 census page with the 1875 map, there were a few names that matched, but not as many as I would have expected. Interestingly, John and his family were listed as "in laws" and "boarding" actually in the Martin Riggs household, as were Mary Greycraft and her brother Randolf. On the 1875 map, R. H. Riggs owned the property directly west of the Wrights.

Moving back to the 1870 Census, things began to make a bit more sense. Apparently, the Greycrafts were a part of the Wright household as were five Wright children, including Francis. At this time John was age 59, so the ages matched, and he lived with his wife Rebecca who was three years older. Most importantly, the names on the adjoining households matched the 1875 map almost exactly – Cleveland, Finch, Dougherty – they were all neighbors. So, John Wright and family occupied the airfield site at least in the 1870s.

The 1860 Census became less focused. The only name on the page that matched either the 1875 or the 1855 map was W. J. Finch, and although his age did not make sense, his infant son was named Orlando, matching the owner of the neighboring farm in 1855. It was likely, then, that the Wrights had been on the airfield property as early as 1860. I was interested to note that John Wright had a daughter, Parmelia, who it appeared married Martin Riggs in whose household the Wrights lived in 1880.

Going back even earlier, the census data seemed to bear out that in the 1840s and early 1850s the same John Wright and his father kept the farm on the eastern side of the township, and marked on the 1855 map. The adjoining entries in the census matched the neighboring farm names, and the names and ages of the children were consistent with the later entries.

All of this had taken up the rest of the afternoon, and it was approaching five o'clock. Pulling up the census records and deciphering the names from the census takers' handwriting, and then examining the maps to find matches, and often not finding them is painstaking and time consuming work.

"Well, I'd say that we've reached a good stopping spot," I suggested as I put my hands on my lower back and tried to stretch the kinks out. "We know for certain that John Wright occupied a farm on the eastern side until after 1855. He then moved out to the western location, probably between 1855 and 1860, where he and his family farmed until sometime between 1875 and 1880. At that time he and his family were living with the Riggs, the in-laws, probably across the street on the adjacent property.

"Now we need to see if we can track down Mr. Hetrick, our burier of treasure. Given the hour, I'd like to start fresh on that in the morning," I said.

The two of them looked at each other and Zach glanced at his watch. I think he was bored, given that he had finished his *Sports Illustrated* long since.

"All right, let's head for the house," Britt said. "So far, so good. Let's keep it that way, Rita."

After I left the office, she led the way and Zach followed a couple of paces behind. As on the way in, I rode in the backseat of the car on the right side, while Britt sat behind Zach and held her gun in her lap as he drove.

"By the way, I'm sorry that she hurt you again when we got home. I thought that keeping her angry with me was a good way to focus her on me."

"That's all right. I'll figure out a way for you to make it up to me," I said.

Chapter 38

The next day we were back in my office by 9 o'clock, having foregone the instructional side trip to the park. Britt seemed a bit more frazzled than she had the day before, and I was on edge as well. I had slept better than I had the first night, but still wasn't as rested as I normally am. Who am I kidding? I felt like crap, and I wasn't looking forward to spending the day with Miss Personality and her tag-along assassin.

I picked up where I left off the prior afternoon. The newspaper articles said that Hetric/Hetrick had lived on the property in a log hut years before. That sounded like it would have pre-dated the Wright's move to the airfield property, and therefore we would be looking back to the 1840s or 1850s. If we were considering the Bonham Road farm, we'd be back to the very early 1800s.

The problem was that there were no census entries for Hetric or Hetrick. I expanded the search to include similar names, and the closest I could come to a match was John Hendricks, who lived about three or four miles north on what is now Todd Road as early as the 1830s. Also dating from the 1830s a farmer named Herrick Brown lived just north of the town of Oxford. The only other reference to a Hetrick in Butler County was a german paper-maker who lived in Hamilton during the 1850s and 1860s.

I spent the entire morning doing searches for connections between these people or their families with the Wrights, or Daniel Fields who owned the airfield property in 1855. In checking the maps I finally noticed, with an accompanying slap to my forehead, that the airfield property was not noted as having an owner on McBride's 1836 map.

I sat back and thought for a moment. If the property were vacant in 1836, then a hermit would be able to squat on the land untroubled. That would probably not be the situation if the land were being actively farmed, unless the owner knew the hermit and permitted him to stay. By 1855 Daniel Fields owned the property which suggested that the hermit was gone. Maybe.

My tired doggy brain finally kicked into gear as I realized that a squatter or hermit would be unlikely to show up in the census data under any circumstances. It would be exactly like the current problem in counting the homeless. "Hetrick the Hermit" probably wouldn't stand up to be counted.

But that left the question; who WAS "Hetrick the Hermit". I could see no obvious connection between an 1830s squatter and any of the people I had identified. There might be something, but if so, I couldn't see it. Both Hendricks and Herrick Brown had successful farms that lasted for many years. I'd done all that I could do in my office. I needed to access the records in the Smith Historical Library to see if there were any further data to be had regarding these people.

Who knows, there might be some defining moment that documented Herrick Brown going off his rocker and moving away from the farm, or establishing that John Hendricks had a deer stand and hunting camp on the property.

I had shifted my opinion back to the airfield property as the likely candidate. The lack of ownership in 1836 had tilted my scales back to the west.

Chapter 39

We went through the usual garbage about being careful and watching what I said and did, but in the end we packed up and had lunch at a picnic table at Hueston Woods State Park. This time we had Jimmy-John's subs and I was rewarded by Zach acknowledging that they were indeed better than Subway, and the fact that I got to eat a better lunch.

We were stalling, waiting for the Smith Library of Regional History to open. A little after 1:30 we arrived, or I should say that I arrived. The Smith Library consists of a couple of rooms at the back of the Lane Public Library in uptown Oxford. It is open in the afternoons Monday through Friday and in the mornings on Thursday and Friday as well. There is a reading area just outside in the main library and Britt found a chair and pretended to read a book while keeping an eye on me. Zach, on the other hand, was in his element perusing the library's copies of various magazines.

I greeted several of the regulars and Elizabeth, the head of the Smith History Library, and went to work. I first checked the Oxford Township names index, a listing of all the names that had been in any public documents over the past hundred and fifty years or so. Volunteers had combed the newspapers, maps, books, licenses, cemetery records, school records, and even old mercantile orders and billing information and had recorded the names and references.

There was a Hetrick listed, and the name appeared in three places, but the dates were mid-1900s and so did not help in the least. John Hendricks was listed as were a number of his children who appeared in school records, but there was nothing to indicate that he had any connection to the property or to the people on whom I was focused. Old Herrick Brown yielded about the same information.

I looked through the Butler County records and came up with a few more Hetricks, Hedricks, Hendricks, Hendricksons, and even an Edrich and an Etterich, but nothing to indicate any relationships of interest or significance to my work.

In short, after an afternoon of plodding through file cards, compendia of names, cemetery records, and the like, I came up with exactly – zilch, zip, nada.

I always tried to get out of the library by about 5 o'clock in the afternoon. Elizabeth is very understanding and very helpful and very capable. She would stay late if I were hot on the trail of some discovery, but I did my best not to inconvenience her. And so, at a few minutes before the hour, I straightened up my notes, packed up my shoulder bag, and said my goodbyes and walked out of the library, preceded by Britt and followed by Zach who did their best to act as if we were not connected in any way.

When we got into the car, I shared my results with the minions of darkness.

"Well, THAT was enlightening," I said sarcastically. "The only thing that I accomplished today was to convince myself that the airport site is the best bet," and I explained my reasoning regarding the lack of ownership in 1836. "As for who 'Hetrick the Hermit' was or where he lived, or what he might have buried, there is nothing I can find. Unless you have something else, some other information that you haven't shared, we're pretty well finished. This is about as dead an end as can be."

"So the high and mighty Dr. Rita Richardson is stumped, eh?" crowed Britt. "All of that 'I'm the pro' and 'Let me do my job' crap, and you struck out! Hah!"

"I told you this was a joke when you gave me the newspaper articles at the outset. We don't know ANYTHING at this point other than John Wright owned a couple of properties in the Oxford Township in the 1800s and that two newspaper articles appeared in 1893 supposedly describing events on the western farmstead. Hell, we don't even know that any of that really happened! Baker could have been telling stories to cadge a couple of free drinks in an uptown bar, or trying to impress his buddies, anything. I tell you, we've got nothing!" I said.

Britt smirked at me from across the back seat of the car. After a moment that she seemed to be savoring, she reached into her backpack and pulled out a folder from which she extracted a single sheet of paper.

"Perhaps this will improve your outlook," she said as she handed me the document.

I put my glasses on and looked down at a photocopy of the directions that had guided the stranger to the rock in 1893! Or, more accurately, the paper held written instructions telling the holder exactly what to do.

"JESUS CHRIST, you have been holding onto this paper from the beginning? What in the hell is the matter with you! How do you expect me to work if you are holding out key pieces of information?" I practically screamed in her face. Britt just smiled. God, I wanted to smack the living shit out of her!

The paper in my hand was a modern copy of the original document.

March 19, 1893

Dear Theodore,

It has been so long. I have thought of you often and fondly, and I hope you are well.

I take pen in hand because my heath is failing.

I have kept your parting token near to my heart these past thirty-three years. It has been our secret bond and for reasons we both know so well, it must remain so. I had thought to hand it down, but after much prayer and contemplation I know that I must return it to you.

Find your way to the farm of an old friend, John Wright, in Oxford, Ohio. Seventy paces from the north wall of the house there is a small watercourse. Turn eastward and take an additional twenty paces. You will find a large rock I know to rest there.

Again, turning to the north, twenty paces further, I have had it buried in a small lock box.

It caused you great pain. Perhaps its return will bring you peace.

Dear Teddy, I always loved you - more's the pity.

Alice

"Does that help you, dear?" Britt asked, her voice like a small child picking at a scab.

"Shut up and let me think," and I sat back and gazed out the car window. We were just passing the airport and I couldn't help but think that somewhere over there, within a few hundred yards was the location we sought.

The letter gave me a lot to think about. Thirty-three years before would have been 1860. What had happened in 1859 or 1860, and how did that connect with 1893, or today?

Chapter 40

I did a lot of thinking, conjecturing really, on Wednesday night. The letter had given me lots to chew on.

What was going on in 1860, and how could it possibly be connected with little, old Oxford, Ohio? I came up with lots of possibilities and nothing tangible to show for it. The Lincoln-Douglas debates had taken place in 1858, previewing the issues that would define the presidential election of 1860. But, the seven debates had all taken place in Illinois as part of the senatorial election that year. Oregon became the 33rd state in 1859. The Comstock Lode was discovered in Virginia City, Nevada. Charles Darwin published his famous treatise, "On the Origin of the Species." John Brown led his debacle of a raid on the federal arsenal at Harpers Ferry, Virginia in October. All in all a pretty reasonable year for history, but nothing that caused me to sit up and take notice, particularly locally.

Of course 1859 saw the Oxford train station open to its first train service on the Cincinnati, Hamilton and Dayton line, extended the following year to Indianapolis. And, the increasingly decrepit west wing of Miami's "Old Main" was abandoned in 1859. All of these things were noteworthy, but again, I found nothing that appeared to connect to the letter or the so-called treasure.

Similarly, 1860 was an important year. Lincoln was elected, South Carolina seceded from the Union, and the Pony Express began operations. The Civil War, or the War of Northern Aggression, depending on your beliefs, did not begin until 1861, so that did not figure into the equation. In the midst of my contemplations, I fell asleep. It had been a long couple of days.

The following morning I heard you whisper, "Stall!" I really didn't have a lot to work with anyway.

Whoever Alice was, it appeared that she and Theodore, or 'Teddy' had parted company in 1859 or 1860 and that she had come to Oxford some time afterward. Subsequently she befriended John Wright or some member of the family. She knew about the rock, and that suggested that it had not recently been uncovered, but had been known for some time. Now, how would a woman know about the existence of an odd boulder on a friend's property? Could this have been some local "lovers' lane" or meeting spot? It would have been one of the few wooded, shady spots on the property then, just as it would be now, a wooded island in the middle of a cornfield.

Theodore had given her a gift of some sort, a 'token' that she had kept for thirty-four years, and it had 'ruined his life' by her estimation. Further, she alludes to some kind of ongoing secret that prohibits her, even thirty-four years later, of passing this token along.

At the end of the letter she asserts that she always loved 'Teddy' and that gave rise to at least one possible explanation. She and Teddy had some kind of fling going and the families wouldn't stand for it. She got sent away, most likely to family and ended up here in Oxford. Teddy gave her a 'going away present' as a token of his undying love, and she kept it. Reading between the lines, ol' Teddy may have given her something else, like maybe 'Little Teddy, Jr.' since she still can't talk about it years later.

It made sense in a melodramatic way, and I began to think of Snidely Whiplash lashing Nell, well, Alice, to the railroad tracks. Even that made sense given the new rail connections. Hah! So there!

Even if all that were true, and I had no idea one way or the other, what good did it do us? I still had no idea who 'Alice' was. It was a common enough name in the time. Trying to identify one specific Alice in the college town of Oxford would be a Herculean task, given that by the 1860s there were FIVE schools, three of which were for women.

Nevertheless, I had my marching instructions – stall. Given the task, that seemed unnecessary. It was going to be a long effort even without dragging my feet. I could think of two avenues to pursue to identify 'Alice' so, when Britt got into the car and asked, "All right, Rita, where to?" I replied, "First stop, Western Campus – Alumnae Office."

Western College was founded in 1853 as Western Female Seminary and it continued until 1974 when it formally became a part of Miami University. It was a worthy institution and graduated a number of accomplished and noted alumnae. Today it was a constant source of confusion among those new to Oxford and Miami because the Western Campus was on the easternmost portion of the Miami grounds. Go figure.

If 'Alice' had come to Oxford around 1860 there was at least a reasonable chance that she might have been enrolled at Western. She could equally have attended the Oxford Female Institute established by John Witherspoon Scott in 1849 or the Oxford Female College which opened its doors in 1856. Combined, the two schools would have had over two-hundred women enrolled in 1860. Roughly five percent of women in the mid-1800s were named 'Alice' so we could narrow the field a bit. Checking the records might give us a clue on the identity of 'Alice', or not. Well, it was a starting place, if not a particularly good one.

A fruitless search of the graduation and enrollment records took most of the morning. We found about the expected number of 'Alice's but in the end, nothing that would seem to connect. I wasn't particularly surprised.

If my 'Romeo and Juliet' scenario had any merit, particularly the part about 'Little Teddy Junior,' then a pregnant Alice was unlikely to show up at one of the Presbyterian schools for women. More likely, she would be married off quickly to some local friend of the family in an arranged marriage, or she would simply be introduced as "Mrs. Doe from the east, whose husband is on a whaling vessel in the Ross Sea." Word would be received sometime later that the ship had gone down with all hands while rounding the Horn, and little Teddy and mother would duly receive the sympathies of the congregation in their 'time of sorrow.' They would further acquire, albeit with some inevitable skepticism, a patina of respectability.

We had lunch at a picnic table at Dogwood Park. This time, at my suggestion we opted for Bagel & Deli. I had my usual; roast beef, smoked cheddar, cream cheese, and jalapenos on a bialy, and a diet Vernor's. Britt was singularly uninspiring with her ham and Swiss on a rye bagel with spicy mustard – woo-hoo, and a diet Coke. I think my zinger about being serially abused wasn't far off the mark. Geez, ham and Swiss at the B & D? My God! Zach opted for a 'Get Swanked' consisting of turkey, meatballs, ½ Colby, ½ Swiss, honey mustard, salt and pepper, on a garlic bagel, and a Dr. Pepper and jalapeno chips.

After lunch, we headed back uptown to the Smith Library, this time to check on death and burial records and obituaries. I was more optimistic about this direction for our research. Alice's letter had said that her health was failing. It was probably pretty bad if she had gone to the trouble of notifying Theodore and telling him to come take his gift back. If so, she may have died soon after, and we could check the records for burials, etc. for someone named Alice in 1893.

The afternoon was spent in the library. Zach had his magazines, and Britt had some book that she pretended to read, probably something like *Lord of the Flies: A How-To for Girls*.

Despite a careful look through the obituaries, and the cemetery records, and the Oxford newspaper social columns – which often told of illnesses, prolonged and otherwise, I came up with a grand total of zero. I could find no evidence that an Alice had passed away in Oxford in 1893.

Finding no evidence didn't really mean much. Then, as now, medical care was better in Cincinnati or Dayton or

Indianapolis and it was likely that she would have traveled, if possible, to obtain better care. Depending on the length of her illness, she could have passed away elsewhere and not occasioned an obituary in Oxford. Similarly, if her family had a cemetery plot somewhere else, she could have been buried in the family plot, again not creating an Oxford record. Or, for that matter, she could have recovered and lived until a building collapsed on her in the earthquake in San Francisco in 1906. Who knows?

So, after a fruitless day, with nothing to show for it, I had 'stalled'. After the obligatory carping and complaining and criticism from Britt, we headed home. I reluctantly told them that tomorrow we might have to visit the site and at least look around.

I expected something, of course, but the first thing that I knew was the clang of metal hitting the garage floor and Zach's feet leaping off the floor and jerking back and forth. Then Britt's window exploded and she was shooting. I had been jotting a note to myself and the only thing I could think to do was to go for her eyes and then grab for the gun.

The rest you know.

Chapter 41

What a difference a week makes.

Last week at this time we were heading into our offices to clean up the end-of-semester mess, and to take a figurative deep breath. The grading and the rush to finish all of the student papers, record finals grades, calculate term grades, and say goodbye to those who are graduating and moving on creates a massive pile up in my office. Em's office always looks like a dumpster behind WalMart, so I'm not sure what she was doing last Monday, exactly. Herding rats? Anyway, last week I was heading in to put papers in files, files in cabinets, answer emails put on hold, and all the rest.

Today we got up and listened to the local news and carefully examined the newspapers for a story about our prior 'guests'. Nothing, so far.

After breakfast we headed into her office so she could show me the maps and the census data and the Google-Earth overhead views. Mostly, though, we were stalling and waiting for the package from "Mr. Big." If experience counted for anything, we wouldn't see the package until afternoon, unless it were sent with special "A.M. Delivery" instructions.

It was a dreary day, temperature in the fifties, overcast and occasionally misting and spitting rain. I gazed out Em's office window and watched the squirrels do squirrely things in the quad around the university seal. The main quad has so many oak and maple and black walnut trees that the campus squirrel population is huge. A few years ago the folks in biology were concerned about inbreeding and created a trapping program – for the squirrels, not the folks in biology. Anyway, they trapped squirrels in the main campus area and took them to Hueston Woods State Park, and they trapped park squirrels and brought them back to campus. My bet is that they just pissed off our little furry friends and that the "tree-rats" hitch-hiked back to their old digs. I've seen no change in squirrel behavior or appearance.

"So, what do you think old Alice buried out there," I asked Em as I watched a couple of rodents play tag up and down a walnut tree. "Had to be something small, and valuable, at least to Theodore, anyway. Jewelry? A locket of some sort?"

"First of all, Alice didn't bury it. She said that she 'had it buried' which means that somebody else did the digging. That worries me. Two people in on a secret treasure means that it is not a secret treasure. What's to keep 'Darryl the Digger' from going back and fetching the booty on his own?"

"Booty?"

"Swag."

"Oh. So you think Alice's booty was swaggy?"

"May have been, but that's part of what we hope to find out. It intrigues me that she would go to the trouble of hiding whatever it was. Why do that? I mean, they had lawyers back then. Go to your lawyer and hand him a sealed box and say, 'I want this delivered to Theodore so-and-so and not Alvin or Simon. Make it so. Here's your fee. See ya!' I mean, who goes to the trouble of having Darryl go out to some out of the way place and bury something? What's the point?"

"For that matter, why not just package it up and ship it to Teddy? She obviously had his address, since she sent him the letter. Why not save everybody the trouble and just send it in the 1893 version of FedEx?" I suggested.

"I can probably answer that one. This thing is one of a kind, and you wouldn't want to risk the chance of losing it. So, the question becomes what would give something that kind of value?"

"Well, it has to be unique. Obviously it is tremendously important to Theodore because she says it caused him great pain and she hopes he'll find peace. A piece of paper, maybe? A deed? A contract that gives her control over some property or asset? That would account for having problems in his life. He gives up access to whatever it was, and she holds it even though he needs it for some purpose?"

"I don't see that. For one thing, if it were a contract or a deed, then a certified copy could be made and notarized, or whatever. She could just mail it."

"Well, how could it be such a big deal? I mean, if you and I had to part ways and I wanted to give you something to remember me by, I suppose I'd want to give you something enduring and priceless, of course, but I can't think of anything that would ruin the rest of my life... Except not seeing you ever again," I added quickly.

"Nice catch. It only hit the floor and bounced a couple of times."

"No, really. There is nothing that would cause me great pain. Let's say I gave you a family heirloom of some sort; Uncle Giuseppe's gold and jewel encrusted moustache trimmer..."

"Uncle Giuseppe had a gold and jewel encrusted moustache?"

"No, but if he did, I would give the trimmer to you as a lovely parting gift."

"You're sweet."

"True, but we digress. Okay, so I might miss it, you know, as it would leave a terrible void above the mantel, but I'm fairly certain that I could get over it with a lot of Wild Turkey and the loving ministrations of a series of lithe, nubile, supportive girl friends."

"Unlikely."

"What? You think I would miss it that much?"

"No, I don't think that you could handle a series of lithe, nubile, girl friends."

"Hmph. Whatever. Point is, I could probably live without whatever it was. I could replace it, or buy another one, or just do without. It wouldn't be the same, but I could soldier on. What's the big deal?"

"Other than the S.T.D. that you got from girlfriend number two?"

"She *said* the doctor gave her a clean bill…"

"Let's think about this in another way, use another word. Somehow his gift to her got him into trouble, say."

"Hey, I like that! That's good! How could you get into trouble by giving someone something?"

"What if it wasn't yours to give?"

"So, he stole something or took something and gave it to Alice? Brilliant!" I said sarcastically. "Here my darling, on our last night together, I want you to take this token of my undying love… a shining symbol of the depth of my feelings for you… which I just swiped from Jared's."

"What if she didn't know it was stolen?"

"She had to. She knew that it had given him great pain, messed up his life. Unless he gave her his OxyContin prescription, in which case it would definitely have caused him great pain…"

"No, she wouldn't have known at the time he gave it to her. She would only have thought of it as a beautiful gift. The life ruining and pain part come later, and only after years can she recognize that. She says that she prayed and thought about it and finally decided to give it back. Oh, and let's also keep in mind that it was something that could be handed down. So, it wasn't a time sensitive thing that would lose value. It was still worth something in 1893, after thirty-four years."

"Okay, cross egg-salad off the list."

She gave me the "I have to put up with you as my spouse?" look, and after a moment said, "Speaking of which, I'm hungry. Let's go to lunch."

"All right, I'm game. Where? Your turn to pick."

"Given the weather, I'm in the mood for the Thai rice-noodle soup at Wild Bistro."

Good choice.

Chapter 42

The package was in Em's departmental mailbox when we returned from lunch. It was a standard FedEx envelope and it wasn't very thick or heavy. We wasted no time in retreating to her office to see what we had.

Em carefully slit the end with her desk pair of scissors, put on a pair of lightweight cotton gloves, and slid the contents onto her work table.

There were four items in the package.

The first was a short, typed note from 'Mr. Big' on a standard 8 ½ by 11 piece of copy paper: "These are the documents. All I have." There was no signature.

The second document was the letter from Alice to Theodore.

The third was a copy of the front of an envelope, postmarked Oakland, California, November 13, 1893:

T. Eckfeldt
Oakland, California

　　　　　　Mr. Jacob B. Eckfeldt
　　　　　　314 Loxley Court
　　　　　　Philadelphia, Pennsylvania

The fourth was the letter itself from Theodore Eckfeldt to Jacob B. Eckfeldt:

November 12, 1893

Dear Jacob,

God knows I tried. The last is hidden on a farm near Oxford, Ohio. Alice has kept it safe all this time. She has gone to her maker. I shan't be far behind. I did my best, but it was the damned dogs. After the first attempt I could never create another chance. Here is Alice's last letter. I beg you to forgive me for the burden I created.

Theodore
Brenner House, Oakland

"Well, what do you make of that?" I asked, after reading through the last letter a couple of times.

No response from Em.

"Earth to Em, come in, Em…"

"Hmmm. Interesting. It seems that Theodore was our mystery man who visited the farm in 1893. The way that I see this is that he got Alice's letter and pretty much immediately dropped everything and headed to Ohio. In those days it would have been a train trip, and it would have taken some time, but anyway, he ends up in Oxford sometime in June.

"So, who knows? He walks or he goes to the livery stable and rents a horse or even a buggy and takes a ride out to the west along Fairfield Road. Now, put yourself in his position. You don't want to bring attention to yourself. From what I can make out on the maps, the Riggs house is pretty close to being directly opposite the place where the rock was. So, what do you do?

"You can go out in the middle of the night, but you are new in town and have no idea of the lay of the land. At the same time, you can't afford to be seen taking too close a look or being too interested. So, if I were he, I'd take a reconnoiter and do a smiling pass-by, just to see what is what, and then I'd come back that night.

"Now if somebody came poking around our place in the middle of the night, what would Sadie and Bea have done?" As Em asked the question, her eyes welled with tears and her voice caught.

Yeah, well, mine too.

"Dog alarm," I concluded for her. "They'd have barked their fool heads off and run out the dog door and raised holy hell until we got up to see what was going on or until whoever or whatever it was took off. Of course, with Sadie it was usually gremlins and imaginary dog-treat thieves."

"No it wasn't! SHE knew. Just because YOU couldn't see them, doesn't mean that they weren't there," Em shot back.

"Okay, okay. The Baker version of Sadie and Bea are on watch, and now that I think of it, there wouldn't be any dog door or fence or chain or anything back then. Farm dogs! Their job was to protect the household from invaders, both two- and four-legged. Teddy comes back and tries to poke around and he's damned lucky if he doesn't get chewed on, or catch a load full of buckshot!" I agreed.

"Yes, and once the dogs are riled up, they're going to be on guard even more than usual. Given what was in the letter, I'd say that Theodore tried to get to the spot and Black Fang and Cerberus wouldn't let him even get close to the sticks," Em said with a very slight upward twist at the edges of her mouth.

"Okay, I'm good with all of that, but at the risk of offending your sensibilities, why doesn't he just shoot the dogs... well, poison anyway?" I offered.

Em glared at me. "If your dog is outside barking like something is going on and you hear a gunshot and a yelp and half the barking stops, what would you do?"

"I'd chase whoever it was to the ends of the earth and beat them to death with my putter! But in 1893, I'd grab my shotgun and chase whoever it was to the ends of the earth and blow their brains out. Okay, I gotcha, but what about poison?"

"Maybe Baker had two dogs? Maybe one eats it all before the other can get his share. I don't know. You'd have to get close or leave the food where they could get to it and not to you. Some dogs are trained not to take food from strangers. Maybe Theodore was just fond of dogs. At any rate, it doesn't happen and he ends up leading Baker to the rock."

"Why? Why not just back off and try again some other time?"

"Again, we'll never know, but I think that is exactly what he did. Could be that he got caught poking around and had to just make the best of it. Could be that he finally figured that he needed to get the exact position anyway, and then he could wait it out. No telling. He's got to feel pretty safe about somebody else digging it up given the distance from the rock. So, he goes and takes a look, with Baker's blessing and plans to come back later. But, he doesn't figure on the tenacity of Lassie and Rin Tin Tin, and finally has to give up."

"You know what this means, of course?"

"Yup. It could still be there."

Chapter 43

Which left, of course, the big question – what was it, "the last one" that Alice had buried, and that Theodore failed to retrieve.

The answer was surprisingly quick in coming.

As Em began to go through her other-worldly, historical spirits incantations, gathering paraphernalia, donning mystical robes, tossing bone fragments and seeking a raven to disembowel, I pulled up Google on her office computer and typed in Theodore Eckfeldt. I expected to get some IMDB reference to a porn star, or "Eckfeldt's Tent and Awning" in Paducah, Kentucky or some such. But, sometimes clean living and dumb luck permit the simple way to work out.

"Uh, Em," I muttered.

She continued the ministrations of her trade.

"Hey! Em!"

"What?" she shot back, annoyed that the figurative pentagram that she was scratching into the linoleum of her office floor had been interrupted.

"I think I found Teddy," I said and thumbed toward the computer screen.

Amidst a considerable amount of spluttering, muttering, and general commentaries about my ancestry, hygiene, underwhelming manly prowess, and general appearance, she gave way to awe and admiration. Not for me, for Teddy and his story.

The very first page you see when you pull up Theodore Eckfeldt on Google tells you all you really need to know. It doesn't take long to figure out the main points. You see, Teddy was a bad boy back in 1858 and 1859. He worked as the night watchman at the United States Mint in Philadelphia, and he was "free-lancing" to produce rare and valuable coins for his own benefit.

That's the gist of it, but it took us three days of digging and cross-referencing, some next-day-air delivery charges, and a number of phone calls to experts to really have a grasp of the matter. Of course, knowing the full story may never be possible.

The Eckfeldt family had been involved with the U.S. Mint almost from its inception. The patriarch of the family was John Jacob Eckfeldt, a Bavarian machinist and blacksmith. He moved to America before the revolution and made dies for the Mint as early as 1783. His son, Adam was Chief Coiner from 1814 to 1839. Adam's son worked in the Mint as assayer, and the grandson, Jacob Bausch Eckfeldt worked in the mint for over sixty years starting in 1865.

Adam also had a nephew, George J. Eckfeldt, who worked in the Mint for over thirty years beginning in 1830. So, in keeping with family tradition, it was just natural, then, that his son Theodore would be employed at the Mint as well. Further, there were other families doing pretty much the same thing, and intermarriages, and offspring and pretty much everybody worked at the Mint. Suffice it to say, that if you had sneezed in any corner of the Philadelphia Mint in the 1800s, somebody named Eckfeldt would have said, 'Gesundheit!'

Anyway, Teddy was coining coins on the "midnight shift" and selling them off through a nearby merchant who acted as a "fence."

But the story gets more complex and bizarre even than that.

Chapter 44

In the 1790s the United States was minting coins to provide a means to conduct business. Nobody would accept paper money because the rampant inflation during and after the Revolutionary War made the government's paper money literally worthless. The silver dollar was one of the coins minted at the time and it was quite popular, particularly in foreign trade. Oddly, foreign merchants would accept silver dollars, but would not accept lesser denominations even though the same weight of silver could be assured.

By 1801, however, a series of conditions forced the United States government to call a halt to the coining of silver dollars. As it turns out, the Spanish milled dollars in circulation at the same time had just a fraction more silver in them. They could be exchanged in the U.S. at a slight premium in value. Further, U.S. silver dollars could be exchanged for the Spanish dollars in the West Indies. The result was that the U.S. silver dollars flowed overseas never to return.

The combination of the drain caused by the dollar's use as a foreign trade medium and losses from the silver premium put the government in a bad position. They needed currency to circulate in the states, and without it the internal commerce of the country was in a bind. They needed an acceptable medium of exchange, not something that was disappearing overseas.

As a result, the government decreed that the U.S. would get out of the silver dollar business. Over four-hundred thousand silver dollars were produced in 1799, but only about half that in the following year. By 1804, only 19,570 U.S. silver dollars were coined. Until 1835 no further silver dollars were created.

In 1832 Andrew Jackson was President of the United States. The government, under "Old Hickory," was anxious to develop international trade with countries in the middle- and far-east. Jackson appointed Edmund Roberts as special agent and sent him on a secret mission to create trade agreements with the governments of Muscat (today, the capital city of Oman near the Straights of Hormuz), Burma, Siam (Thailand), Cochin-China (Viet Nam), Sumatra, Malaya, Borneo, and Japan.

Roberts returned with tentative agreements with the Sultan of Muscat and the King of Siam, and the treaties were ratified by Congress in the fall of 1834. In preparing to return with the signed agreements to Muscat and Siam, Roberts explained to the State Department that it was customary for gifts to be given as part of the protocol in the eastern countries. He went on to complain that the gifts we had been giving were cheap and were making us look bad.

One of the gift suggestions Roberts made was a complete set of U.S. currency in a nice box. The President agreed and directed the Mint to provide them. When you look at it, it makes sense. For just a few coins and a couple of bucks for a nice box, you have a classy gift.

At this point, though, things begin to unravel. Nobody specified what coins were to be included. As a result, the people at the Mint decided to include a silver dollar, even though there were none being minted in 1834. Instead of just selecting an existing silver dollar from the specimens that must have been held at the Mint, they decided to strike new coins. No one has ever been able to explain why.

Back in 1804, the last year in which silver dollars had been produced at the Mint, there had been 19,570 created. However, they all bore the date 1803! As an economy measure, although against the law which called for all coins to bear the year of their minting, it was common practice at the Mint to use dies until they literally wore out. This saved on the cost of metal and engraving in the creation of a new die.

So, for a reason that nobody has been able to fathom, and in a fashion that strongly suggests something fishy, in 1835 the people at the Mint created a new 1804 silver dollar die. They then proceeded to create eight brand new 1804 silver dollars to be included in the gift sets requested by Edmund Roberts.

Roberts took four of the boxes with him on his next voyage, in 1835, and reported that he delivered one set to the Sultan of Muscat that fall, and a second set to the King of Siam the following spring. However, Roberts fell ill with dysentery and died before he could make contact with the Emperors of Cochin-China or Japan, and the records show that the remaining two gift boxes were returned to the U.S. State Department.

An interesting side note is that the story of Anna and the King of Siam, depicted in the musical *The King and I,* is about part of this trade mission.

By various routes and means the eight 1804 dollars found their way into the hands of private individuals, and have since been carefully hoarded as rare specimens in noted coin collections.

The dies sat there in the Mint's storage rooms, unused, until 1858 when a new set of 1804 dollars appeared on the scene. It is unclear who was responsible for the actual coining of the new specimens. It is hard to believe that George Eckfeldt was unaware, given his position as Foreman of the Engraving Department, but it eventually came out that Theodore Eckfeldt was the individual who sold several of the coins onto the open market. Other coins of lesser denominations were also being created on the sly and collectors and observers were beginning to question Mint practices.

In all, five 1804 silver dollars were coined in 1858. Four of the five were eventually recovered by Mint officials, and three of the coins were destroyed. The fourth, for no sensible reason, was kept in the Mint collection. This specific coin was clearly an illegal attempt on the part of the coiner, and an imperfect one at that. The original eight coins, like the legitimate silver dollars that preceded them, had lettering around the edges. This version had smooth edges. Further, careful examination showed that this coin had been struck over a coin that had been minted earlier, not a blank planchette which was the normal practice. Traces of the design of a Swiss Bern five franc "Shooting Thaler" coin can be seen. Why such a coin would be kept as part of the Mint collection is unfathomable.

The fifth coin was never found!

Despite being caught red-, or at least silver-handed, Theodore was kept on in his position of night watchman at the Mint, and things were generally hushed up. But, whoever was behind the "midnight minting" put forth another effort in 1859, and a new set of 1804 silver dollars was struck, this time with the appropriate lettering around the edge. They had learned their lesson and had improved their work. Still, there were slight differences between these coins and the 1835 originals, most notably a missing curl from the head of Lady Liberty. Thus, there are three different versions of the coin.

By 1860 questions were being raised about the existence of further 1804 dollars, although no public response was made by Mint officials. Theodore, however, lost his job about this time. A year later, representatives of the prestigious Boston Numismatic Society again pressed James Pollock, Director of the Mint of the United States, as to the status of the 1804 silver dollar, noting that several had been offered for sale.

In his letter of reply, Director Pollock assured that all was well at the Mint, but inadvertently confirmed that post-dated currency had been created by avowing that such practices wouldn't happen again.

By 1878, as more of the "midnight" versions of the 1804 dollars surfaced, the outcry became too much to ignore and the practices and policies of the Mint were roundly criticized. The role of at least some of the members of the Eckfeldt family came to public light.

Chapter 45

After three days of piecing together the story of the "midnight minters" we were at home Wednesday evening preparing dinner and discussing Teddy and what we believed to be the missing 1804 dollar.

I took a sip of Wild Turkey to prepare myself for the ordeal, and then used the flat of a chef's knife to flatten a couple of cloves of fresh garlic. As I picked the garlic "paper" off the remains and began to use the edge of the knife to cream the rest into a paste, I asked Em, "So, you figure that Alice's keepsake was the missing 'Class II' dollar, eh?"

She did not look up from her computer screen there on the kitchen counter. "Makes sense. Of course it could be something else, but it feels right. It could certainly be valuable enough in today's terms to be a motive, even for murder."

"How much would it bring? It is not like you could just have an auction at Christie's or whatever, or could you?"

"With something like this it would all depend on the believability of the provenance. If you could show the connections and thereby prove its authenticity, it could be worth millions! One of the original eight was sold at public auction in 1999 and set the world record for the price of a coin at that time, at $4.14 million."

"Well, okay. That was over ten years ago, so this one would go for more?"

"Hard to say… As I said, provenance is everything. What we have in terms of the letters and the timing makes for as good a history as some of the other specimens, but certainly not all. The quality of the coin and its characteristics would also play a big role. If Alice carried it around in her purse and used it to crack walnuts, that would diminish the value, of course," Em opined, looking over the top of her glasses.

I had rubbed the bottom of an old, wooden salad bowl with the garlic paste, and was now rolling a lemon back and forth across the cutting board to break up the pulp inside and make it easier to juice. I cut the lemon in half and squeezed the juice of both halves carefully into the bowl, picking out the one escapee pip.

"I'm guessing that the fifth coin is going to be like the 'Class II' specimen at the Mint. If so, I'd think that would go a long way to convincing people that it's genuine. Since they used a 'Shooting Thaler' as a blank for the one, it makes sense to me that they would use the same method for all five. Why would you go to the trouble if you had access to the regular blank disks the Mint had on hand? Even with all the underhanded stuff going on, I don't think they could get away with just stealing the silver. There were records and assays and accounting to be dealt with. If you just walked in off the street with a bag full of your own coins, you avoid all that hassle."

"Uh-huh. Logical, but for all we know, there were lots of coins around at the time with the same weight and size. For that matter, they could have used an 1803 dollar or one of the Spanish milled dollars. But, I wouldn't be surprised to see another Swiss five-franc piece as the blank, and if so,

257

you're right. That would add credence to its authenticity. Of course if I were going to make a counterfeit version, I'd probably go buy a mediocre quality 'Shooting Thaler' and use it as a blank, for exactly that reason."

"Spoil sport."

Em paused as I buried my head in the refrigerator to search for the Lea & Perrins Worcestershire Sauce. There are some items where you just have to buy the old, original product, and Lea & Perrins is one of them. Sorry, French's, it just ain't the same.

I added several dashes to the bowl and brought out a whisk.

She continued, "There's another interesting question, and that is how a 'Class II' would be perceived by the numismatics folks. The coin that went for four million bucks was one of the original eight. The 'Class II' and 'Class III' coins have not been tested in the market for a while. One could make a good argument that they are 'illegitimate' and therefore should be worth far less. As a matter of fact, the owners of the 'Class I' coins made exactly that argument and tried to have the Mint recall the others and declare them as counterfeit."

I located my Wild Turkey and, wiping my hands on a dish towel, took another swig. "Well, from what I could gather from my reading over the past couple of days, all of the damned things are bogus to some extent. They should never have been made in the first place. If the people at the Mint had asked for clarification or for permission to create a new, post-dated coin, they'd have been turned down cold. So, I don't see how any of them can gripe. So there!"

"Well, yes, but at least the 'Class I' can claim some sort of legitimacy on the basis of being ordered by the President and the Department of State. The others were clearly being created on the 'black market'. Em swirled the dry white wine in her glass and took a small sip. It was another of our small vineyard favorites, Flora Springs Pinot Grigio 2008.

"The counterfeit question is another interesting angle. There are some who claim that all the coins are counterfeit and should be confiscated. Others argue that the coins cannot, by definition, be counterfeit because they were struck at the Mint using the actual dies owned by the government. So far, anyway, there hasn't been any move on the part of the government to take action against the owners of 1804 dollars. It's a pretty neat bucket of worms."

I squeezed a dollop of Grey Poupon mustard into the mixture with its gratifying mini-farting sound and whisked some more.

"I'd think that the long-lost, fifth 'Class II' might actually bring more! Think of it. It is truly one of a kind. It is notorious. And, what with the buried treasure in Oxford, Ohio bit, it makes it more collectable than ever. Price is going up!"

"Maybe… Interesting to find out."

"And, what's to keep 'Mr. Big' from announcing the find of the century and doing the whole public auction thing? Why NOT play up the letters and the rock and all the rest? Build the publicity and pump up the action."

I hovered over the salad bowl with a half-opened tin of anchovies in my hands. Em looked at me like I had just grown another head.

"You are not usually this dense. Are you feeling well?" she asked, the great concern in her voice only adding to the depth of her sarcasm.

"Wha-at?"

"It is buried on Miami property, you dolt. HE doesn't own it. Not only that, but if he uses the letters to support the provenance, then the location comes out and he loses. Miami, or more properly, the State of Ohio probably wins. He can't afford to tell the story. NOW do you see?"

"Well, rat poop on a stick!" I grumped, and went back to my anchovies, taking a fork and separating the little fishy fillets, and pouring the oil into the mix.

"Actually, it isn't that simple, but the effect is pretty much the same. Legally, it would depend on whether the item were declared a 'treasure trove' or 'abandoned property'. Historically, money or coins that were purposely hidden but where the original owner cannot be expected to return or be discovered, constitute a 'treasure trove'. Common law generally supports the claim of the finder. However, if the finder doesn't have permission to be on the property, then the laws of trespass apply and the 'treasure' belongs to the owner of the property. To make it more complex, if the original owner or heir can be found, assuming the item was properly bequeathed, then it belongs to them. And beyond all that, some countries and states have passed laws that simply confiscate anything found. Bottom line, 'Mr. Big' would have a helluva time in court, with no guarantees at all of walking away with the coin," Em lectured.

"I'm beginning to see why 'Mr. Big' went all 'Dark-side' on this. At this rate he's gonna end up owing money," I said as I began cutting a few thin slices of Kentucky country ham into julienne strips. The real recipe probably called for Serrano ham, but this was pretty close and a lot less expensive.

"Don't forget the taxes; becomes part of adjusted gross income."

"Geez! The next time I find a buried treasure, I'm just going to cover it back up and hope that nobody saw!"

"Good idea."

I added the ham and some freshly ground black pepper and a little juice from the green olives I would use to top off the salad.

"Dinner is almost ready."

Working quickly now, I pulled a bag of roughly torn iceberg lettuce from the cooler and emptied it into the wooden bowl and drizzled a bit of extra-virgin olive oil. I began to toss the lettuce gently with the dressing. Two plates and forks from the freezer, and a mound of salad on each, topped with a handful of green olives, and shredded Romano. A loaf of crusty bread from the oven, and butter that had been softening as I worked, and voila! The Richardson version of Tampa's famous Columbia Restaurant 1905 Salad!

"You are my treasure," Em purred.

"Durned right!" I responded graciously, as I topped off both of our drinks and sat.

Chapter 46

Em and I had changed places. She was at the sink and I was sitting at the counter. We have this agreement. The chef for the evening is absolved of clean-up duty.

"I don't get it. I can see that 'Biggie Rat' wants to keep things quiet and recover the loot on the sly. That way he avoids all of the pesky little problems of rightful ownership and all. But, then, what the hell does he do with it? Display it as part of his shot-glasses-from-every-state collection because he's missing South Dakota?

"If he wants to sell it, he has to show the provenance, and that means the letters. Other folks can find the John Wright farm, too. Miami's property. He's caught between a rock and a hard place, both literally and figuratively."

Em just rolled her eyes.

"So, really – what does he do with it? I suppose he could sell it to some unscrupulous numismatist somewhere, somebody who doesn't care about the niceties of ownership or sources or whatever, but that just begs the question. I mean, then what does the corrupt coin collector do with it? Just sit and look at it?"

"Well, really, what does any collector do with a coin or a baseball card or any collectable for that matter? They hoard it. They take it out occasionally and 'ooh and aah' and take great satisfaction in that they own it and nobody else does. They look at appraisals and sales prices of like items and either smile at its increasing value or worry over its decline," Em philosophized.

"That's pretty weird."

"Really? How many golf balls do you have in the hall closet? About one-hundred?"

Em referred to my collection of logo balls, one from each course I have played over the years.

"Well, that's different," I protested.

"How? You probably spent an average of what, five dollars on each ball? That's about five-hundred dollars that you have invested in a golf ball collection. And where are they? In the hall closet in egg cartons. When was the last time you took them out and chipped and putted down memory lane? Hmmm?"

"Well, I moved them to get to the Christmas wrapping paper," I temporized.

"I rest my case," she said as she dried her hands on the dish towel.

"Hey, I didn't kill anybody to add to my collection!"

"I've seen you play. It is just a matter of time."

"Hmph. Nice! Give a girl her 1905 salad and once the meal is over, bam! It's back to spousal abuse. One minute I'm a 'treasure' and the next, my highest virtues are impugned." I stuck out my lower lip and tried to look pitiful. Didn't work.

Em just said, "Yep" and walked into the den. I followed like the whipped cur I was.

"You know, about what you were saying before dinner? I wonder what would happen if our 'Mr. Big' were the actual heir?" I suggested.

"Now THAT'S an interesting thought!" Em replied.

You just keep thinking, Butch. That's what you're good at.

Chapter 47

Thursday morning was a lot like Christmas. It was a bright, sunny day with a few stray cirrus wisps setting off a gorgeous sky. The forecast was for low to mid-eighties. We were on our way to Cincinnati in a Miami University van to pick up 'the pig' and then we were going treasure hunting!

At least Em called it 'the pig.' In reality it was a ground penetrating radar or GPR system. Em called it 'the pig' after the truffle-hunting pigs in Europe. In the right hands it kind of snuffled around under the ground and found things that were worth a lot of money. It looked a lot more like a three-wheeled baby stroller than a pig, but so what. Where baby would have been, there was a metallic box, roughly the size of a case of beer. Between the handlebars there was a display screen kind of like that of a depth-finder. You wheel it along and it beeps and whirrs and shows fuzzy pictures with all kinds of cool colors and somehow tells you what is beneath the ground and where.

It is actually electromagnetic and its efficiency and sensitivity and depth of effective operation and all of that depended on the nature of the soil or rock, the amount of moisture in the soil, the electrical conductivity of the substrata and all sorts of arcane and technical things that I really don't care about. I feel the same way about fish finders and GPS units and cell phones. I don't really care how they work as long as I can talk to the fish.

Anyway, Em had used 'the pig' before on historical and archeological digs and swore by the darned thing. It also had a built-in GPS and obviously a compass feature that allows the operator to map out a search grid and stick to it. It records the findings and the position for future recall; all kinds of bells and whistles.

I asked Em why we didn't just use a metal detector and I got 'the look' in return. The bottom line of it all was that she was comfortable using 'the pig' and that was that. She had confidence in it. Period.

Personally, I had my coat hangers, and I was happy as a clam. You see, I can find objects underground by dowsing.

No, I am NOT kidding. I don't profess to understand it, but I do know that it works. I can find pipes and metal objects and water. Never tried it with a body, but I have demonstrated it over and over with the other things. Works like a charm.

I would never have believed it, either. A couple of houses ago we had a septic system that was in need of pumping. Since we had bought an existing home, we didn't know exactly where the tank or the leaching field was. We called a plumber and he came out and asked where the access to the tank was. We told him we had no idea. So, he asked me for a coat hanger.

Now, I figured that he was going to straighten it out and use it as a probe, poking holes in the yard as he searched. Not even close. He got out a pair of pliers and cut and bent the hanger into two L-shaped pieces. He held one loosely in each hand so that one part of the wire was vertical and the other part of the L pointed out in front of him. At this point, I suggested that I really didn't think it fair for me to be paying him eighty or one hundred dollars an hour to have him play games in my back yard. He was an old guy, a grizzled veteran of many a septic-skirmish, and he just said, "Sonny, you don't know what you are talkin' about. Watch and learn."

About forty-five seconds later he found the outflow pipe, and thirty seconds after that he found the septic tank. He handed me the hangers and said, "I dunno how it works. It jest does." So, I tried it. He was right.

When you cross over something the two Ls of hanger swing toward each other and cross. As you continue past, they separate and go back to being roughly parallel. You can even do it with one hanger. As you pass over a pipe, let's say, it will swing toward the pipe. You turn about ninety degrees toward the pipe and continue walking and as you pass over it, the hanger will swing in the other direction. By zig-zagging along you can map out the pipe or electrical line or whatever.

We used to do demonstrations as a parlor trick at parties. Folks would bet drinks that it was all a crock. By the time the evening was over, I'd be snockered and they'd be scratching their heads, but convinced because they had done it themselves.

I seem to recall watching some program on the History Channel or some such a few years ago. Apparently, some researchers decided to test this phenomenon. The set up at a local university, I think it was Cornell. There was a quadrangle with a walkway around it. It was winter and the whole area was covered with snow. They buried a quarter in the snow at this one spot along the walkway. They gave anybody who came by the two ell-shaped hangers and explained how to hold them and simply said, "Walk the path all the way around the quad, and if you think that anything is happening, just stop in place and count to twenty, and then go on." They had a video camera going so they could record the whole deal. Some incredible number like ninety-four percent of the thousand or so participants stopped within two feet of the quarter.

I got my hangers. Em can play with 'the pig' all she wants.

We picked up 'the pig' from a dealer down in Cincinnati. The place looked exactly like you'd think it would. It was a dumpy little industrial park building in Tri-county just down from the Bobcat dealership. Convenient, you could find it and then dig it out all in one easy trip. They had a showroom to display the latest and greatest underground viewing devices of various sizes, shapes, and complexity. Rob came out from behind the counter to greet us. He was wearing a uniform of industrial blue pants, black work shoes, and a white, long-sleeved logo shirt. We knew it was Rob because his shirt said so.

Anyway, after signing the obligatory rental papers, and signing away our first born, and assuring Rob that Em did, in fact, know how to use the device, and no, thank you, we did not need a refresher course for an additional two hundred dollars, and no we did not need to upgrade to the next model, and no we did not need the collision insurance, and we would bring it back full of gas, we loaded it into the back of the van and started back toward Oxford.

269

The collision insurance and gas part didn't really happen, but close.

By about 10:30 we were parked on a flat spot on the southeast corner of Riggs and Fairfield, had unloaded 'the pig' and were beginning the actual search. Em was merrily focused on the screen as she pushed the contraption along a Cartesian grid and I was working a spiral pattern.

We had a friendly wager on who would find it. The stakes don't really matter because Em never pays up when she loses, anyway.

Chapter 48

Mid-morning the following Monday we sat at the dining-room table, two cups of freshly brewed coffee steaming away between us.

Dead center of the table was an ivory colored jeweler's cloth, and on it was a slightly tarnished Class II 1804 silver dollar!

"It is a pretty thing," Em ventured.

"So is a coral snake," I grumped.

"Hmmm."

We sat and just looked at it silently for a time. After all that we had been through, it was surreal that here we were, item in hand. It was hard to actually believe that we had done it.

"Rogers and Clark," I muttered.

"Hunh?'

"Rogers and Clark. They must have felt the same kind of thing when they came over the last rise and saw the Pacific for the first time."

"Absurd. This whole thing has taken just two weeks, and really it was just following a map and using a little creativity and know-how. It's not that big a deal," Em argued.

"Nope.   Maybe, Sir Henry Stanley tracking down Livingstone in darkest Africa in 1871?"

"The way this thing is so twisted around, I wouldn't be surprised if Livingstone had the damned coin at some point," Em suggested.

"Well, we won't have it for much longer, either.   Are you ready to make the call?"

"I want this all to be over, so I guess so."

"Okay, let's do it."

Em picked up the phone, switched it to speaker and hit the autodial for 'Mr. Big.' We waited as it rang twice.

"Ah, Dr. Richardson?"

I couldn't help myself, "You were expecting Dr. Livingstone, maybe?"

"What?"

Giving me 'the look' again, Em cut in quickly. "Never mind. We have good news. We have the coin. It is sitting on the table in front of us."

'Mr. Big' sighed, I couldn't tell out of pleasure or relief. "Ahhh.   Well, that IS good news.   I was beginning to wonder if I would hear from you at all. It has been eleven days," he said with a chiding tone.

"Yeah, you know how it is. The Reds had a home stand and I needed to rearrange my sock drawer. Who gives a rat what you think or how impatient you've been. Here's the deal. You want the fifth 1804 silver dollar. We want our cut; one million dollars."

"Out of the question," he instantly shot back.

"Well, you know what? That's just fine. The coin disappears again. I'm sure we can find another buyer for considerably more than a million. We know what it is, now. We know what it is worth, and so do you. We figure we can EASILY sell it for two or three times what we are asking from you. So, you don't like the deal, go play in the snow."

Em, the 'good cop' added, "You have the original letters, and I am sure they can be authenticated. That gives you a much better position in the market. The provenance will be carefully scrutinized, as I am sure you know. With the coin in your possession, and your connection you have a better claim to the property than some outsider." As she said this she raised her eyebrows and shrugged, as if to say 'who knows?'

I could sense indecision from the other end, and decided to poke him in the eye again.

"You know what, I've had just about enough of this! There's another option. We walk into the Miami University President's office this afternoon and we plop the damned coin down on his desk and say, 'Hey, prez – lookee what we found!' We want to donate it to the school. We come out looking like heroes, we get all sorts of celebrity status, everybody loves us, we get raises, and all

273

the grant money we ask for in perpetuity… Life is grand! Sucks being YOU, but what do we care? Whaddya think about them apples, pal?"

"You can't do that!" he said forcefully.

"Oh, yeah? Watch me."

"You forget your vulnerability," he said with some confidence.

Oh no, I hadn't. Nor had Em.

"First, there is the matter of the police. I expect that you would find it very uncomfortable to have them investigate the events of two weeks ago."

Em's turn, "Why, we have no idea to what you could be referring. What events?"

I helpfully offered, "You want the Oxford Police Department number? I have it right here."

It had been eleven days and we had watched the Cincinnati newspapers religiously every day, dreading the headline, 'M.U. PROFS MURDER FOUR" and at minimum expecting "Four Bodies Found in OTR: Police Suspect Gang Violence" or some such. What we had seen was, nothing. Either the civic-minded citizens who had found the car and guns and bodies had decided to provide a quiet graveside service and burial, that is, hidden the bodies… or, the car was still sitting there, undisturbed, where we left it… or, the police were investigating and keeping it all quiet so they could leap out and yell, 'Surprise!' as they arrested us. But, so far, there was no news at all.

"I may be forced to make that call, although I would do so reluctantly," he threatened.

"And what are you going to tell them?" I asked. "Hi! I'm an anonymous tipster, and I just thought that you would want to know that four young people mysteriously disappeared from the home of two of your leading professors. They had no prior connection with the Richardsons, and nobody saw them together, and there is no evidence, but I just thought you'd like to know. Yep, that's gonna work."

"Perhaps not. But you continue to ignore your second point of vulnerability. I have the advantage of you. At any time of my choosing I can appear out of nowhere and have either or both of you kidnapped or killed. As you are aware, I have done it before," he said coldly.

"That's right. And that brings us back to the deal. One million dollars, in cash, twenties and fifties. You hand over the money and we hand over the coin. Everybody wins."

It seemed like an eternity. I could hear the wheels grinding at the other end of the line. Finally, he replied, "It will take some time to get the money."

Em responded, "Take your time. Call us on this phone when you have it."

I added, "Have a nice day! Bye!"

Chapter 49

He called back on Thursday afternoon.

I answered on speaker, "O.P.D., Sergeant Callahan, make my day."

"Dr. Richardson?"

"Yeah," I said resignedly. "What gave me away?"

"You know you are not as humorous as you believe yourself to be?"

"Awww. Why do I always get the tough crowds?"

Em decided that enough was enough. "We are listening, and by the way, I agree with you about J.D.."

Man! Everybody's a critic.

"I have the money."

"All right," Em said. "Tomorrow night at two a.m. we will meet on the twelfth green at the Indian Ridge Golf Club. It is three miles south of Oxford on U.S. 27. We will exchange the coin for the money there. You will, of course, come alone. If we see anyone else, we will abandon the meet. Are the instructions clear?"

"Perfectly, but why, may I ask, did you select such an odd location, and at such a horrific hour? Why not meet in a public place at a civilized time, say Cincinnati's Fountain Square at noon?"

"We thought about that. First and foremost, we don't trust you. In a crowd you could have any number of hired assistants who could do a quick mugging, hand off the package, and be gone before anyone could react. What could we do, go to the police? Second, and we think you'll agree, we do not want to be seen making this transaction. Obviously, we do not want someone remembering that they saw us together," Em explained in her best professorial tone.

"So, to avoid being seen together we needed to make it at a secluded spot, and in the dark. Think about it. How many places can you think of that are safe from patrolling police, or a random drive-by spectator? It is a rural golf course. The twelfth green is in the middle of the course, out of sight of the clubhouse and just about everything else in the world," I went on. "If you park your car at one of the lots nearby on 27, and hike in, the police will have no reason to interrupt us."

"Yes, I can see your points," he agreed reluctantly.

"So, two a.m. Friday morning," insisted Em.

"I do not like it, but I shall be there."

"Oh, and one other thing… Bring the original documents. They are the only identification that we have that will prove we are dealing with you in person. You can't afford to put the provenance in someone else's hands. Without it you have nothing, and you know it."

"I see that my confidence in you was not misplaced. I shall bring the documents," and he rung off.

277

"Geez, Em, what is it with you two and the double negatives?"

Chapter 50

I backed in on the east side of the empty furniture store that adjoined the Indian Ridge property and the Derickson place, and checked my watch. It was a couple of minutes past ten p.m. I was early, as intended. It hadn't been dark all that long, and I wanted to be on location first. I figured on sitting up on a high point above the thirteenth green where I could watch the entire hillside and most of the approaches to the twelfth. Unless he came up out of the dense underbrush just below the green, I'd see him walking in, and whether he was alone.

My parking spot was protected on two sides by trees, and the building itself blocked the car from being seen from 27. The mounds along the driveway into the golf course protected me on that side.

I had played with the lights of the 'beater' rental I was driving. It wasn't the same one we had used before, but it was close enough to be a member of the 'family'. The back-up lights were disconnected, as was the interior light. The license itself had been doctored with duct tape.

It was a beautiful night. The forecast had been for possible showers late in the afternoon, but as usual the weather had split and both north and south of Oxford had gotten rain, but we were left dry. The temperature was in the mid-sixties and there was a light breeze out of the northwest pushing the full moon in and out of the clouds. It would have been a wonderful setting for a midnight stroll or an adventurous tryst, but not tonight.

279

My mouth was dry and my heart was beating hard. My shoulders and neck had knotted up to the point that I could feel the hair on the back of my head. To put it bluntly I was scared out of my wits. I didn't trust 'Mr. Big' any more than I trust the billing from our HMO.

I eased the car door shut and locked it, then stood a moment in the shadows and listened and scouted all around for signs of activity: people, dogs, vehicles, anything. I didn't want to be surprised, not even a little. As I watched, I nervously put my hand into my pocket and fingered the soft jeweler's bag wrapped tightly around the prize.

I was wearing dark clothing and I carried a small backpack with a six-inch Maglite and a bottle of water. The Browning 9mm automatic, I kept in my pocket.

Em and I had said our goodbyes earlier. We had discussed this night in great detail and had agreed that it made no sense to expose both of us at the exchange. If he saw only one of us, it could be a deterrent to foul play, as the other would be out of his reach, who knows where. It was not a pleasant farewell. It is a hard thing to let go when you know that it may be the last time, ever.

As another buffalo herd of clouds grazed their way across the moon, I took advantage of the darkness and slipped along the trees and the cart barn, around the edge of the empty parking lot and across to the burned-out hull of the clubhouse.

The State Fire Marshal and the police had ruled it arson when the clubhouse had burned a year earlier. They had cleaned up the site some, and the ubiquitous yellow tape surrounded what was left, warning people to stay out. Frankly, I had no desire to go in. Now that I thought of it, I didn't have much desire to go into the place when it had been whole. As a member I never understood why we needed a seven-thousand square foot monument for a clubhouse.

I paused for a few moments and again surveyed my surroundings. The silver-white light of the moon flowed across the corduroy landscape below me. Shadows from the clouds stalked across the fairways, merged with darker patches of woods and passed on. I could hear traffic from the highway a hundred yards behind me, a truck shifting up through its gears in its blue-collar percussion. A long way off to the north a dog barked, but he didn't sound as if his heart was in it. Again, sensing nothing, I moved with the darkness across the hillside below the practice green and found my spot in the hollow below the brow of the hill that crested the thirteenth green.

I waited… And wondered what the next few hours would bring.

Chapter 51

Watching is hard work. It takes a lot of energy to concentrate, to use your senses at their peak and to stay still. You wonder, did that shadow move? Was that sound the same as it was a moment ago? Could he have seen me? Is he coming up behind me? Is there more than one of them? You move your eyes to keep them from locking on shadow or light and to keep your peripheral vision going.

At least that was how it affected me.

Several eternities later I thought I caught the swish of footsteps in the grass behind me on the ridge. Then I heard it more clearly. The sound was coming from the direction of the clubhouse and would pass behind me along the first hole. I flattened on the hillside and peered through the tall grass that bordered the left side of the first fairway. There he was! As he passed me he was moving slowly and carefully, headed for the gap in the high grass that would lead onto the twelfth fairway. If you didn't know the course, that would be the most logical route to find your way to the twelfth green.

I waited for several more minutes of intense watching and listening, but gained no sense that he had brought someone with him.

Finally, I straightened and walked down the hill on the cart path along the thirteenth that would lead me to the rendezvous.

He was standing at the front edge of the green as I approached. He, too, was wearing dark clothing, what looked to be a matte black windshirt of some sort, and a dark baseball cap with no discernable insignia. Beside him on the skirt of the green was a medium size, dark duffle bag.

He was shorter than my height by a few inches, and seemed to be of moderate build. It was hard to tell given the windshirt, but he didn't appear to be either emaciated or grossly overweight. I couldn't guess an age. Might have been anywhere from forty to seventy. What I could see of his face in the shifting moonlight was suggestive of sharp features and light colored eyes. If anything he looked a little like the actor Kevin McCarthy. It was not a kindly face.

"So, Dr. Richardson, where is your wife? I expected both of you at our meeting," he said with something of an edge to his voice.

I cleared my throat, not trusting that I would be able to speak, "Well, you know how it is. We don't have a DVR and there was a 'House' rerun... And besides, it was my turn to deal with the trash."

Before he could respond, I turned away from him and walked a few steps away from the green and toward the wooded area to the right side of the fairway, "Let's move over here where we are a little more under cover."

I took off my backpack and knelt and began to open it.

"Hold it! What are you doing there?" he rasped. I now had no doubt that he was 'Mr. Big'. I had heard that rasp on the other end of the phone on the first call.

283

"Look, Buster, I figured that you would want to see what you are buying. And I sure as hell want to see the color of your money. Now, if you want to stand out here in the middle of the golf course and start shining a flashlight around, we might as well set off a rescue flare and call 911. I expect that the cops can be here in about five minutes.

"I have a little Maglite in the backpack so you can look at what you need to see inside the pack, and I can do the same. Okay, or do you have some better idea?" I asked testily.

"I, too, have a flashlight, but your arrangements are well reasoned. Shall we begin?"

I took off the dark leather driving glove on my right hand and reached into my pocket to retrieve the single coin it its bag. "You've been waiting longer than I have, so here you go," and held it out to him.

He reminded me of nothing so much as Gollum from *the Lord of the Rings*. He had finally acquired his 'precious'. He quickly knelt and hunched over the open backpack, put both hands inside and turned on the light. For several long moments he gazed, spellbound, into the protected confines of the bag. As I had checked earlier in our darkened closet at home, very little light escaped. He sank back a little on his heels in relief and appeared to be turning the coin over and over in his hands.

He looked back at me and said in a hushed tone, "It really is the fifth coin. I can hardly believe it. The fifth coin... I've done it."

I didn't say anything, but I thought that was a bit condescending on his part. I would have given Em some credit, after all.

He stood from his kneeling position as if rising from prayer in church.

I took this opportunity to satisfy my curiosity. "Can I ask you something? There are a few things we don't understand... If you don't mind."

He shrugged.

"First, I'd like to know why Theodore was passing poorly made Class II dollars when shortly after, they were making the much-improved Class IIIs. And, what was the story with Alice, and why Oxford? And what is your connection to all of this? Or, do you even know any of this stuff? "

For the next few minutes he filled me in, taking great pleasure in proving that he was superior in knowledge, social position and power. He finished his story, and said in a condescending tone, as if he were Scrooge supposing that Bob Cratchit would be taking Christmas day off, "And now, you'll be wanting to see your commission."

He unzipped the duffle and reached inside, and as he did, I said, "Un-unh. Unzip it all the way."

He shrugged and opened the bag from one end to the other. Well, it looked like it was filled with banded stacks of money, anyway. He selected one band, apparently at random, and started to hand it to me, but I shook my head and said, "Let's try that packet in the corner."

285

"Of course," and he handed both to me.

It was my turn to kneel and use the cover of the backpack to inspect the money. I twisted the Maglite and shone it on the first stack which I riffled with my other hand. Fifties. I didn't count them, but they looked real to me, and a full band. I repeated the action with the second stack. Twenties, again real enough.

As I was doing this I asked, "Oh, one last question: why didn't you just come to us straight up? Em could have worked for you legitimately." I turned off the flash and looked up, my night vision corrupted by the light, but not so corrupted that I couldn't see that he was holding the twin of the 9mm automatic in my pocket. It was pointed directly at my face.

"Because I would have had to share," he said simply. "This way it costs me nothing."

The gun was no more than three feet in front of my eyes.

I gulped, "Before you pull the trigger, there is one more thing."

"Yes, there always is, isn't there?"

"There were more than five Class IIs made!" I stammered.

"Impossible! DuBois was emphatic that only the fifth coin remained!"

"Look, if you'll let me get up, I have proof. There weren't just five, there were nine. DuBois was misquoted. What he said was that there were five still missing," I insisted.

"Besides, with all that had happened and all the lies and cover-ups, what makes you think that DuBois would tell the truth? He and his family were in it up to their necks."

He began to waiver the tiniest bit. He hesitated, and finally said, "Yes, that could be so. The Pattersons and the DuBois had been stealing from the Mint from the beginning. Get up. Slowly. Now, where is this proof?" He carefully kept his distance, the gun trained squarely on me.

I stood, my knees groaning and back creaking as I tried to straighten up. "May I reach into my pocket?"

He motioned with his gun for me to go ahead.

"I have two pieces of proof for you. Here's the first," I said as I slowly and carefully handed him a folded piece of paper.

He shook it open and glanced down at it in the moonlight. "What is this, I can't make it out."

"Well, if you'd like to look at it inside the backpack…"

"Just tell me."

I took a deep breath, and sighed, "It's a print of a photo showing the five coins side by side, including the one you have, my wife's hand, and the front page of today's newspaper."

"Hmmm. And the other piece of evidence?"

I repeated my move from a moment ago and took a second jeweler's bag from my pocket and handed it across to him.

Even in the moonlight he could see the draped bust of a second 1804 silver dollar.

"I would not have believed it. Where are the others?"

"Not here."

"No, I would not expect that. However, I would expect that your wife will know," and he raised his gun to fire.

I threw myself to my left and down as the shattering boom destroyed the stillness of the night, and much of 'Mr. Big's' head disappeared.

It's a good thing that golf courses are soft. I rolled over and started to reach for my own gun, but then got a better look at what had been his head, and decided it wasn't necessary. Shaking, I pushed myself up to an unsteady but upright position.

I looked over to my right as the foliage parted and Em emerged, the shotgun her father had left her draped professionally over her arm and pointed at the ground.

"That went well, don't you think?" she asked, and then took two paces and kicked 'Mr. Big' soundly in the ass.

Chapter 52

After a deep breath or two, we worked quickly. Who knew whether the shotgun blast had been noticed by anyone or if it had, whether they had done anything about it? At any rate, we had no intention of hanging around until the first foursome came along in the morning.

While Em kept watch, I put on my gloves again and went through 'Mr. Big's' pockets. I emptied the contents into the duffle. I removed his watch and a ring. Standing over the body, I dropped seven Oxycodone tablets and after a moment's thought, took one of the bands of twenty dollar bills, unzipped his pants and stuck the packet halfway in.

Em glanced at what I was doing, and simply said, "Nice touch."

One last careful look around. Em donned the backpack, and I picked up the duffle bag.

"Have you got the shotgun shell?" I asked.

"Of course."

"Let's go."

The cloud cover was increasing and in the darkness it provided we moved quickly but carefully. Across the swale to the left of the twelfth green, to the trees to the right of the thirteenth tee, then to the tall grass that separates thirteen and fourteen. From the tall rough behind fourteen tee to the hillside below the practice green and then to the shadow of the clubhouse.

Just as we were about to make the final dash across the open space to the fence and bushes at the edge of the Derickson property, beams of light played across upper level of the clubhouse ruins. My heart leapt to my throat. Where could we run? We could go cross-country if we had to, but that would take time. As soon as they found the body they'd have dogs and all the rest. They'd find the car in no time. Game over.

I was just making up my mind that if it came to it, I'd give myself up and give Em a chance to make a clean getaway. The lights swung around, hitting the trees, more or less following our route back to the car. We could hear the tires on the asphalt as the car retreated back down the drive. A minute later we saw the police cruiser with 'Sherriff' markings pass under a light on its way toward Oxford.

I needed to use the bathroom.

We waited another few minutes, listening, and then made our way back to the car. We kept the lights off and crept out from behind the building. When we could see no traffic on U.S. 27 or Stillwell Beckett, we turned left onto 27 and headed south, away from Oxford. After about a mile, again seeing no traffic, we turned right on Stillwell Road and made our way to Riley, then Riggs Road and back home.

It was just a little past three a.m.

We pulled the rental car into the garage, closed the overhead door, turned off the engine and just sat.

"J.D.,, can we NOT have to do that again? Please?"

I sat back in the driver's seat, my knuckles white on the steering wheel to keep my hands from shaking.

"Can you think of any way that we could have avoided this?"

She paused. "No, not really. He didn't give us any choice, other than to die."

"No. He wasn't going to give up, and he wasn't going to keep his side of the deal."

"Did you think he would?"

I sighed, "No, but I almost wish he had." I arched my back and rolled my shoulders. "But, that is why I played a few holes on the back nine earlier this evening, and why you rode in the cart, and why you sat there in the woods for six hours."

"Trust but verify."

I nodded in agreement and then turned and looked her in the eye, "Em, thank you."

"You're the only husband I've got. It would take me a lot of effort to break in a new one."

We got out of the car. Em stripped to her bare skin and disappeared into the house, only to return a minute or two later with a couple of large, heavy-duty, plastic trash bags, and saints be praised – my purple cup filled with ice and Wild Turkey! God, I love that woman!

I traded my black driving gloves for a pair of cotton gardening gloves and began transferring the money from the duffle into one of the trash bags. 'Mr. Big's' personal items and the two 1804 dollars went into the second bag. When I was done, Em took both and disappeared into the house. I took her clothes and put them into the duffle, and stripped down and followed suit with my own. My fifty-five gallon drum trash burner was going to get a workout in the morning.

Finally, I unzipped the knapsack to retrieve the two stacks of bills and the Maglite before adding the pack to the duffle.

"What the hell?" I exclaimed. There in the bottom of the pack were seven assorted golf balls. Em had made the most of her wait in the woods. As I said, I love that woman.

Chapter 53

We had showered and dressed, and sat in the living room, neither of us figuring on getting much sleep. Outside it began to rain.

Em settled back in her chair with a cup of coffee. "With the wind and the rustling of the leaves, I couldn't hear most of what you two said."

I got up and retrieved his wallet from the dining room table and tossed it in her lap. "Look at the license."

Em pulled it out of the wallet, glanced at it and then looked back at me. "Well, I'll be damned!"

The name on the Pennsylvania license read: John A. Eckfeldt.

"His great-grandfather was John M. Eckfeldt, Chief Coiner of the San Francisco Mint, and Theodore's brother," I explained.

"And according to the census data, Theodore lived in Oakland, in the Brenner household in the 1880s. That matches with the return address on Theodore's letter to Jacob, that and the fact that Brenner was employed as a gold melter," Em added.

"Yep. Brenner was married to Kate… Eckfeldt, Teddy's older sister. Brenner moved to California from Philadelphia to work for John M. I don't know if they were married in Philly or if they met later. At any rate, when

Theodore left town, he went to live with his sister and brother-in-law in Oakland.

"In 1860 things were beginning to heat up at the Mint in Philadelphia. Teddy had gotten caught with his hand in the cookie jar, not once but twice. The family figured it was in everybody's best interests to banish him to the west coast. They weren't very happy with ol' Teddy, you see, because he pretty much messed up what had been a sweet deal until then.

"Almost the entire family was in on it, and they weren't even very apologetic about it. They were post-dating, minting coins from earlier years, and selling them on the collector's market for up to one hundred times face value. It wasn't just dollars, but all sorts of other coins as well. The odd thing is that the Class II dollars were never meant to be sold. The 'midnight minters' were just setting up the dies and getting organized, so they used whatever they had on hand to correct the alignment and perfect the method; hence, the Shooting Thaler as a blank.

"Rather than just disposing of the Class II specimens, which is what the family intended, Teddy decided to make a little profit on the side for himself," I concluded.

"So, he jumped the gun, and messed up by alerting the collectors that these fakes were on the market. The fact that they were so clearly not the same as the original Class I version, raised hell!" Em observed.

"That's about it. Peoples' eyebrows were already raised when the Class IIIs began to show up, and they were carefully scrutinized, looking for the smallest of details to prove them 'fakes'. That was the beginning of the end. The party was about over, even though the family or families, I should say, continued to try to cover up the whole deal."

I sipped at my Wild Turkey and continued, "But, that's not the whole story. You were right about Teddy and Alice, or at least on the right track. Alice's last name was Patterson. She was the daughter of Dr. Robert Maskell Patterson, Mint Director from 1835 to 1851. By the way, his sister, Martha married into the DuBois family and later one of the Dubois married an Eckfeldt. Suffice it to say, they were all entwined.

"Anyway, Teddy was from the wrong side of the Eckfeldt clan, but that didn't keep him and the young daughter of the past Mint Director from falling in love. Well, that just wouldn't do, and when Teddy ran afoul of the family on the Class II deal, that clinched it. It was proof that Teddy was no good, and he and Alice had to be separated. They decided to ship him off to California to report to his older brother. Some of the family believed that Teddy was trying to raise money so that he and Alice could run off, and that was why he was freelancing in the first place. So, about this time, Alice turns up pregnant, and she gets shipped off to live with cousin Andrew O. Patterson."

"So that explains how the coin ruined Theodore's life," Em interjected.

"Yup, although I don't think the family was having any of the Teddy-Alice connection one way or another," I mused.

"And until his letter to Jacob in 1893, I don't think that anyone knew what had happened to the fifth coin."

"And, A.O. Patterson lived in Oxford. Patterson Place on Western Campus! Of course! And, Patterson Avenue! He was a Presbyterian minister as I recall, and he had a son who gave the land in town for the Presbyterian Church."

"'Mr. Big' didn't know anything about Alice or the baby after that, only what was in her letter. Theodore made his play for the coin in 1893, but the combination of his failing health and Baker's watchdogs shot that chance, and he went back to California and died later that year.

"So, there things sat until this spring. 'Mr. Big's father died, and in a lock box in his bank, there is an envelope with the letters in it. 'Biggie' does a quick Google search and connects the dots. He is 'heir' to the last 1804 dollar! And it's a good thing for him. He's with the Division of Bank Examinations in Pennsylvania, and he's had this little scam going. Everything was okay until recently. What with the economy and all, he can't juggle assets fast enough to cover up. So, if he doesn't come up with a few million by the end of the fiscal year in June, he's going to be exposed and he'll end up with a long jail term."

Em picked up, "That explains how they would know so much about us. The guy is a bank examiner, or whatever. He'd have access to financial records, bank records, credit card information, tax returns, you name it."

"And, he'd probably come across some pretty seedy characters in his investigations – people who would be willing to do whatever it took to avoid prosecution. Enter the 'Fab Four'. Anyway, he knows the coin was buried somewhere west of Oxford, but he doesn't know where so he needs somebody who knows about research and finding such things."

"Me."

"You. But he doesn't have time to screw around with court cases and disputed ownership, and tax liabilities and all of that. He needs a pile of money and he needs it now. If he goes about it all legal and above board, the publicity and the delay are gonna kill him. In the end, he didn't see any way but to force us to work for him."

Em shook her head, "So this all comes down to an asshole crook, who is the great-grandson of an asshole crook, who hires four other asshole crooks to pressure us to come up with a multi-million dollar bank bailout?"

"That sums it up nicely," I agreed. "Kind of reminds you of Congress, doesn't it?"

Chapter 54

I awoke for no apparent reason, to see that it was light out. I had apparently dozed off at some point as the adrenalin in my system was replaced by ethanol. Given my druthers, I'd just as soon stick with the ethanol in the future. I had a half of a sore throat, and a half of a head-ache, and I was half nauseated, and my neck and shoulders hurt like hell. Pretty standard.

I creaked my way out of the chair and went to the window. It looked like we had gotten a fair amount of rain overnight. I hoped so, because it would help to confuse the area around the twelfth green and muddle the evidence a little.

Not seeing Em, I called for her, but got no response. I found her in the garage, carefully cleaning her father's shotgun.

"Morning, sleepyhead," she greeted me cheerfully.

Obviously, she'd had her coffee already. I just growled in response.

"There's fresh coffee, and I poured your juice for you."

This time my mumbled growl sounded the tiniest bit like "thank you."

"Last night, right after we got home, you said something about almost wishing that he had kept his part of the bargain. Do you?"

I painfully sat on the doorstep, resigned that we were going to have a conversation whether I wanted to or not. Em talks to me when I am trying to read in bed before going to sleep. She talks to me when I want to listen to the news on the radio. Whenever it is least convenient, she must have a conversation. "Do I what?"

"Wish that Eckfeldt had been straight with us and just made the exchange and left?"

I thought about it for a minute. "Yes, I think that would have been a lot better. For one thing, there wouldn't be another dead body beside the twelfth green."

"You mean there was another one?"

It was my turn to give HER 'the look.'

"I hope we get away with it. I hope that nobody was out for a two a.m. stroll and saw us. I hope that we didn't leave a trail. I hope that he didn't leave a note with HIS lawyer. I hope that you didn't leave your purse at the scene. I have a lot of hopes and a lot of misgivings, so yeah, I wish that it didn't have to happen."

"Hon, he really didn't leave us any choice. He was going to kill you, and then he was going to come after me."

"I know, but you asked. I wish that he had taken the coin and left."

"Well, maybe. I might have shot him just for Sadie's sake."

"Now THAT I believe."

Em was wiping down the wooden stock of the shotgun and beginning to put away the cleaning supplies.

"If he had walked away, how long do you think?"

I rose from the step and turned to head back into the house. "No way to tell. Maybe forever. It was a damned good fake."

Chapter 55

From the moment that we first read about Teddy on Google, we knew that we needed a 'plan b'. 'Mr. Big' wasn't going to leave us alone just because we came back and said, 'sorry, dude, we can't find it.' And, Em will tell you, the odds were very much against us finding Alice's buried treasure. Sure, it could have been there, but there was every reason for it not to be.

The rock isn't there. Who knows what happened to it? Baker could have found the treasure box after all, and seeing a single 1804 silver dollar, he might easily have just said, 'big deal' to himself and put it in his pocket. For all we know, the person Alice delegated to bury it may have kept it. And, as Em said at the outset, LOTS of people know of the story.

WE certainly never found it. It could still be out there, but I'd bet against.

While Em dug deeply into the Eckfeldts and the 1804 dollar at the beginning of the prior week, I took my thumbnail knowledge and got on the phone to talk with a good friend on the engineering faculty here at Miami, Ron Hawthorne. I had some weird idea about buying an 1803 dollar in good condition and then making a ceramic mold from it, changing the 3 to a 4, and a few other things, and voila, casting an 1804 silver dollar. So, I started asking all kinds of questions about mold making and how quickly it could be done, and Ron about floored me with his response.

"Why go to all that trouble? Rapid prototyping can build whatever you want in a few hours."

We had a somewhat lengthy discussion during which I'm afraid I lied shamelessly. I told him that Em had a deadline looming on an important grant proposal. She was going to develop a display for the Smithsonian Museum detailing the history of 'trade dollars' and the U.S. currency at the beginning of the nineteenth century. I convinced him that if we could show the replica currency in a mock up of the 'King of Siam' display case, that it would vastly improve our chances of nailing down the grant. Ron worried that what we were talking about could be considered counterfeiting. I assured him that the coin would lack edge lettering and would, therefore, be easily recognized as a fake. Finally, he agreed to make the coin.

I hated to lie to him, and I think that deep down he knew that something fishy was going on. Ultimately, though, I suspect that the combination of our friendship, Em's reputation and mine, and his own desire to show off some of his new engineering toys cemented the deal.

Despite Ron's assurances that he could work from photographs, I wasn't so sure. I spent the rest of the day on the telephone and finally tracked down a specimen of an 1801 silver dollar in a numismatist's shop in Dayton. By paying cash, I was able to get the price down to a little over fifteen-hundred dollars for what the dealer said was a coin in 'fine' condition.

Close examination of the available photographs, and having used all sorts of laser measurements of the 1801 specimen I had provided, Ron began creating the computer data that would direct the process. He was like a little kid at Christmas getting to play with a coveted toy for the first time. The process is called direct metal laser sintering, or DMLS, of course. What it amounts to is that a layer of very fine powdered metal alloy is laid down and a computer then directs powerful pinpoint lasers to intersect at specific points. Where the beams intersect, they melt the metal. Then another layer of metal dust and more laser melting, and so forth. The end result is a three-dimensional model of whatever you wanted to make. DMLS is used to make one-of-a-kind metal alloy parts for space vehicles, prototypes for automobile parts, and on and on. It is very accurate and can literally be accomplished in a few hours, once the data files are loaded. Actually, it took Ron a couple of days because he wasn't satisfied with the early attempts, and because I challenged him to make a couple of different shooting Thaler versions. In all, we came up with five serviceable specimens by the end of last week.

When we failed to find the lockbox or Alice's coin on the airport property, we were forced to go to 'plan b'.

Chapter 56

Over the next few days there was a frenzy of press coverage surrounding the golf club murder. There was much speculation that it was a drug deal gone wrong. There was speculation that it was a gang confrontation. There was speculation that it was a professional hit and that organized crime was putting out a warning of some sort. There was speculation that the dead body was somehow related to the arson from a year before.

In short, there was a great deal of speculation, posturing, official announcements and all the normal claptrap that goes on in such cases. The Oxford Township Police were "following up on important leads". The Butler County Sheriff proclaimed that budget cutbacks were at fault, and pointed the finger at the County Commissioners.

The lack of identification on the body was making things difficult, apparently. I was surprised that they hadn't found his car already.

There were also a number of poor taste jokes, of course. One accused Stevie Williams. One joke had the first foursome discovering the body because one player's ball had ended up wedged by the corpse. The player says, 'Oh, my God!' and his partner says, "Quit your complaining, it could have been in the hazard.'

Em and I missed a lot of it because we had decided to take a weekend trip to Pennsylvania. By Saturday evening we were in Harrisburg. We pulled up to a U.S. Postal Service drop box in a nondescript industrial area. We made sure that the last pick-up time was early afternoon and that there was no weekend pickup. We deposited four carefully packaged and labeled boxes addressed to the head of the Pennsylvania Department of Banking. The four boxes contained nine-hundred, eighty-seven thousand dollars. I had stuffed two thousand into 'Mr. Big's' pants and Em had insisted that we mail an envelope with nine thousand dollars in it to the local no-kill animal shelter. We had spent about two thousand on a new freezer and a replacement chair, plus assorted repair supplies. I figured I could sell the 1891 dollar back for about what I paid.

The boxes were helpfully labeled with Mr. John A. Eckfeldt as the sender. The timing would have been tight, but he could have mailed the boxes and still made it to Oxford in time.

When we pulled back into the garage on Sunday night, we were exhausted from the long drive on top of the events of the past weeks.

A quart container of left-over Brunswick stew from the freezer got nuked it until it glowed. We added a couple of Marx bagels and trudged our way through dinner.

As we were finishing, Em looked up and said, "Okay, are you going to say it?"

"Say what?" I responded, genuinely perplexed.

"I am not just going to sit around and wait for you to rub my nose in it!"

NOW I knew what she was talking about. "Why, I have no idea what you are talking about," I said in my most innocent voice.

"Bullshit! Now's your last chance, buster."

"Yes, dear," I said meekly. "Are you going to pay up?"

"Hell no! You didn't find the strong box."

"True."

While Em had wheeled 'the pig' around the northwestern part of the airport property, I had wandered off. I had a little theory of my own. On the 1836 Oxford Township map it showed two branches of a stream or run-off on the property. It had dawned on me that if someone were to live on the property they would have to have water. That meant either a well, or a cistern, or they were hauling water quite a ways. So, while Em was using her ground penetrating radar, I coat-hanger dowsed over the more southerly branch.

"Well, then."

"So you are saying that Hettrick the Hermit's Hoard doesn't count?"

"Of course it doesn't! It wasn't what we were looking for!"

"The hell you say! It was what I was looking for!"

"Well, I'm not paying up."

"There's a surprise."

The small wooden chest was badly deteriorated, only a few crumbles of rotted wood and some cloth and leather and hardware remained. But the contents hadn't suffered too badly. We unearthed over a thousand coins of all denominations. Mostly there were half-cents, large cents, all variety of dimes and quarters. Here and there we found a few quarter, half and full eagles as well. The dates ranged from 1793 up to about 1845, but we hadn't had time to catalog all of them, yet.

Em glared at me for a moment, and the phone rang.

I could only hear half the conversation.

"Hello. Oh, hi Debbie... Um hmm... Sure... Tell me about her... Oh, that's sad... Are you sure?... Wow, basset and springer?... That's quite a mix... How old?... About seven o'clock?... Okay, see you then. Bye."

She put the phone down and turned to me, tears in her eyes. "Deb is going to bring Maggie-Joy by to introduce us tomorrow night. Her family has to move and can't keep her. She sounds like quite a girl."

Author's Notes

I have attempted to be as historically and otherwise accurate as possible in the creation of this book.

1.   The 1804 dollar is a reality.   Much of the information in this book comes from The Fantastic 1804 Dollar, by Eric P. Newman and Kenneth E. Bressett, Whitman Publishing Company, Racine, WI, 1962.   There are fifteen known specimens including the eight original "Class I", the one "Class II" in the Mint Collection, and six "Class III" coins.   There is no way of knowing how many "Class III" coins were created.   Further, the fifth "Class II" is still missing, according to William E. DuBois, Curator of Numismatics of the Mint Cabinet in 1878.

2.   The two newspaper stories about the visitor, the Wright farm, the rock and the purported treasure are real.   I do not suggest that they are accurate, only that the stories appeared in the Oxford and Hamilton newspapers in June, 1893.

3.   The property is at the Riggs Road end of the Miami University airport.   The copse of trees is there and having asked permission, I have searched.   There is no longer a rock of the description at the location.

4.   The movement of the Wright family from the eastern portion of Oxford Township to the western site is accurate, as are all the other property and map references.

5.   The historical Eckfeldt, Brenner, Patterson, and Dubois characters are all real.   The relationship between Alice and Theodore is a total fabrication. There was an Alice Patterson who lived in Oxford in the late 1800s and early 1900s, but there is no connection whatsoever to the Philadelphia Patterson family or the Mint.

6.   Theodore did move to California and lived with his sister and brother-in-law. He died in 1893, by sheer coincidence.

7.   The John A. Eckfeldt in the novel is fictitious.

8.   Sadie, sadly is no longer with us. She died of cancer over a year ago. "Maggie-Joy" is a wonderful dog, as described.

9.   So far as I know, no treasure has been found on the airport property.

10.   The descriptions of the golf course, our home, the airport property, mileages, sight lines, and all other locations and details are as accurate as I could make them, (including the Columbia 1905 salad recipe).

DWR, Oxford, 2011